CRAVING A KING

The Heart Craves Without Caution

LOUISE LENNOX

#HappyBlackRomance

Development Editing by Lauren Helms with Forever Write PR

Copy Editing by Sydnee Thompson with Shades of Sydnee

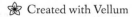 Created with Vellum

To Kelali, My Sexy High-handed African King.

Chapter One

PREPARATION

Ella

𝒶t the insistence of an insufferable sovereign, I am placing my life on hold for thirty days.

King Kofi Ajyei is practically forcing me to come to Africa. He says I need to "absorb the culture" before I propose how my charter school network, Revolution Academies, may serve his Ashanti villages. My schools teach students the inner workings of law and public policy along with reading, writing, and arithmetic. I'm only tolerating his command because having an impact on public education in West Africa will be a dream come true for me and my organization. If he chooses us.

I'm pissed because this is not how the bidding process works! When I told him my status as a UN-approved contractor requires me to submit a proposal, not pitch it to him personally in his country, he scoffed. When I told him that no potential contractor would put their entire business and life on hold to live in another country for a "maybe," he laughed! When I flat out told him no, he overnighted first-class plane tickets and accommodations at a five-star beach resort in Accra. When I threatened to send them back, he threatened to tell the UN I was not negotiating in good faith. Checkmate.

So here I am, ten hours before my flight to Africa with nothing of consequence packed.

Why do I always wait until the last minute?

Whether I'm going on a weekend jaunt to Kiawah Island's beaches or a 16-day Mediterranean cruise, I inevitably leave packing to the day before. Thirty-day trips to Africa will now join the list.

I started at five p.m. Three hours and three glasses of Merlot later, I've only packed my hair products. This is actually a feat within itself, since my hair is an entire mood. Generally, I keep my hair in two-strand twists or braids that fall just below my shoulders. But something about going to Africa makes me want to wear my afro full and free. Plus, arriving in West Africa with braids is like bringing sand to the beach—the art of hair braiding is an integral part of West African culture. I plan to leave the continent with amazing braids. However, this decision has forced me to ensure I have all tools, creams, gels, conditioners, rods, and co-washes needed to tame the beast. Between that and the wine, the hours flew by!

I hear my doorbell ringing—must be my girl Maya. As usual, I called her to come and rescue me from myself at the 11th hour. I put my glass down and rush to the door.

"Hey, girl!" I say with a bit too much energy.

"Hey, lush!" Maya grins as I let her in. Even after eight on a Sunday night, she is stunning. "Ella, how do you plan to get anything done knee-deep into a bottle of wine?" I shrug my shoulders and close the door behind her.

I've known Maya for 15 years, since our first day at Spelman. She, like me, is an only child, and we hit it off the moment we met. She was my roommate, and even then, I was awestruck by her beauty. At six feet tall and 130 pounds soaking wet, she's never ignored. Her skin is the color of onyx and smooth as silk. She has wide-set, almond-shaped eyes with defining flecks of hazel and a brilliant smile. Her jet-black hair is as long as mine, but always blown out and never in its natural coils, so it falls to the middle of her back. I've always thought she looked like Naomi Campbell, which is an appropriate comparison since she modeled in Paris and Milan for six seasons. Currently, she teaches African studies at Emory University. Not bad for an orphan that spent her childhood in the foster system. She's an inspiration. Even now, she looks like a model in a bright green shift that would be too short if she were in heels. Instead, she paired it with brown Louboutin flats the same shade as her skin. *I wonder where she got them.*

I giggle and close the door behind her. "I'm not a lush! Well...at least not yet. I'm sure to be drunk if I have another glass of wine, though." I grab both of her wrists and drag her into my room. "I need an intervention, Maya! I literally have no clothes. And my flight leaves at six tomorrow morning!"

Maya rolls her eyes. "If you come to the gym with me and work off 10 pounds, you can raid my closet in times of crisis! But since you refuse, I guess your beautiful size eight ass will have to shop your own closet. Now, let's see..."

Maya immediately starts going through the clothes in my closet. The closet is my favorite thing in the house. I bought this house a little over a year ago in Atlanta's North Decatur suburb after a devastating breakup with the love of my life, Marcus Banks. The house is on my favorite street, Ponce de Leon, but everyone just calls it Ponce. I designed every inch of the 4,000-square-foot space myself. Transforming the home became my therapy. It took 16 months to renovate and update the historic home into my personal retreat.

The smooth, whitewashed gray-and-blue interiors flow from the front door to the patio out back. My closet is no different. It has whitewashed Oak barn double doors, and the interior has beautiful blue walls. Blue is my absolute favorite color. There are rows of light gray marble-topped dressers and quartz shelving. Every purse and shoe lines up from lightest to darkest. My clothes hang on wooden hangers beneath the shoes and bags. I took special care to color coordinate clothes with shoes. *Just the kind of obsessive-compulsive thing someone does when rebounding from a bad breakup.*

Maya takes me out of my thoughts. "So, when you say you have *literally* nothing to wear, what you really mean is you have *way* too much."

"I know," I respond, "it's overwhelming." Adding to my anxiety is the sight of Maya pacing in and out of my closet at an urgent speed, throwing items on my bed and pointing to suitcases, gesturing for me to begin folding and packing.

"OK, let's focus." Maya's eyes narrow in on something in my closet, and she walks to the back. Her mumbled voice continues to speak, "Since you are going to Ghana to meet with parliament's Speaker of the House, you need to look fierce and in control. I'm thinking lots of bold colors: reds, magentas, fuchsias, and oranges. I also want you in some sort of heel every day." She steps out of the closet with a handful of items. "You know my motto: if you're under five-nine, you always need a heel!"

My favorite pair of high-waisted fuchsia Max Mara pants hit my bed. I've had those pants since I graduated from law school almost eight years ago. They were the first designer piece I bought with my new salary and always make me feel like a million bucks. Before I started my initial career as a corporate attorney, I never even knew who Max Mara was. My mentors in the office quickly schooled me.

She follows the pants with a matching silk camisole and four-inch nude Jimmy Choo strappy heels. It's another choice that reminds me I'm no longer the shy, plump girl at Spelman; I'm a beautiful boss. They are the sexiest shoes I own. When those hit the bed, I know I definitely don't like the way this is going.

"Maya, I want to be comfortable. It's Africa *in July*. How about some nice sundresses and leather thong sandals? If it's a business luncheon, I'll throw a linen blazer and some pumps on. Plus, he's not just Speaker of the Ghanaian Parliament. I've found out that he's actually styled as a king." I throw that last piece of information in to slow this *What Not to Wear* episode down. "I don't want him to get the wrong impression of me from the way I dress." Maya knows that unlike her, I hate the spotlight. It works; she marches back out with no items to toss at me.

"Right. God forbid he realizes you actually like to have fun. Also, if he's truly royal, you definitely cannot afford to blend into the background with sundresses. You have to shine brighter than anyone else around. But wait, let's establish what you mean by 'king'? Please elaborate."

I recall the conversation my Morehouse Brother, Adom Annan, and I had two weeks earlier. Morehouse is the brother school of my alma mater, Spelman College. During the first week of orientation, we are all assigned a sibling of the opposite sex, and Adom was mine. We have been inseparable ever since. Coincidentally, Adom is Kofi's cousin, though they don't seem to be very close. Luckily, Adom is like family to me and prepped me for my visit.

"Adom and Google are the extent of my research; he's the head of the Ashanti tribe. Apparently, he sits on the Ashanti throne, which is actually a Golden Stool. I'm still not sure what all his ranks and titles mean. Adom's explanation was short and not very in depth. But if the way he ordered me to Ghana is any indication, he's definitely accustomed to being in charge."

Maya places her hands on her hips and releases a sharp breath. "So, wait...he's the Asantehene? Why didn't Adom ever tell us his cousin was African royalty?"

My mouth flies open in shock. "You know what that is?! Adom told me his official title, but I still have no earthly idea what he was talking about. *I also can't pronounce it.*"

Maya takes a seat on my bed and gestures for me to sit beside her. "Well duh. Of course you don't! But if you asked your brilliant best friend that studies Africa for a living, you could have easily found out." Exasperated, Maya stretches the full length of her body over the covers. "Did I tell you how much I love this big ass bed? California King! I don't know why I don't have one yet."

"Only every time you come over." I roll my eyes. She's so easily distracted.

I guess I could have asked her about Kofi, but sometimes I forget Maya is a professor. She's a member of the Black jet-set and rarely in the states. Plus, between my hectic work schedule and her weekend jaunts to Paris, I rarely see her anymore.

"Girl, If I knew the title existed before lunch with Adom, I would have asked you about the title. But since you're here now, tell me: how big of a deal is he? Adom said Kofi becoming speaker of the Ghanaian Parliament means nothing compared to his role as Asantehene."

"And he's right! Let me put it this way...The President of Ghana technically looks to him for direction."

I shake my head. "How so, Maya? He's president of the entire country. Kofi is..." I use air quotes to emphasize my amusement. "...*King of the Ashanti*." I mean, come on—it sounds like he made the title up. It reminds me of the rapper T.I.'s self-made title, *King of the South!*" I laugh at my reference.

"You can laugh if you want to, silly girl, but the President of Ghana is Ashanti, and so are 11 million other Ghanaians. He and his family have ruled a little over a third of the Ghanaian population for close to five centuries. It's the largest tribe in the country."

"Oh," I deadpan. "Well, I'm glad I decided to defer to Adom and address Kofi as king in all our communications."

"Communications? Hold on, I'm intrigued." Maya stands, grabs the iPhone out of her Chanel tote, and begins typing away. I know exactly what she is doing. She is Googling him. "Oh my! That's him? He doesn't look anything like Adom. He's fine and chocolate. While Adom is fine and buttery." She shoves the phone in my face for emphasis. "No wonder you're three sheets to the wind over what to pack; this man is a hunk."

"That's not it at all." *A blatant lie.* "I simply want to ensure I'm dressed appropriately for every situation." I stand up and begin blindly folding and packing the items thrown on the bed earlier. Maya gives me a look of total disbelief and decides not to challenge me. Instead, she opts to head back into my closet.

"OK, well, where are you staying?"

"The Westin at Labadi Beach. He chose it and arranged the

reservation after I specifically told him I wasn't coming. He's a domineering prick. Nevertheless, I did research the hotel—it has a nice lounge and poolside bar that hosts live music in the evenings."

Maya continues to rummage through the back of my closet. "Hmm, OK, so we do need nice flowy dresses for that." She emerges with three sundresses: one in a colorful print, and two silk dresses in more muted colors. "What else is on the itinerary?"

I join her in the closet. It's getting late, and my energy and sobriety are waning. "Well, meetings of course, and a festival called the Ak-was-i-dae?" Maya's eyebrows shoot up. She takes a seat on one of my marine blue velvet ottomans, clutching an oyster-shaped Judith Leiber clutch.

"The Asantehene is escorting you to the Akwasidae? Girl, we won't even try to pack for that; I'll connect you with my girl Mawuli. She has a bespoke shop in Accra; I'll send over your measurements and she will put something together for you." Before I can protest, her phone is out and she's starting to text numbers. I bend down in front of her, placing my hands on her knees.

"Is this really necessary?"

Maya grabs my shoulders. "Ella, after hearing all you've told me, there are three things I know without a shadow of a doubt."

She dramatically stands up and begins to count off her fingers. "One, you're not ready for all the fabulous historic luxury this man is about to introduce you to. But you deserve it. Two, if you're walking around Kumasi and Accra with a king, nothing in your closet is going to cut it. We can pack some things here, but then I'm calling Mawuli and the Chanel Atelier to pull some strings. You will need things sent. They will be at the Westin day after tomorrow. And three, this man is interested in building more than schools with you. I think you're interviewing for more than one job, ma'am. The other being his queen."

I roll my eyes. "OK, Professor Taylor, the first two on your list, yeah, okay, I'll give you those. But that last one is just crazy. Please pass me some of those jeans behind you." Maya obliges and grabs a few T-shirts and more silk bras and panties than I can count before following me out of the closet. I add the last few pieces to my over-flowing suitcase before sitting on the bed. Maya sighs and gives me an entreating look.

"Ella, listen. This man is not only a king—he's a politician soon running for re-election to parliament. He has major things going on. Girl, he would not waste his time parading you through Kumasi or presenting you at Akwasidae if you did not pique his interest. Akwasidae is a cultural celebration of the Ashanti. It's hard to convey the significance, but I'm sure he'll be more than happy to explain it once he meets you. Trust me, it's like the biggest freaking Easter parade you've ever seen."

I shrug. "He probably just wants to share his culture so I can design better schools for him." I point a finger at Maya. "Let me remind you of why I'm traveling to Kumasi in the first place. I'm trying to spread our education model globally, not to become a queen. Plus, what would an Ashanti king want with me?"

"Girl, just like you, he probably Google stalked you and is in love." We both bust out laughing at her comments, falling over each other.

"I did kind of cyberstalk him. You are talking crazy with this love affair, though. I'm not strikingly beautiful like you or half as interest-ing. I'm just Ella Jenkins, impeccably dressed, good hair, great tits. Amazing nonprofit CEO." I smile, but Maya doesn't. "Plus, you know I have self-diagnosed trust issues. Now is not the time to try and overcome that barrier playing around with a king."

"Before that Marcus fiasco, you didn't have those issues and you always knew your worth. Now, you sell yourself short. I hate him for that. But I'm also grateful you're going on this trip. Who better to remind you of the queen you are than an actual king!"

"Maya, what would I do without you reminding me how great I am?"

She shakes her head. "I don't know. I'm tempted to get on the plane with you and make sure you don't miss your shot at having all kinds of amazing sex with that fine ass man." She lets out an exaggerated sigh. "I just have to trust all I've taught you will be enough."

I throw a pillow at her and laugh. "I think we've done as much as we are going to get done. That pillow is calling my name." She gives me a side-eye, knowing I'm changing the subject. "Thank you for coming to help."

"Are you kicking me out?" *She knows better.*

"Well, I'm not saying you've got to go home, but..." I laugh and grab her in a big hug. "I'm just kidding! I love you, girl. You can always take me to the airport at 4 a.m. We can have a sleepover." I arch both eyebrows.

Maya shakes her head and grabs her bag, beginning to walk to the door. "No thank you!" She spins around and grabs me forcefully by my shoulders to make me face her. "I love you, too, and you better call me every day." I pull her to me, and we hug again. Part of me wishes she could go with me. Once I let her go, she turns to leave, but pauses.

"And Ella, I saw your face when I mentioned Marcus. Please use this time to finally get over him and under that fine ass king!"

Chapter Two

DISTRACTION

Kofi

*A*ccra nightclubs are not what they used to be.

The music is uninspiring, the VIP service is deficient, and most of all, the women are way too eager to jump in my bed. Senya is mad as a hatter for wanting to spend his birthday here, and impetuous for insisting I accompany him. I am king of the Ashanti. It is unbecoming for me to take shots surrounded by half-clothed temptresses to the rhythms of the most generic brand of Afrobeat music.

There is sure to be some unflattering picture of me in the press if I make even the slightest misstep. My reputation as an international playboy is finally starting to die down. My last tryst ended disastrously. At one point I had to increase palace security and increase my security detail by three men besides my head of royal affairs. The same Senya who I somehow allowed to cajole me into this morass.

I look down at my phone and see it is 2:00 am. Time to go. I check my email and see a name that makes my heart skip a beat. Ella Jenkins. The beautiful CEO that will spearhead the construction and operation of public schools in my village. Half the reason I gave in so easily to Senya tonight was to distract myself from thoughts of her. I am not sure if she will arrive tonight as planned. I demanded her visit from Atlanta weeks ago, and she balked. I sent the tickets anyway, but she did not respond. Finally, I sent a harmless threat to call the UN about her negotiating practices and she responded with a simple OK. However, she has sent no further communication. I open the email hoping she is not telling me to go to hell and build my own damn schools.

> DEAR YOUR MAJESTY,
> THANK YOU FOR THE FIRST-CLASS ACCOMMODATIONS, THOUGH I STILL FIND THIS TRIP UNNECESSARY AND YOUR INSISTENCE UPON IT HIGH-HANDED. I AM DETERMINED TO MAKE THE BEST OF IT AND PROVIDE YOU WITH AN UNPARALLELED PROPOSAL FOR PUBLIC SCHOOLING IN KUMASI.
> YOURS IN THE WORK,
> ELLA JENKINS
> CEO, REVOLUTION ACADEMIES

Thank God. Judging by her email, she is enjoying first-class, which means she is on the plane. It is apparent my request still irritates her. However, irritations can be easily overcome. Now more than ever, I am ready to go to my hotel and prepare for her arrival.

I look to my right and notice the woman sitting next to me sipping the 5th drink I ordered for her tonight. I slip my phone in my pocket and stand... too quickly. I've had way too much to drink. I quickly sit back down, and my booth mate places her hand on my thigh. I implore my body not to react. This is ridiculous. Senya should know better than to place me in this situation. However, as my best friend, he would never come into this situation without me. He's nowhere to be found, and I am trapped in VIP with a relentless woman. All night she comes and goes. She has found more creative ways to push her pleasant rump into my face than a stripper giving a lap dance. It is exasperating. She is pretty, but unappealing.

Comfort- I believe that's her name- has done everything but flat-out beg me to take her home. She uses what I call bottom barrel lines- I've never been inside the palace. What's it like? I have heard them all before. I bite my tongue and nod like an idiot. I dare not tell her I do not live there. I do not tell her that women who see the inside of the palace have an expiration period of thirty days. It is really my royal fuck pad. No woman goes there to live happily ever after. I live at my private residence in the forest, hidden from royal groupies. My home is my haven and only those who truly know me have the privilege of visiting. This woman does not care to know me or the cause I live for. No, she wants prestige, title, and money. Little does she know, a night with me will not guarantee her any of those things.

Comfort scoots closer to me on the velvet couch. She is sitting so close she could dry hump my thigh in this darkness and no one would notice. I glance over and finally spot Senya getting friendly with two women I'm sure he's taking back to his room tonight. No one is coming back with me. I need to leave Accra without a woman I will only have to ghost within a month.

Determined to break away, I turn and smile at Comfort before scooting a few inches away. She stares at me, never blinking, and grabs my dick. She could have slapped me across my face, and I would be less shocked. I go still. My jaw clenches and I inhale deeply as she massages the growing bulge between my legs. After a weak campaign of resistance, my dick wakes up. I resign myself to how this evening is likely to play out. The sooner we start, the sooner I can send her on her way and go to bed.

I remove her hand and stand. She looks up at me with a frantic glare. Apparently, the dick-grab is her go-to move. She set a goal to fuck the king tonight, and now she has no back-up plan. I discreetly adjust myself and exhale. She will do. She's worked hard to get this shot. Her little pouty mouth will do well wrapped around my dick.

"Comfort gather your things. I'm taking you to my suite."

She doesn't move. "A hotel? Why not the palace? Do I look like a whore?"

I should turn around and leave right now. Not only is she thirsty. She's stupid. I bet Ella is not stupid. Ella will be here tonight.

I take another look at her incredible body and give Comfort one more chance. Through gritted teeth, I respond. "The seat of the Ashanti kingdom is in Kumasi. It is not here in Accra. So, I am a visitor to your town. I am staying in a suite on Labadi Beach, you are welcome to join me... or not... it is up to you."

Her eyes shine bright and the corner of her lips turn up into a sly smile. Licking her lips, she tosses a long weave behind her back before standing. I inspect her and realize she's wearing the equivalent to a napkin. I can almost see what makes her a woman from the front of her little gold dress. She turns as I guide her out of the VIP area, and I notice her dress does a worse job covering her ass. The four-inch heels she is wearing don't help my restraint. She definitely came to play.

Once we get outside, my Range Rover pulls up and she frowns. "I thought you rode in a Maybach?"

Here we go again. She should just not speak at this point. I roll my eyes. "Why would you think that?"

She ignores my exasperation. "Whenever the Tattler or bloggers cover you in London, you are always stepping out of a Black Maybach." Her eyes take on a greedy gleam. "I was hoping to ride in it. I wanted a picture for the gram." She comes closer to rub her hand up and down my arm. She pokes out her bottom lip, resembling a spoiled child. "Is there any way you can switch cars? They will bring you whatever you ask for, right? You're the king."

I shake my head. She can walk for all I care. This woman is crazy if she thinks I'm texting Senya to call for a Benz from the royal fleet. I should tell her I do not want to fuck her that badly. But I refrain, because that would be harsh. According to the palace public relations team; I need to be less harsh in public. I squeeze the bridge of my nose and take a deep breath before I address her.

"Yes, I could do that. But that would be impractical. You are free to take any vehicle you like home. I am sure Uber has quite the variety. You can use the royal account." I am proud of myself. I said how I feel without saying how I really feel. The communication coaching is paying off.

Undeterred, she rubs up against me. The motion reminds me of a cat mewling for its milk. I have some milk she can drink. Her voice purrs against my ear. "Men who do whatever I want..." She takes my hand and places it on her juicy ass. Fuck! "Get me to do whatever they want." I shake my head and pull out my phone to text Senya.

This is dumb, but between the alcohol in my system and amount of ass in my hands, my dick has reached the point of no return. This will only take a few minutes. I walk Comfort around the corner into the mouth of an alley. I look around, ensuring no paparazzi are slinking in the shadows before pulling her into me. I grind my now full-blown erection into her soft body. She closes her eyes and whimpers.

I pause and place my mouth close to her ear. "What do you want from me, Comfort?"

She opens her eyes and faces me with full confidence. "I want you to fuck me until I'm a member of your thirty-day club." So, she knows the rules. Her forwardness turns my entire body into a raging hard-on. I cradle her head in my hand and grab a handful of ass with the other. Taking a fistful of hair, I pull her into a rough kiss. I devour, lick, bite, and suck until I hear moans of pleasure come from the back of her throat. Then I take a soft bite of her neck before pulling away. She giggles and adjusts her dress.

"Are we going to make it to the hotel?" She asks with a smirk that says she has no plans to do so. Her eyes are inky pools of lust. Her coppery skin is perspiring. I say nothing and walk her back around the building to the front of the club. The Maybach pulls up and I extend my hand; inviting her to enter the car. Suddenly Senya pops out of the shadows with two women in tow. He stops Comfort in her tracks before she can enter the car and shoves an electronic NDA in her face. My man is always on duty. As she signs the iPad, he reminds her she can never speak of tonight. She shrugs and giddily enters the car.

Once inside, she takes two obligatory selfies. I ensure I'm nowhere near her camera and after three clicks; I tell her to put the phone away. She complies. Senya knocks on the window and I roll it down. He talks in hushed tones.

"I'm driving the Range and my guests to the hotel. You have a royal fleet driver. Roll the partition up before you play around and turn on music loud enough to muffle your new friend. She looks like a screamer."

I smirk and nod before rolling up the window,

I turn to my right, and my guest is staring at me with crossed legs. "Come here," I command. She quickly crosses the massive back seat to climb on top of me. Her dress rides all the way up her ass. Now I see she has on a little black thong. My weakness. My fingers grab the thin piece of fabric between her full cheeks and pull it up against her pussy and ass with one strong jerk.

"Your majesty" She moans from the sensation. I continue, and do it twice more, before moving my fingers forward to sample the moisture, I know is waiting for me. I insert two fingers into her soaking wet center and confirm she's hot and ready for whatever. But I don't shag in cars. That's just disrespectful. A blowjob is another matter entirely.

"On your knees." I rasp. I unbuckle my black jeans and pull out my dick. Her eyes go wide as she drops to her knees. Her wet mouth devours my dick in one swift motion. She comes up slowly, dragging her tongue over my rod. Then she uses her spit to slide her hands over my shaft while her mouth moves in the opposite direction. The drive to my hotel is fifteen minutes. She requested a Maybach. Now let's see if she can maneuver inside one.

She takes me back into her mouth and pushes me to the back of her throat. I put my hand on the back of her head and thrust into her face. As I zone out my thoughts drift away from this vixen who only wants to say she had sex with a king. They settle on Ella, the woman that will help me build a kingdom.

Chapter Three

ARRIVAL

Ella

Against my better judgment, I am on the flight Kofi booked for me.

Shockingly, the flight to Ghana is better than I expected. I was nervous about traveling alone, but everything is running impeccably smooth. A friendly flight attendant greeted me as I boarded the plane. Her name is Grace and she helped calm my nerves. Then she showed me to a seat more comfortable than any chair I have at home. Grace brought me wine, silk pajamas, crisp linens, and a full gourmet menu for my direct flight into Accra. The flight has been in progress for an hour now and I feel good.

Now that I'm comfortable I take a moment to observe the luxury around me. I notice everything about this trip is over the top, causing my mind to wander to Kofi. While I've found myself annoyed with his overall pushy behavior, he spared no expense for my travels. My manners overruled any annoyance while I was in a cab on my way to the airport. That's when I looked at my ticket reservation and noticed I had first class accommodations. I immediately sent a thank-you email.

All I really want to do is sleep, but the amenities keep me awake for most of the trip. Even though it is early in the morning, I sample at least four bottles of wine and get ahead on some of the work I will miss while in Ghana. For lunch, I choose filet mignon served with roasted fennel and potatoes that are to die for, and after I eat, I catch up on *Insecure* episodes. When I finally drift off to sleep, there are less than two hours left in the flight and I wake to the voice of our captain.

"We are approaching Accra and will land in 20 minutes. The current time in Accra is 9:51 p.m., and the weather is partly cloudy with a temperature of 28 degrees Celsius, 82 degrees Fahrenheit. Please stay seated and buckled until the seat belt sign is turned off. All electronics should be placed in airplane mode. Thank you, and welcome to Accra."

Shit. I'm here. *What am I doing?* I have no idea how to interact with this man, but I refuse to blow this contract. From our two phone calls and dozen emails, I've deduced he's an arrogant ass. If what the tabloids say is true, he's with a different woman every month. I have no patience for a man like that, so I am not worried about falling for this arrogant, yet gorgeous, ass. I spent eight years of my life trying to build something with a man like that, and it was a disaster. I won't be pushed around, and Kofi doesn't strike me as a man who is used to not getting his way. I just hope these next thirty days go smoother than I expect them to go.

Once we land, I quickly head to the restroom to freshen up my face and hair. I'm wearing my softest pair of skinny jeans and a blue linen off-the-shoulder blouse that billows when I walk. Once in the restroom, I swap my sneakers for a pair of Louboutin espadrilles and take my hair down from the silk scarf it's wrapped in. My afro full of curls tumbles down and frames my face, free-falling to the bottom of my neck. One quick facewash and lip-gloss swipe later, and I am ready to meet a king.

I quickly get through customs. Kofi has arranged for me to have a private screening generally reserved for diplomats. Once my passport is stamped, I head to baggage claim and wait for my six bags to arrive on the conveyer belt. Twenty minutes later, I realize my Louis Vuitton duffle bag containing all of my underwear, hair products, and toiletries is missing from the belt. Luckily, I have two backup pairs of panties in my carry-on luggage. Now my annoyance is at full capacity. I need to file a claim, but I don't want to keep whoever is here to pick me up waiting. I decide to meet my escort first and then circle back to customer service.

As I head to ground transportation, I look for someone holding a sign with my name, and sure enough, there he is. He is impossible to miss. The man is head and tails above every other person I see and with an American NFL linebacker build. He's holding a sign with my name printed under the official Ghanaian government seal and looks rather imposing.

As I approach, I notice his skin is the color of the free trade coffee beans I brew every morning. His muscles are clad in an all-white linen suit. As I reach him, he unleashes a kilowatt smile made of pearly white teeth that somewhat relaxes me. I smile back and try not to stare at the mountain in front of me. He extends a hand I'm sure could snap me in two, and I oblige him a handshake. If this is what all the men in Ghana look like, I should have moved here long ago.

"Hello, Ms. Jenkins. Welcome to Accra; I am Senya." I stumble at his accent. It's part British and part West African. I wonder if he spent a significant amount of time in the U.K. He grabs my bags and waits a second, expecting a command. I clear my throat and stop staring long enough to answer.

"Umm no, I'm good; the bags will be all. Well, unless you can make the airline find my lost luggage. That reminds me...I need to go to customer service and file a claim. That bag is pretty expensive, and it contains vital items."

He relaxes a bit and nods, instantly sharing my frustration. "That is unacceptable for first-class travel. I will be sure to properly file a complaint from our office on your behalf. I assure you anything that is missing, we can replace."

He promises a lot to be a transportation company representative.

"You can replace it?" I tilt my head to one side and give him an inquisitive look. "Hotel transportation has come a long way if you can find or replace lost luggage."

He laughs at my statement and gestures for me to follow him as we walk toward the airport exit doors. "No Ms. Jenkins, I am his majesty's chief of staff, or what our culture calls 'the right hand of the king.' We are here to escort you to your lodgings. We will be glad to take you wherever you need to go and replace your belongings. We want you to have everything you need to be comfortable."

"OH!" I pause. I remember that title from *Game of Thrones.* Somehow, I think what he is talking about goes deeper than that. He does not notice my pause and keeps walking. I skip a bit faster to catch back up with him and I half shout at his back. "Did you just say we? Who else is here?"

He half turns to me, never breaking a step. "His majesty is also with me, but he is waiting at the car. He did not want to draw attention in the airport; otherwise, I'm sure he would come in to fetch you himself. Please do not think him rude."

I shake my head and swallow the fact that the king found it worth his time to come and pick me up from the airport. Maybe all the nonsense Maya was saying about him being interested in more than my schools is true. If that's the case, I need to turn around and grab a flight back to Atlanta. But I can't. So instead I continue to walk toward 30 days of uncertainty. "Of course not. I appreciate him coming at all. I'm surprised he'd come all this way to escort me to my hotel."

He stops his deliberate stride to look back and say, "Yes, it's surprising indeed." He readjusts my luggage on his shoulder and turns to continue out the doors into the parking lot. It's so dark I don't really want to keep following him as we get farther and farther away from the airport and all other cars. But I also do not want to be stranded at the airport. So, I begin following him into the night.

Before we get much farther, I reach out and touch his back, asking him to stop. He turns. "Umm, before we get to him, can you tell me a little more about him?" I start to absentmindedly fluff my Afro, a nervous habit I hate. "Like, is there anything I should know? How does he like to be addressed? Should I bow or something? Women curtsy, right?"

Even in the dark, I see a smile hint at the corners of his mouth. "Bow?!" Now he does laugh. "No, Ms. Jenkins, we don't bow or curtsy. This is not the British monarchy. Just wait for him to address you, which he will. Then he will extend his hand and you will shake it. That's it."

I give a nervous laugh. I hate nervous laughter. "Yes, of course. I know I'm not in Britain. I just really want to make a good impression. This contract is very important. He wants to ensure all Ashanti children have a strong public school option, and I know we are the best organization to make that happen. I don't want to offend him before I even get a chance to show him what I can do for him."

Senya smirks. "I wouldn't worry about your impression, Ms. Jenkins. I think he will be pleased." He looks at me intently as he speaks. "Kofi is a good king. He can be very sharp in his speech and distant in his demeanor. You will need thick skin at the start. But, once you get past his façade, you will quickly realize how great the man inside is. Just don't disrespect him. That will make him angry. That is never good." I nod at his words, trying to make sense of them. I start to ask a probing question, but he interrupts and starts to walk again. "Now we must really get going. He also hates to be kept waiting." I follow.

Finally, we approach a black Range Rover parked indiscreetly at the edge of the parking lot. It is so dark; I hardly make out the vehicle. I squint and see there are two other black SUVs parked in spots across from the Range Rover. As I approach, men exit the vehicles. Alarmed at their presence, I pause. Senya still leading me, looks back and motions for me to come. Once closer, I see King Kofi Ajyei leaning against the back passenger-side door. He holds his right hand up in a gesture that triggers the men return to their vehicles.

He possesses an unwavering stature. I willingly advance toward a jet-black God with evidenced divinity until we are face to face. His presence takes the air surrounding us. The contour of his body peeks through black jeans and a tightly fitted black T-shirt. What would be soft is hard. His smile radiates raw power. His dimples project perfection. His stare makes me pant. His mouth promises a directive. I stumble, knowing if commanded, I will worship his body right now on this hot asphalt. He extends his hand to me, which I grab, latching on, but I don't shake his hand in return, as I'm completely enamored by this man. He looks down at my hand and grins. This king is used to being held onto. Covering my hand with his, he leans down, allowing his deep voice to kiss my ear.

"I'm Kofi. Welcome to Ghana."

Chapter Four

CONFUSION

Kofi

"It is a pleasure to meet you, your majesty. I'm Ella."

Her name and voice are music to my ears. Her high cheek bones, wild hair, deep-set hazel eyes, and flawless caramel complexion make her irresistible. Senya must have set a brisk pace from the airport, because her breathing is labored and there is perspiration at the top of her full cleavage. Her breasts slightly heave with her breathing. My body responds before my mind can register and enforce self-control. I want to take her in every way a man can take the female form. However, that is not wise, and kings, if nothing else, are expected to be wise. Conversely, I feel like a complete idiot for inviting her here. All she has said so far is her name, and my mind is already kissing those sweet full lips.

Get yourself together, Kofi! Shake it off.

This is ridiculous. I am rubbing the top of her hand like I have never seen a beautiful woman before.

I clear my throat. "Please join me." I finally release her soft hand and guide her into the vehicle. I relish the opportunity to touch her again, even if it is just the small of her back and a skim of her waist. I close the door behind her and nod at Senya as he loads her luggage into the trunk of the car. He smiles knowingly and nods back. Once I enter and sit next to her on the back seat, I immediately toy with the idea of closing the small distance between us. I want to touch her again. Plus, she smells like a piece of citrus fruit. It is an aphrodisiac, hypnotizing me and inviting me in. Small talk is the best distraction.

"How was your flight?" I ask as Senya settles into the driver's seat. He answers for her.

"The airport lost a very expensive piece of Ms. Jenkins' luggage. I am certain losing it has dimmed her travel experience. I know it would wreck mine." They share a knowing laugh before he continues. "I can take her tomorrow to replace the bag and whatever else she needs." His words stir a foolish jealousy in me. First of all, why is he speaking for her? To add insult to injury, he knows of her needs before I do. This is why I wanted to pick her up personally. It was only on *his* advice that I did not, and now here they are sharing inside jokes.

"Oh no, that's all right," Ella protests. "I'm sure the hotel will have the basics I need until my luggage is found."

Senya chuckles. "I wouldn't be so sure." A look of displeasure falls upon her face.

"Why? Are five-star Westin hotels in Accra not as accommodating as others across the world? I assure you, I've stayed in 52 Starwood hotels across 45 countries, and they are all pretty much the same."

Senya can't resist. "Ahh, but I bet none of those fine establishments were on this continent. This is your first time in Africa, is it not?" Ella tenses. It is clear she does not like being wrong or corrected.

"I assure you this Westin will be like none other you experienced."

I exchange glances with Senya through the rearview mirror. He arches his eyebrows at me and subtly shrugs his shoulders. I glare back and shift in my seat as I fumble pensively with the gold tribal bracelet that has been passed down from one Asantehene to the other since time immemorial. I finally look over to her. She looks at me, waiting for an explanation of the disparities between hotel amenities in African and Western nations.

"Ella..." *I must approach this topic lightly.* "You are absolutely right. I once stayed at the Accra Westin, and it does have top-notch amenities." Her face softens, looking relieved that she was correct in her assumption. "What Senya is trying to convey is that the Westin amenities will not matter, because you are not staying there. You're staying at my personal home right outside of Kumasi. It is called Bonbiri. It is near the Tafo village and it is my favorite place in the world." I pause, waiting for a reaction. It comes to her eyes first like fire and lightning.

"The hell I am!" she thunders. "I'm not staying in your home. What the hell is going on here?! You are completely crazy if you think I'm going home with you." I suspected she might be concerned with the prospect and was prepared to make concessions to accommodate her, but this disrespect cannot be tolerated. I am a head of state! No one talks to me like this. Least of all some woman from America who I only barely know. I turn and face her full-on.

"Mind your tongue. This insolence will not be tolerated. Express your concerns with respect. I am the chief of the largest ethnic group in Ghana." My hands clench into fists. I cannot help it. Nothing gets under my skin faster than disrespect.

If she is chased by my statement, she does not show it. Instead, she turns and jabs her finger directly in my face as she barks a response. "And who are you to demand my respect when you clearly don't respect me at all?"

"Did I not just tell you I am the Asantehene?!" My statement is several decibels louder than I intended. I also hear my Ghanaian accent take over my speech. Without a doubt, I am beside myself with anger. "I am king of the Ashanti, and you, Ms. Jenkins, are treading on thin ice."

"So, you *are* a king! I'm glad that's finally clear."

"That is what I just said. Is it not?"

She shakes her head. "Forget it. What you need to know is that I skate on thin ice for the hell of it. As a matter of fact, I lick thin ice! It's called a snow cone and I love them!" *Why is she so disrespectful?*

"Excuse me?" I shout as I close the physical distance between us. "Do I look like a snow cone to you? This ice is not one that will go down your throat easily. I promise that when you swallow it, *Wahala!*" *Did I just say that out loud? And in Twi?* I am boiling. "Who do you think you are—?" Before I complete my statement, she is cutting me off.

"And another thing!" *Oh great, there's another thing.* "I don't care about your damn title. I don't even know what it means! But by the looks of it, asshole must be somewhere in that definition. Senya, pull over. I can handle myself from here."

Senya looks at me through the rearview mirror. "Your highness?"

Ella bangs her fist against the door. "You don't need his permission to stop the car. I don't feel safe." Her voice cracks slightly. Senya stops the car immediately, and before I can do anything, she jumps out and slams the door. I roll the window down, but before I can speak, she pokes her head in and turns to Senya. "Please release the trunk and I will be on my way."

Senya steps out to assist Ella. He tries to calm her down.

"Please, Ms. Jenkins, you cannot stand here on the side of the road in Accra waiting for a Lyft. This is not Atlanta. This is dangerous and stupid."

She is incredulous at his statement. "Oh, you mean dangerous like two men I don't know who were trusted to take me to my hotel but instead change the plan once I'm locked in their car? And stupid like me actually letting them take me to a home in the forest without my express permission?" Senya sighs, and I swear I hear that traitor mutter, "Touché" before opening the trunk and grabbing her bags.

He's a coward. He knows full well we cannot leave her on the side of the road. The press will eat me alive. Plus, her wild diatribe did slightly turn my heart away from anger at her disrespectful words and toward empathy I did not know I was capable of having for such an infuriating creature. She has a point. At the end of it all, Senya and I are two strange men taking her to a place she is not familiar with and was not aware she was going. I didn't take into account how problematic that might be.

I unbuckle my seat belt and walk out to meet her. "Ella," I start warily. Her eyes shoot me a promise of slow death if I come any closer. It is cute. "You will have to excuse our behavior." Senya shoots me a look and mouths, "your behavior" while pointing at me from behind her back. He's right. He told me this was a bad idea from the start, but I would not hear his reason. I told him she'd be honored to stay at the Asantehene's private home instead of some hotel. He tried to assure me that would not be the case. I believe his exact words were, *"I doubt she even knows what an Asantehene is."*

"We...I mean...I... mean you no harm. I honestly thought you would be more comfortable staying in my private home. It is near three of the villages I want to show you. For the purpose of your trip, it is actually more convenient than a hotel at the center of Accra. And as soon as it is known you are my guest; the press will give you no rest. I use my home to get away from all that."

I think I see her eyes lightly soften. It is not much, but it is better than rage. "I see," she starts, "so, it's not my safety and comfort you are concerned about, it's your own?"

My God! Does the disrespect ever end? I control my anger. "Please enlighten me—how is that the case?"

"King Ajyei—" she starts.

"Please call me Kofi," I interject.

"Your majesty," she fires back, "I'd rather not. King Ajyei, no one knows who I am or cares about me checking into my lovely room at the Westin to finally rest on my heavenly bed after a 20-hour day." She moves closer to me until she is so far into my personal space, I can smell her citrus scent again. "No, king, they care about you. They know you." She points at my chest. The tip of her finger touches me slightly.

"Therefore, what you are really saying is that it is more convenient for you to have me stay at Bonbiri with you, so that you do not have to deal with any of the craziness that comes with your title. But you see, I am not royalty. I am a Black woman whose mama ain't raise no fool. If you think I'm staying in your home, in the middle of a forest, with you, a man I do not know and who is undoubtedly used to having his way with women, you, sir, are mistaken."

Incredible! She honestly thinks this is about me wanting to sleep with her. I may have fantasized about it once or twice while watching her TED Talk videos online, but I would never disrespect a woman by tricking her into my bed. I would never need to. Furthermore, after this drive from the airport, I no longer want to. I rub my hands back and forth through my hair and speak.

"OK, Ella. It seems you have made your mind up about me without knowing me at all. However offended I am by your insinuations, I do want you to have a comfortable and enjoyable trip while here in Ghana. How about a compromise? Since we do not know the status of a hotel room for you at the moment, why don't you stay at my home, and I will stay at the palace in Kumasi."

She looks at me through the narrowed slits of her eyes. "There's a palace in Kumasi?! You mean to tell me you could have acted like a gentleman and decided on these separate living arrangements ahead of time?"

"Yes, Ella. There is a palace. I am a king, after all. However, I promise it is much more comfortable in my home far away from all the pomp and circumstance. Nevertheless, you can stay there along with my cook Akua—she will serve you. I am sure you will be most comfortable. Everyone that visits Bonbiri loves it." I see the wheels of her mind turning. Her face turns from defiance to annoyance and finally settles at resignation. Thank the ancestors! I am ready to get off the side of this road. What if someone sees us?! We look like we are taking her hostage, for God's sake!

"Love it?" she counters. "What I love is honesty, and what you just pulled on me was not honest. Nevertheless..." She sighs and throws up both hands. "I will stay at your home, *without you*, for one night. But I expect to be in a hotel by tomorrow night. Is that clear?"

"Yes, yes, whatever you say. Now, let's return to the car. Senya, please return Ms. Jenkins' luggage to the trunk." As I attempt to guide her to the passenger side of the car and open the back door, she stops me.

"I'm fully capable of letting myself into the car." The look she gives me is as cold as the thin ice she happily skates and licks on. She enters my Range Rover and slams the door. Slamming doors is a serious pet peeve of mine, but I decide to excuse the infraction. I walk over to the driver side and hop in.

"We are all set, Senya. You may start the drive and, hopefully, we can all get to our *separate* destinations without any more interruptions."

Ella snickers. "As long as you boys don't have any more surprises, we should be good." She rubs her eyes and yawns.

"Good." My clipped tone is only a ripple of the volcanic rage boiling inside me. We ride the rest of the way to Bonbiri in silence. I no longer want to close the physical distance on the back seat between us. I am grateful for it.

She falls asleep about ten minutes into the ride, and I reluctantly look over. She looks soft and vulnerable. Great! Now, I want to hold her in my arms and rock her to sleep. She is exasperating and exhilarating all at once. I don't know if I want to curse her or cover her in soft kisses. I will take care not to give into either temptation. Senya warned me this could get messy. I'm determined for it not to.

Chapter Five

HOSPITALITY

Ella

I fake sleep on the ride to his home to ensure *King Ajyei* doesn't say another word to me.

I can't believe he had the audacity to speak to me the way he did, when he is the one clearly in the wrong. I won't even dare to think what he called me in Twi. He just yelled out "Wahala" in the middle of his diatribe. I will make sure I look that up later. All of this trouble, when he could have just quickly agreed to stay in his palace if he really wanted me to avoid a hotel. Clearly, he was only interested in things going his way.

I bet he is just trying to get into my pants! *Sophisticated playboy chief with a woman for every occasion!* The passages I read in the tabloids come rushing back to my memory. Any grown man knows you don't bring a woman you just met to sleep in your home without her knowledge unless she's a woman you think will sleep with you for a contract. Well, I'm not the one. He's probably played this same game before. Rushing oblivious women to cabins in the forest when they think they're going to a hotel, or worse...HOME! Oh my God! What if he's a rapist?! King or not, my hotel better be rebooked and ready for me tomorrow, or I'm on the first plane back to Atlanta.

We pull up to a steep driveway and proceed up a gravel drive for at least a half a mile. I sit up and take note. *How in the hell will I be able to escape down this driveway if I need to?* Only a SUV can even make it up here, and there's no guarantee Uber will even find it. The sight of Bonbiri halts my emergency planning. It is a breathtaking cabin, if you can even call it that. Remodeling my own home has me addicted to *Architectural Digest*, HGTV, and the HOUZZ website, but I've never seen anything like his home.

First off, it's perched on a hill. When we arrive at the top, light breaks out from every angle to fully illuminate the home. It is made entirely of mahogany wood and glass. There are too many windows to count, and it is massive! It is modern, but woodsy. The second floor has wraparound decks, and the roof is hard lines of steel. It truly is a work of art. Without thinking, I gasp. "Beautiful."

Kofi stirs and brushes my hand. "Thank you, I am pleased you like it," he whispers. Now that he's calm, I hear the precise British accent he shares with Senya again.

I snatch my hand away. Owner of a beautiful oasis or not, he's still on my shit list.

Once Senya stops the car, he and Kofi hop out. Kofi comes to my door and immediately offers his hand. I bypass it and jump out. He smirks. Senya grabs my bags and I follow Kofi to the door. The doors are massive stone carvings. They remind me of something from Tudor castles of the past. Totally over the top. Next, I'm eye level with lion head door knockers and I cannot resist laughing.

"What is causing you to laugh?" Kofi asks as he leads me into a foyer that is half the size of my entire apartment.

I try to contain my merriment. "I'm sorry, but the entrance to your house is so intense. The stone-carved doors are a bit medieval. But your door knockers..." My laughter returns. "Lion heads? Really? They're so on the nose. It's like a scene from the movie *Coming to America*. What's next? A lionskin rug?"

He looks perplexed. "Fortunately, I have never viewed *Coming to America*, so I cannot confirm nor deny the comparison." His jaw hardens. "However, I think you are trying to tell me my door knockers are gauche?"

Who the hell uses the word gauche? "We will have to fix that. Everyone must see *Coming to America* at least once! I can't believe you've never heard of it."

He shuts the door and turns to me. His jaw is still tense, and his eyes are penetrating my soul. "You misunderstand. I know of Eddie Murphy's movie. I just refuse to see it. It is a mockery of African culture. It contributes to misguided views of my homeland. I refuse to support propaganda passed off as comedy. I certainly hope it is not your view of Africa. You cannot build schools in a community that you view as a joke." He turns on his heel and throws a command over his shoulder, "Come." We walk farther into his home past the foyer. However, I still have so much to say. So, I say it to his back.

"How is it propaganda if it's true? You literally have lion heads as door knockers to your home. That is something you would see in that movie. Where's the lie? It is because I understand the diversity of Africa that I can laugh at the satire of *Coming to America* and sepa-rate the wheat from the tare." He pauses and turns to finally face me. I seize the moment. "You, sir, take yourself too seriously." I brush by him and turn in the direction of the stairs ahead of me. "Now, will you please just show me my room for the night? I assume the rooms are upstairs." I start toward the staircase.

As I move up the stairs that seem to go on forever, he follows me. He let me have the *Coming to America* battle, but I have a feeling that will not be our last skirmish. We arrive at the first landing and he pauses at the stairs. "We will continue up the stairs—there are two rooms to the right and one on the left. You can pick whichever one you like. They are all en suite." The massive steel-roped staircase seems to float in the air. Once we reach the top, I turn and inadvertently bump into his large frame. He smells like musk, nutmeg, and cinnamon. So this is what African royalty smells like. Up close his skin is as smooth as a Hershey bar and undoubtedly just as sweet. I want to take a bite of him. "This way, Ella." He passes me on the top step and begins to lead the way. He opens a door just ahead to our right.

"This is your first choice. I call it the rainforest."

I can see why. The walls are draped in mossy green fabrics and the bed boasts blue and gray silk linens. The paintings are of villagers at the river fishing and swimming, along with colorful abstract paintings of animals in the forest. It is a captivating room.

"This is beautiful, your majesty. Did you design it yourself?"

He nods as he closes the door. "I did. I designed every space in this home, because it's mine. It doesn't belong to Ghana or the Ashanti. It belongs to me. I purchased the land and building materials with the money my mother left me at her death. My mother's family was very rich, as my grandfather invested in Nigerian oil fields. I invested the rest of the money, which makes up the fortune I currently have." He continues down the hall to the next room with a wistful look. "I thought about all the things she loved about Africa when designing it. The rainforest, the desert, and the river. Come. Let me show you the Sahara room."

Kofi starts to resemble an actual human being with every step we take. In this moment, he certainly isn't a man who is trying to seduce me at his sex pad in the woods. He is a sovereign allowing me to stay in the place he deems as a tribute to his mother. As we come to the Sahara room, he opens the door and I can see it is even more beautiful than the rainforest room.

"Oh my!" I gasp. "Your majesty, I've never seen shades of gold and red like this before. Where do you source your textiles?"

"Please, Ella, call me Kofi." He gives me a mischievous look as he comes closer to tease. "What do you know of textiles?"

"Well...King." I clear my throat. No matter how informal he tries to be with me, I am not ready to be informal with him. "I too have a home I designed and call my own in Atlanta. It's my little piece of heaven. I picked everything down to the table linens. So, I understand your effort and appreciate it. It's like a peek into who you truly are. That's how my home is for me, and also why I don't let just anyone in."

"Ahh!" He steps closer to me and places his hands on my shoulders. So close, I think he might kiss me. Instead, he speaks. "So maybe you can understand the gravity of my gesture? I was genuinely attempting to honor you by inviting you to stay in my home. I never thought it would offend."

This man has got some serious game. I will not fall for it. "Maybe, I understand that. Maybe I don't. The jury is still out." I pull away from his hands. "Please show me the last room. Since you've shown me the desert and the rainforest, the river is the last one, right?"

He gestures for me to leave the room before him. "Yes, the river room is last. Come."

During the walk down this long hallway, I am getting a good look at his ass and thighs. In his black jeans, I can see that both are rock hard and full of power. I start to think of the possible effect of that force on my body. I need to stop. We are most definitely not going there. As he approaches the cedar barn door on his left, he turns to address me.

"The river room is my favorite. My mother and I used to walk by the river for hours. To this day, the water is my favorite place to be."

We step in and I exhale a deep breath. Every shade of blue is represented in the wall coverings, bed linens, and even the floor tile. The floors are colored such a deep gray they look blue. There are also small fish tanks in between the tiles of the floor, so it looks like I am walking on water as the fish swim under my feet. "King, this is magnificent. May I stay in this room, please?"

He looks into my eyes. "Of course, Ella. You may have whatever you want. I am sure all the toiletries you may need are in the bathroom. I just want you happy while you are here."

I chuckle. "Why are you so concerned about my happiness? Is it really so I can build excellent schools for you? I assure you this is not how the client-contractor relationship generally progresses. It is I that needs to impress you."

He does not laugh. "No. Never try to impress me. It is an impossible task. I will always expect more. As for your happiness, between exiting the car and walking to this room, it became of interest to me."

I clear my throat. "And why is that, King?"

"Well, Ella, the jury is still out."

With that, he crashes his body into mine and kisses me like I have never been kissed before. It starts tentative and gentle. His full lips are soft and asking my permission to go further with every touch. My mind says to stop this, but my body craves it, so I allow it. Opening my mouth, I invite him in to explore and make himself comfortable. The wall starts to tumble down as we give into the passion that sparked the moment we laid eyes on each other. The kiss chips at my resolve bit by bit before finally taking me to the river.

Chapter Six

CORRECTION

Kofi

The kiss with Ella last night was a mistake.

    I let my lips write a check I am most certainly not ready to cash. Now it may be awkward. But I could not resist. The sight of her makes me want to take her against the nearest wall and screw her until she passes out from the pleasure. She is equally infuriating and sexy. The way her teeth captured my bottom lip while I was kissing her was a direct display of her power over me. But then, she parted her lips so readily and let me set the pace as I devoured her. For a moment, Ella yielded power. She is a walking contradiction. Hard and soft. Sweet and spicy. Fetching and fightable.

    I wish I could figure out which side of her is making me lose my mind! Even now I am lying in this bed thinking about how her full breasts pressed into me during that kiss. I swear she tried to grind the sweet spot at the center of her body into mine. She definitely felt the bulge between my legs last night—no way she missed it. I was rock hard! Shit! There is no way I make it through my morning shower without rubbing one out. The fact that I sleep naked is no help. I feel my hand creeping toward my dick already. Ever since I started researching Ella, watching the videos of her speeches and looking at her pictures, I jack off more than a teenager. But it cannot go further.

From this moment on, I will be the ultimate host. After the abrupt kiss, she admitted it was silly for Senya and me to drive to the palace in town when I was already at my home. So, I got permission to stay in my own damn house! Unbelievable. She is infuriating and she thinks way too much of herself, but I love it. It just makes me want to get her in bed even more. Just imagining her sweet hazel eyes looking up at me while she swallows me in that sweet caramel mouth of hers makes me want to go wake her up so we can live out my fantasy.

Instead, I will continue my plan today and show her the best Kumasi has to offer. The Manhyia Palace Museum will give her a great lesson in Ashanti customs and history. Then, my palace in Kumasi will expose her to the seat of our government. The marketplace will give her a chance to see our artisans at work, and I have a surprise for her there. I want her to fall in love with this place so she will build her schools here and stay. Well, at least stay for a year after the launch to ensure the implementation is smooth. The future of my people depends on well-educated youth. I cannot afford to mess this up. Damn! I should have kept it 100 percent professional. A romantic entanglement is a harbinger for heartbreak, and breaking her heart is the surest way to run her and her school network back to Atlanta. This situation is stressful.

The running stream outside my window always calms me down. I call this home Bonbiri because of its location near the former Bonbiri game reserve. When I want to think without the noise and distractions of Kumasi or Accra, I come here and bring only my cook Akua and my right hand, Senya.

"Your majesty, I have breakfast ready downstairs if you and your guest are ready." I know that sweet voice anywhere. I grab the robe by my bed and head to the door.

I am not hungry, but I know Akua will not take no for an answer. She is like a second mother to me. She has served my family for over

60 years. My mother passed away 25 years ago, when I was only twelve.

"Auntie." I open the door and usher her in. "You speak as if you expected my guest to be in here with me." I close the door behind her.

"Well, I saw you two kissing last night as I was passing to my room, and I just thought..."

"Auntie, were you spying on me?!" I feign offense.

Already that one kiss is causing mischief. I keep my romantic interests separate from my home life. Away from Akua. Hopefully, Ella and I can go back to a friendly business relationship and pretend the kiss never happened.

She laughs at my expense. "You know I don't sleep. And I still see everything. Well, if she's not here, where is she staying?"

I nod to my right. "The river room."

"Ahh OK, well, I will set the table for breakfast in an hour." She grabs the side of my face with her hands. "I'm even making your favorite fish stew for lunch!" She turns to leave but changes her mind.

"Osei Kofi..." She pauses for effect, and I straighten to attention. Few have the privilege of calling me by my full name. Those who do use it only for serious conversation. "Tell me more about this woman you invited here. She's staying for a month?" Ahh, the old woman wants information. I knew my favorite fish stew at one o' clock in the afternoon would cost me something.

I playfully narrow my eyes at her. "Hmmm. You know a lot of information for someone that does not spy." I told no one but Senya of my plans. If he is Akua's source, I will have words for him this morning.

"I accidentally overheard you on the phone a few weeks ago, giving some directions to Senya about a woman named Ella. I believe you told him to ensure her transportation and that she should have comfortable accommodations for her monthlong stay? Where is she from that you need to accommodate her for a month?" Akua raises her right eyebrow as if to say, *gotcha!*

"She is an American." I say nothing more and we reenter my

bedroom. Her expression informs me that I am in for a lecture. I take a seat in a nearby chair.

"Kofi Ajyei, how long do you plan to act like you only have business interests with the American?"

"Excuse me?"

She is digging too deeply. I have no desire to share with Akua that I have replayed Ella Jenkins' TED Talk, "What About the Children," at least 100 times since I Googled her school network. The woman is extraordinary. She is a bronze goddess that speaks like a warrior. Obsessively, I watch her full lips and dream of possessing them with my own. I will admit to no one that I stroke myself watching her give that damn speech over and over again. I will not share that my passion has ruined more than a few sets of satin sheets. I combust from the intensity of her eyes and the bounce of her hips when she glides across the stage. For 30 minutes, she commands an army and I, a king, want to be her soldier.

"Senya told me about your ride out here last night. The Kofi Ajyei I know would have driven her straight to that Westin and been done with it. You avoid drama like the plague. Yet, you still brought her here. The place you come to escape drama. I don't have to remind you that if you get involved with this woman, there will be trouble. You will marry an Ashanti. Our queen should be of pure blood. Running around and giving that young woman false hopes will be an unnecessary disruption."

I stand. "I assure you, Auntie, I know more than anyone the expectation that I marry Ashanti. However, no law says that I have to." I soften my voice and take her hands. "Auntie, I promise it is just one kiss. I do not even know why I did it, but it will be the last kiss between us. I am interested in nothing more than protecting Ashanti business interests." She does not look convinced. I don't want her worried or, worse yet, curious. "Her name is Ella Jenkins, and she is the founder and chief executive officer of Revolution Academies. Her network of schools secured a position on the UN's list of approved school vendors. Kumasi will select her network to fulfill our Promise Grant."

"Ah, yes! The grant to build free public schools in town."

"And don't forget the surrounding villages," I add.

Akua's face alights with joy. "I'm so glad you are determined to serve all Ashanti and not just the rich. Your name will be praised long after your works."

"I do not need praise, Auntie. Just a fully educated people."

Akua means well. She herself was from the bush and made her way to the city. She impressed my grandmother 60 years ago when she showed up with a fresh bowl of rice and the same fish stew she will prepare today. "I'm keeping her close because I do not want too many outside influences on Ella as she plans our schools' launch."

"You've already decided to go with her network?"

"Well yes, she's the best."

"Does she know this?"

"That she's the best?" I arch my eyebrow and give a half smile. "She has founded the most public charter schools throughout the urban cities in the U.S., and with the highest success rate."

"No." Auntie does not engage my silliness. "Does she know that you have already chosen her network, and that she really did not need to come here to win your favor?"

"Of course not. But in all fairness, she does not seem to know much about Kumasi, let alone our people. I think we can both get a better feel for each other's vision if she breathes in African air and understands our ways before finalizing her proposal. Plus, I do not need her to launch from Atlanta and come by once or twice a year. I need her here at least a year to ensure the schools get proper implementation. So, Ghana must woo her."

"Will Ghana woo her, or will you?"

The question floors me. Will Ghana woo her, or will I? Sometimes, I feel like I am Ghana. My whole life has been planned out for me and I lead 11 million Ghanaians. But I am more than Ghana, and Ella may need more than Ghana to stay. But I am not sure I am ready to share anything else other than my homeland with her. If it takes any part of me to woo her, it will be a lost cause. Auntie knows that.

"Auntie! Do not be daft." I start to rub the back of my neck. My exasperation is on full display. "I just met the woman. The kiss was just a gesture that all men try with beautiful women. I honestly think her schools are what Kumasi needs. She only has to first understand why her school network needs Kumasi. What better place to do that than Bonbiri? I want to show her the real Ghana, not the tourist attractions and gleaming lights of Accra."

My eyes plead with her to let it go. "Auntie, I must shower and dress. Ella and I have a long day in front of us. Please wake Senya as well and let him know to join us for breakfast."

Akua relents. "OK, just be careful. You tend to break hearts without even realizing it. I'd hate for the villages to lose out on an amazing opportunity because of misplaced passion and hurt feelings."

I let the mild scolding stand; she needs to rest. "OK, Auntie, I promise to be good. Now go and take some rest before you serve breakfast. You look tired."

"I think it is me who has tired you." She gives a light chuckle as she shuffles out the door.

When she leaves, I am alone with my thoughts, and her words sit with me. I cannot afford to lose the opportunity to build the best free schools in Kumasi and surrounding Ashanti lands. I invited Ella here on a whim, and I will have to be extra careful not to screw it up, which is what I usually do with women. They always want more than I am willing to give. I never want the emotional responsibility of a relationship. I do not have the time. I am a king that is not yet ready for a queen. I rule an empire of 11 million Ashanti. At this point, all I want is a nice dinner, conversation, and a good shag. Something we both can enjoy. I tell women that. It is fine for about three months, and then it gets stupid.

Women ask too many questions and demand too many answers. They think they have a right to my thoughts and want more and more of my time. Small things start getting left at the palace. Security is shooing a stranger away from palace gates. Games start to be played for which there is no rule book. If it gets really bad, our whole relationship ends up in Ghanaian and British papers. Then I am labeled a "playboy" that uses women. Or as one woman impolitely put it, "*international fuckboi*." The scandals seem like bad dreams, and I always wake up wondering how I got there. After it all ends, I always have one less friend in the world.

Maybe that is just an excuse to not deal with the real reason I push love away. The responsibility of being everything to someone is far too heavy. I learned that lesson early, at 12. I thought a son's love could save my mother from the demons that lurked in her mind, but I failed. It is safer not to be a lifeline. It is much easier not to care.

With Ella, I will keep all of our time and activities mission driven. I will have to crave her from afar. I have no time for love, and she does not strike me as the type to be down for dinner and a good bang. We will change Kumasi together as nothing more than comrades in the fight to educate Ashanti children. Maybe if I am lucky, we will do it as good friends.

Chapter Seven

INSTIGATION

Kofi

*A*fter my shower, I decide to let Ella know about breakfast and our plans for the day. Hopefully, she's not still asleep. I am eager to see her, and that is not good.

As I approach her door, I start to imagine what she looks like lying in her bed. Maybe I will knock, and she will tell me to enter while safely under covers. Or maybe she is just stepping out of the shower and will have to quickly grab a robe. Steam will rise from her skin, and her hair will be damp with dew and perfume.

When I reach her door, I am overtaken by nerves. Is it too early to be at her door? After a couple minutes deliberating, I decide a king can do what he likes in his own home. She is my guest and I need to keep her apprised of our schedule.

I knock and am kept waiting for several minutes when I turn to leave. *Maybe this really was a bad idea.* Just then, she breathlessly answers the door. She is sweating and visibly exerted. When she sees me, she arches her eyebrows and removes an AirPod from her ear. "OH! Good morning, your majesty. I am finishing up a Pilates work-out. Can I help you with something?"

I am at a loss for words. She is a vision in a white sports bra with black leggings. I can see that she is full at the top and bottom, and I want to bury my face between the strong thighs she just finished bending and contorting. Her face is flushed, and her hair is tied in a pile on top of her head. She has lovely high cheekbones, but what really mesmerizes me is her stomach. It is not super muscular, but it is lightly toned. It looks like a region that is soft as a pillow, connecting her supple breasts to her waist. I want to rest my hand there and rub back and forth before kissing a trail down into her valley.

"Your majesty?" She interrupts my naughty thoughts. I hope she did not notice me drooling all over her like a young teenager who just entered puberty.

"We get started with our days early: breakfast is promptly at eight in the morning every day. Don't be late and be ready for the day," I say gruffly. "We have a long day ahead of us."

She looks at me intensely, like she is weighing something on her mind before speaking. "Why don't you come in and tell me what the plans are?"

I clear my throat a little too loudly. "Ehh? You want me to enter your room?"

She laughs. "Yes, your majesty, I don't bite. And I'll be sure to avoid your lips."

So, she is thinking about our kiss, too. I wonder if she touched herself last night thinking about my body pressed into hers and my lips in places I have yet to explore. Just the thought that she may have been next door getting herself off at the thought of me while I was getting off at the thought of her makes me nearly come inside my damn robe. I should have gotten dressed before coming over.

"Thank you for the assurances." As soon as I walk into the room, I notice she has an outfit made up of silk. That will not do. "You know Ella, you may want to rethink your outfit for today. Silk does not breathe well in African heat."

She looks over at her outfit and smirks. "My best friend Maya warned me of that. I should have listened. Hopefully some of the things she sent over will arrive tomorrow and I will have more choices. I do believe I have a linen dress that will work."

As she starts to move toward her closet, I am overtaken by her lovely citrus scent. "You smell like a peachy orange. I've never smelled a scent like that before."

She stops to turn to me and blushes. "It's a custom fragrance. You have a good nose, King; it is peach and orange flavors, but also with a hint of vanilla."

I move closer to her without thinking. She is magnetic. "Well, your scent is intoxicating. May I ask a favor of you?"

She turns her head to the side and gives me a look of intrigue. "It depends on what it is, King."

I chuckle. "Nothing that grand. I know we talked about this before, but I need you to stop with the 'your majesty' or 'king.' Kofi is fine."

"AH! I see. Well, to be honest...your majesty," she continues cautiously, "I'd like to keep a level of formality between us as we work out how my organization can serve your people. You're a king, aren't you? I'll address you as one as a sign of respect."

I needlessly grab her hand and begin to circle her palm. "So...you respect me?"

She looks down at my thumb working its magic inside her hand before looking me directly in the eye. "I do."

"But you do not respect my wishes?"

"Not that one."

I smile and release her hand before walking over and sitting in an armchair. "Well, how about this one. Now that you have stayed here at my home and see how incredibly comfortable it is, why don't you continue to stay here for the duration of your trip."

She walks over to me and opens her mouth to protest, but I politely shush her before continuing. "You now know I am a perfect gentleman and that we are not alone. It will be easier to conduct our business and daily outings if we have the same home base. I promise you will not get better food and hospitality than Akua's."

She leans against the end table next to my chair and eyes me curiously. "Outings?"

"Yes, outings. I plan to show you the best Ghana has to offer. I want you to meet the community and discover what makes the Ashanti heartbeat. Then you can truly propose a school plan that will meet our needs. Today, I plan to take you to the Manhyia Palace Museum to learn some history. Then Manhyia Palace, which is the seat of Ashanti government and my home in Kumasi. We will also visit the marketplace to start putting faces to your plans. How does that sound?"

She slowly nods her head. "That sounds manageable. However, we will have to go another day. I have plans to meet with the Tarkwa village chief's representative today."

I abruptly shift in my seat. Her answer throws me for a loop. The Tarkwa chief is Kwabena Owusu. I definitely don't want her spending time with any of the Owusus alone. They could ruin everything, especially his daughter, Abena. They are also rumored to be crooks. Their business dealings are not always proper. Nevertheless, I try to sound calm, but I fail. "Who's the representative you're meeting with?" My voice booms.

She shifts in her seat. Raising my voice has made her uncomfortable. I must do a better job hiding my displeasure. "The chief's son, Thomas Owusu. He reached out to Adom. He sounded excited about what Revolution Academies could do for Tarkwa in particular. He invited me to the village today."

Of course. My cousin and Thomas were friendly in school. I, on the other hand, have never trusted Thomas. I'm not exactly fond of my cousin Adom, either. However, if he's her friend, I will manage. I do wonder if they were ever more than friends.

"You're not here for 24 hours and you already have a date?"

She smirks. "It's not a date. I only have 30 days to put together a proposal that will convince you I'm the one you should choose. I need to gather as much information as possible."

I nod. Foolish woman. She is spending time with my subordinate's son, when she could spend all of her time with the only man able to give her what she wants. "I think since I'm the one that makes the final decision, it is keener to spend time with me and not the son of a chief that has no real decision-making power."

Her nostrils flare. "Are you insinuating I don't know how to conduct my business? I ensure you I have opened new schools in 44 communities. It's not just about winning over the man in charge. The community has to also invest."

I raise my hands in surrender. I hate that I always seem to offend her. "I mean no offense. I'm just disappointed. I was excited about today. But we have all month to explore Kumasi. Just be careful. Thomas is no gentleman. He's a slimy piece of jackal manure."

She laughs. "A piece of what?"

She's not used to my way of cursing. "I do not use actual curse words —I find them to be too crass for my station. Instead, I create my own."

Ella nods. "I see, *well*, I'll keep your warning in mind. He can't be too bad if Adom is friends with him."

I decide to not delve into the subject of my cousin and his judgement in choosing acquaintances. "Very well. Please look at your calendar and let me know when you have time for me."

She exhales a breath. "Of course. I will do so with all haste, your majesty."

Now she's mocking me. The little minx! "Wonderful." I lift from the chair, feeling the need to give her space and privacy. "I'll let you start your day. About my request: will you stay here for the rest of your time in Kumasi?" I touch her arm, passing by toward the door.

She follows me. "Yes, I'll stay as long as it makes sense."

I pause at the door and look deep into her eyes. "Ella, you're the first thing that has made sense here in a long time. I fear that could last forever."

I lean toward her and take her into a kiss that makes everything around me explode into a burst of stars. I find her mouth to be an even more willing participant than it was last night. I take my time and let the tip of my tongue brush her bottom lip, teasing the corners of her mouth with small nips in between. She tastes like a ripe peach, and I grab the back of her head with a strong but gentle push to capture even more of her mouth.

When I hear small moans of pleasure, I lose myself. I wrap her legs around me and carry her to the door, pressing her body up against it. Now I have access to her whole body, and we are both grateful. I gently start to rub her nipples through the thin sports bra, feeling as they harden between my fingers. She grabs my hands and roughly massages her breasts, commanding my movements. Another moan escapes her throat and I happily obey. As I repeatedly roll my hands over her taut breasts, I keep control of the kiss until I am ready to pass the baton to her.

When I do, she takes it with ease, licking my neck before greedily riding me through her now-damp workout pants and my opening robe. She is chasing a release that I am more than glad to give her. I try to focus on something else, because I refuse to be the type of man that shoots cum all over her pants against a door. As she said earlier, I am a king; I will have my release in my shower as I replay this moment over and over again.

That, however, is easier said than done. All I can focus on is her soft breasts, her full ass, and the softest lips I have ever kissed. After what seems like hours of pleasure, she begins to collapse into me, falling against my hard body and finally catching the release she needs.

When she comes down, all I hear is my name, "Kofi," fall from her lips. I gently drop my hands and start the process of physically letting her go. My ending kisses on her cheeks and forehead signal to her that it is time to climb down, and she opens her eyes. She looks overtaken and sated—a look I decide will become her natural state of being while with me. I want her thinking about me making her cum while she is with that jackal today.

As I leave her room, I call over my shoulder, "Remember to switch your outfit for a fabric that breathes. The African heat is unforgiving."

She smirks before closing the door behind me. I hear her as she walks away from the door. "Yes, your majesty."

Chapter Eight

ADHESION

Ella

I've been in Ghana for a week, and all I have accomplished is an increasing attraction to Kofi.

Since our first kiss on the night I arrived, our craving for each other has grown every day. That kiss was electric and shocked my sleeping lady parts awake. Once I realized it was tugging at my heart too, I broke away from him. I felt myself falling into something I am not able to control. I even asked him to stay at Bonbiri that night. Suddenly, I did not want him far.

What is this man doing to me? Giving into these cravings is both incredibly stupid and just plain incredible. I barely know him, but he feels like home. I'm here to secure a multi-year contract, not an international affair. Not that he would know that. None of my actions have said I'm here to launch schools for his nation's children and then leave. Instead, they're saying, "please, take me as your lover." I continue to stay in his home, where I allow him to kiss me whenever he's inclined. Lately, we've set up pointless meetings that end with us dry humping against doors, walls, and chairs. Whatever —I am grateful for the long-overdue orgasms, no matter how they are achieved.

I'm very aware he might think I'm another one of his rumored concubines. He probably won't even give me the contract; West Africans can be notoriously close-minded about women and their sexuality. He was absolutely right about Thomas Owusu being handsy. I spent my first full day in Africa dodging his advances as he showed me around the village. He was relentless.

I spent the rest of the week avoiding Kofi's plans to take me on a daytrip to Kumasi. I know if we spend an entire day together it is going to end in sex, something we will not be able to ignore. I've literally visited every public and private school in the Ashanti region to dodge him. Now, on day nine, I'm out of excuses.

Kofi presents as the king of respectability and control, but I know better. He always finds an excuse to touch me. He gets close enough for the tension to turn into smoldering kisses. He comes to my room at 7 a.m. every morning to invite me to breakfast and check if I need anything. He has servants for that. The more I think about it, this is all a bit too much. Today, I am reestablishing our relationship with the proper amount of distance. No personal conversations, no being in the room alone, and no sleeping next door. I'll have to renege on my favor and book a hotel room. It's the only way.

It was the same with Marcus. In the beginning, we couldn't keep our hands off each other. I met Marcus as a 21-year-old with limited sexual experience. I had one fumbling experience at nineteen with Adom, and we decided to never try that shit again. My parents are pastors, so my upbringing was pretty religious. I was taught that abstinence is the way, the truth, and the light. When he assured me I wouldn't burn in hell for sex, it opened a whole new world to me. I was devoted to him. He was smart, arrogant, and a natural leader. I was like a moth to a flame. He controlled my career and social life. He told me what to major in, he talked me into going to law school with him...he even managed to have our first jobs at the same firm. Everything centered around him. I vowed to never do that dumb shit again. I've been doing only what I want ever since then. I'm not giving that up for anyone, not even a king who makes me feel like I'm freefalling. His touch makes me melt, and I lose my whole mind as soon as he calls my name. But it's time to focus on the business at hand; the foolishness has to stop.

After my shower, I start to ponder what I will wear for today's events. We'll be in the center of Kumasi for most of the day, and I'd like to make a good impression on the community. I'm glad I took the time to unpack my suitcases and hang my clothes. I settle on a thin cotton kente sundress, a pair of bright purple wedges, and giant 14-karat gold hoops for my ears. It's too hot for all this hair, so I decide to put it up in a bun. My curls hang in the front and frame my face. I'm pleased with my reflection in the mirror. I opt for a light tinted mois-turizer, blush, and bright pink lips. Anything more will surely melt in the African sun.

I put a few essentials in my LV backpack and head downstairs for breakfast. As I approach the kitchen, I hear loud and happy voices.

"Auntie, have you managed to get Kofi to admit to his crush on the American?" I hear Senya tease. I have not seen him much since I arrived. He took me out the second day for me to get some essentials and a cell phone that will work out here without enormous usage fees. Since then, he's been scarce. "You should have seen how accom-modating our king was the first night she arrived! He even got *out of the car* and begged the American to come to his home."

"Enough, Senya," I hear Kofi shoot off. "Why have I not fired you after all these years? Nothing but foolishness leaves your mouth."

"Oh, hush," I hear a sweet voice cluck. "You keep him because he's your brother. Since the moment Senya showed up as a hungry little boy at our kitchen door, you have been inseparable. Senya, it is foolish to talk about crushes. The king knows he has no time for such foolishness. It would be a disaster for our kingdom. No American woman will turn our Asantehene's head."

Instantly, I want to turn on my heel and fake sick for the day. Every morning, Akua greets me with a death stare and leaves while Kofi and I share breakfast. I can only imagine what she must think of me. I come into her nephew's house under the pretense of a business deal, and I'm kissing him before I rest my head the first night.

Instead, I take a deep breath, put my big girl panties on, and stalk into the kitchen, head held high.

"Hello, everyone!" I sing the words as I pass by the seat Kofi is pulling out for me. "I hope everyone is having a wonderful morning." I head straight to Kofi's Auntie Akua. I will not allow her to ignore me today. She is standing against the stove. "Good morning, Akua."

She looks at me like I have two heads, and neither one particularly pleases her. "Hello," she stoically replies. But I am undeterred.

"I've heard you be referred to as 'auntie'...I didn't know you were Kofi's aunt as well as his cook."

She chuckles. "I'm his Auntie, not his aunt." She turns and begins to place a divine-smelling stew into a bowl along with some plantains for me.

"Oh! What's the difference?"

Senya graciously answers. "We call all older women that are close as family or serve our families 'auntie.' It's a term of endearment. We rarely use the word 'aunt' in the sense that Americans do."

"Oh, I see." I feel out of place. Akua's stare makes me feel like I crashed a party no one invited me to. Except Kofi did invite me, and after this exchange, I cannot for the life of me figure out why. Right now, I wish I were sitting happy with my full complimentary breakfast at the hotel overlooking Labadi Beach. I clearly know nothing about him or his people. I should have prepared more.

Akua continues. "I don't expect you to know our customs after a little over a week in Ghana. You're from an entirely different world."

Is Akua throwing shade? It sounds like she is not interested in serving me anything but a flight back to Atlanta. But why? A hand touches the small of my back, and a rush of heat hits between my thighs. Kofi has come to guide me back to the seat he originally pulled out for me. *This is what I get for not taking the seat he pulled out earlier*. I am grateful for the save.

Kofi takes the seat next to mine. "That is why Ella is here, Auntie.

For me to teach her everything she needs to know. When I finish with her, she will practically be Ashanti." His eyes never leave my lips as he speaks. His erotic stare makes me question what method he's contemplating for my Ashanti conversion. I can't resist smiling back. *I'm intrigued.*

Akua walks from the stove and places my bowl in front of me. "No one can practically be Ashanti, your majesty. It's not something you practice. Either you are or you are not." Senya chuckles at Akua's words.

Now that was definitely a jab. "You know, I'm not that hungry, your majesty. If you and Senya are finished, I'm ready when you are."

Akua looks directly at me with an icy glower. "They have not finished eating because they are gentlemen and waited for you to come downstairs to eat. You awake so much later than we do. You know hotels have wake-up calls to help with that." That's it! I'm not going to a hotel. I'm staying here just to irritate her. Plus, if I leave, she will think she has run me out.

I continue talking to Kofi as I rise from my seat. "Well, please eat. I'll take a walk around the grounds."

Kofi rises and begins to follow me. "I'm not that hungry, either. We should be on our way. We have many events and limited time." He turns his glance to Senya. A quick nod commands him to abandon his plate. "Auntie, we will be eating all of our meals out today. Please take this day to rest."

Akua looks completely dejected. "But I am making peanut butter soup and chicken for lunch!"

Kofi goes over to kiss her cheek. "I know, but I will eat it tomorrow. I promise." Akua gives him a pitiful look.

I almost feel bad for taking her boys from her. It's obvious she lives to feed them and showers them with the type of love only a mother can give. But then I remember how she came for my throat a moment earlier and decide she'll live.

Once we're in the car, Kofi is quiet. His mind is elsewhere, and I decide not to disturb him. Who knows the thoughts of a king? He looks as if the weight of 11 million people is on his mind. The ride isn't long, but I nap anyway. Twenty minutes later, we arrive at a beautiful structure with the sign *'Manhyia Palace Museum'* out front. The moment we arrive, Kofi perks up. He hops out the truck and walks over to open my door.

"Come, Ella." He offers his hand and I take it. "I am excited to show you who we were and are as a people."

Once my feet hit the ground, his hand automatically moves to the small of my back. It is a possessive move that I like. Marcus used to do the same move, but it always felt constricting. With Kofi, it feels freeing. "I'm eager to learn, your majesty."

He smiles. "Please call me Kofi."

I smirk. "I will not." Teasing him about this point of concern has quickly become my favorite pastime.

He turns to face me. He is so close our noses and pelvises touch. "Oh yes, your promise, but you know you broke that promise a few minutes later. Remember?"

I blush. I am in the middle of West Africa, in the arms of a king, blushing! Who am I right now?! "Yes, your majesty, I definitely remember, but I was under the influence of an incredible orgasm."

He chuckles. "Oh, is that so?" His eyes change from playful to dark storms of lust.

"I will remember that you cannot be trusted to keep your promises when I put you under my spell." Kofi looks around cautiously to ensure we are alone before he kisses the tip of my nose with a chaste peck. He steps back, turns, and reaches behind for my hand. Once our hands touch, Kofi steals another quick glance and winks. "Come, Ella, let's go inside."

Chapter Nine

PROGRESSION

Ella

The Manhyia Palace Museum is an old royal residence which has been converted into the Ashanti cultural center.

As we walk hand in hand to the entrance, I spot two marble lions flanking the porch and chuckle to myself, remembering my *Coming to America* comments from last week. Kofi has to admit that West Africans use lions to decorate quite a bit. He looks at me curiously, but I decide not to share the source of my glee. He didn't take the jokes well the first time.

Once inside, Kofi is the ultimate tour guide. I see a menagerie of animals the Asantehenes of the past kept on the grounds, and amazing plants indigenous to the area. Kofi names each plant as well as its medicinal qualities and importance to his people. I am impressed and slightly turned on. His voice has the weight of a Ghanaian king. The British voice coverup from his schooling days disappears when he talks about the Ashanti.

"Do you know that my royal surname is Asante?" He leads me to a bench, and we take a seat. The bench is small and forces our thighs to touch. It's hard to focus on the cultural lesson.

"No, I did not. Is that where your title stems from?"

He smiles. "The name signifies that I am in the royal lineage. It's actually a common name for those with any blood connections to the royal line. For example, it is also my mother's family name. Though our families are connected by members that are like six or seven times removed." He chuckles. "I thought my title might be easier for you to pronounce now that you know the base word, Asante."

"Asante-hene," I say it proudly. "You're right. Except, it seems most people don't call you that?"

He nods. "Yes, that's my ceremonial title. Most call me 'King' or 'Your majesty.' Other chiefs will often call me chief, because I am essentially their chief and the only one that outranks them. I often-times refer to myself that way also."

"Adom was the one that told me to address you as 'your majesty' and not Asantehene. He advised that no one calls you that." Kofi tenses at the sound of his cousin's name.

"How did you come to know Adom?"

"Of course you know Adom went to Morehouse, the male histori-cally Black college in Atlanta? Well, I attended the female histori-cally Black college Spelman, across the street. Every year, the two schools hold a brother-sister exchange during the first week of orien-tation. They line us up and whoever ends up beside you is your brother or sister. I ended up next to Adom."

Kofi looks puzzled. "So, what does the pairing actually mean?"

"It means that someone cares for you and has your back, without romantic interests, while you're in college and afterwards. Like a real sibling."

Kofi lifts his head and gives a skeptical look. "So, you mean these brothers and sisters never end up in bed together?"

I laugh. "Of course they do, but it's not as common as you think. It's actually kind of frowned upon. It's good to just have a platonic friend that will always be there for you."

Kofi's demeanor turns suspicious. "Did you and Adom sleep together?"

This conversation is starting to cross a line, but I don't want him thinking I've slept with his cousin. I also don't want to admit why I care what he thinks at all. "Adom and I slept together one drunken night sophomore year and never tried again." I laugh at the memory. "I don't even remember it. It is like it never happened. Plus, he's always been infatuated with my best friend Maya."

He cocks his head slightly to the side. "Maya?"

"Yes, Dr. Maya Taylor. Ironically, she's a professor of African studies. She also prepped me quite a bit for this trip. She's a true beauty. She modeled in Paris for six seasons. Adom has always thought the sun rises and sets on her. I think she likes him, too. They fight like cats and dogs. Yet, they always want to be around each other. It's very frustrating."

"Hmmm..." Kofi weighs my words before speaking. "I asked Adom about you before you came. He seemed very possessive, like you belonged to him. He would not give me much information. Granted, we have not talked much over the past 15 years, but still, it was odd."

I shrug. "Yeah, he does that with most men that show interest in me. It's just what he does. He never thinks anyone is good enough."

"Well, I am the best." He reaches out and strokes my hair before twirling a curl. "He should be pleased; I am definitely a better choice than him. You must be the reason he insisted on staying in Atlanta for school. Our grandfather wanted him at Oxford with me."

I teasingly bat his hand away. "I told you we are just friends. Are you jealous, King?"

"Always." He says it a little too quickly. I decide to change the subject to something lighter.

"How is it you and Adom are first cousins with such opposite complexions? It surprised me when I saw a picture of you."

He laughs. "People always asked us that in boarding school. To be honest, they were always more shocked about Adom's light-skinned complexion than my ebony skin. They expected a man from

Ghana to have black skin. However, what they did not know is that our grandmother is Egyptian."

My eyes widen. Kofi and Adom are part Egyptian. Kofi's beautiful body is the full African continent in the flesh. "Really! That is fascinating. Isn't it odd for your grandfather to have married a non-Ashanti woman?

He nods. "Well, as chief he had more latitude than my paternal grandfather had as king. He chose who he loved, and our people loved her. At least, that is what I'm told. I never met her," He pauses. "She died giving birth Adom's mother." He averts his eyes. He is sad. I can tell he misses a grandmother he never met. He grieves the missed opportunity. I shift the conversation again.

I nod and reach out for his hand. "So, what about your love life? Any friends, girlfriends, friends with benefits?"

He shifts uncomfortably in the seat. "I am sure you have seen the tabloids."

"Yes, but now I want to hear the truth, from you."

"Oh, it is mostly true. I do not have time for relationships, and I'm no good at them. My reign is what is most important. I want to add to the honor of the Ashanti. I have 11 million people to take care of. I do not see how a significant other can fit into this life."

So, he's not a fan of relationships, either. That's one thing we have in common. "I understand. I don't have time for relationships, either. But unlike me, aren't you bound by custom to produce an heir?"

He sighs and rubs his hands over his face. "Yes, but I have time. I am only 37. Eventually I will enter into a marriage and fulfill my duty to our people."

He sees marriage as a duty, not an act of love. How romantic.

"May I ask you one more question?"

He stands and places his hands in his pockets before leaning on the bench. "Sure."

"Have you ever had your heart broken? Or do you only break them?"

He pauses. "Yes, my mother broke my heart, but I do not want to talk about that."

OK. Mommy issues. I'll leave that alone.

He looks at me carefully. "What about you? Who is the man that has made you close your heart?"

I laugh. "It's that obvious, huh?"

He laughs and nods his head. "Instead of staying with me at a royal residence, you tried to walk to Accra from the side of a road." He pauses for effect. "In a country you know nothing about. I figure there is a story that begins and ends with an idiot."

"His name was Marcus. We were college sweethearts. He was my first love. But as I grew up, my priorities changed. The superficial goals he held so dear were ridiculous to me. I could not care about vacation homes and Range Rovers when illiteracy runs so rampant in urban communities. That's why I started securing funding and building excellent schools. I appreciate nice things, but they don't define me. Anyway, long story short, Marcus proposed with a ridiculously expensive three-carat solitaire from Cartier at my annual Eradicate Child Illiteracy fundraiser. Honestly, I was uncomfortable with his overt display of wealth at a charity event, but I accepted. Two weeks later, I found him screwing his secretary. *What a cliché.* I refused to speak to him for weeks."

Kofi's face transforms into complete confusion. "Wait! He proposed to you in front of all those people, just to cheat on you two weeks later. What did you do?"

"Well, I refused to see him at first, and he didn't take that well. Suddenly, I, the woman he professed to want to spend the rest of his life with, was a selfish whore that never knew how to properly make love or take care of him anyway. You know, what hurt most was that I secretly always thought those things. Back then I never thought I was good enough for him. I was constantly waiting for the other shoe to drop. Apparently, it was a cheap shoe named Keisha that gave him his coffee every morning along with a blow job."

Kofi nods. "I am sorry that happened to you. He was an idiot."

He sits back on the bench next to me. *He's too close.* "I knew any man that would let you go had to be. Do you feel you are fully healed form that experience?"

I pause to think. "I'm definitely over him. But the experience as a whole changed me forever. I'm never sharing my life on that level again. It's too painful to unravel yourself from a partnership of that magnitude when it all crashes and burns." I laugh. "You know, I think you reminded me of him too much at first. You're both alpha males, gorgeous, and high-handed. But..."

He stares at me intensely. "But we're different?"

I nod. "Yes. There's an empathy and need to care about others that makes you vastly different."

He offers his hand to me and I take it to stand up. "Well, any man that broke your heart is a fool. You called your best friend a true beauty. I cannot imagine a beauty that surpasses you." He kisses the back of my knuckles before softly rubbing them as we begin to walk. "You are the most beautiful woman I ever laid eyes on. So much so, I used to obsessively watch your TED Talk presentation and stare. I listened, too. Your ideas about education are brilliant. Your work is commendable."

There's no way I'm making it back to America without having sex with this man. He talks and looks way too good. He's trouble. Maybe if we just give in and do it once, we can get it out of our systems.

He leads me back inside the museum to see wax figures that are set up to reenact scenes of governance from the past. We feed peacocks in the indoor courtyards. He even allows me to touch and hold some of the most precious Ashanti artifacts. It's a privilege most don't ever have.

We walk out of the museum talking and laughing in an easy manner. A total shift from the anger of our first night together.

Kofi squeezes my hand. "I hope you enjoyed the museum, Ella. It is just a taste of the rich Ashanti culture and heritage."

"I did, your majesty. Where are we headed next?"

"My home in Kumasi, the new Manhyia Palace. Lunch is waiting for us there. It is a short walk from here."

I look down at my watch, thinking it could not possibly be lunch time. I'm shocked to see it is 2:30.

"OH my. I didn't even realize we spent our whole morning here. It certainly hasn't felt like five hours."

He rubs the center of my back as we continue to walk. "That is because time flies when having fun with beautiful company." My heart skips a beat. He drops gems like that constantly. When we visited the gold room earlier and I remarked how beautiful each piece was, he reminded me that their beauty did not rival mine. Maybe I can relax and just be with him. I don't have to be his queen. I don't want to be. Maybe I can just enjoy his sweet and loving nature while I am in Ghana. *Maybe I will be able to enjoy his body, too.* I start to daydream before I remember I'm here to secure a contract, not a lover. *Back to business, Ella!*

When we arrive at the modern palace, lunch is jollof rice and ground nut stew. The spices and flavors are so delicious that I eat two servings. I pat my bloated belly over the thin cotton fabric covering it. "Hats off to the chef. This is delicious."

Kofi looks pleased. "Glad you enjoy it. I like feeding you." He leans back in his chair and studies me for a second, raking his eyes over my body. "Tell me, Ella: who feeds you at home, in Atlanta?"

"Ahem." I almost choke on the water I am drinking. "Excuse me?"

"Who feeds you at home?"

"Your majesty, I live alone. I feed myself. I'm actually a rather good cook."

He chuckles, but it feels facetious. "Oh, I am certain you are, but what about your body? Who feeds that work of art? Who satisfies you sexually in Atlanta? I know you avoid relationships. But like me, you have needs. How do you meet them? Do you touch yourself, or is there someone to do that for you?"

I place my glass down on the table and push my chair back. How dare he ask such a sexual question? I can't afford for him to not take me seriously.

"That is a highly inappropriate question." I glare at him without blinking once. "What makes you think you can talk under my clothes?"

"Inappropriate!" He guffaws before standing and slowly walking over to my side of the table. He stands behind me and leans into my ear so that only I can hear him, and not the servants starting to clear our meal. "You don't deem me inappropriate when I allow you to dry hump my dick so your neglected body gets some release."

I turn around in my chair and face him head on. The nerve! He is infuriating and so full of himself. How could I ever think he was worth daydreaming about? I stand up. "Though I thank you for the service..." I begin before he interrupts me by placing a finger on my lips. It is wildly erotic and eviscerating all at once.

"No thank you is necessary. I'll call you my queen as I give you only the pleasure a king can provide you. A pleasure I hope to repeat over and over again. Making you come is my new favorite thing. Next time I want to feel that waterfall over my hard, naked dick or in my mouth so I can swallow your pleasure whole. Your panties continually steal that privilege from me."

I'm so wet. I can feel the moisture pool between my legs. My body clenches tight and betrays me with every wicked word he speaks. Yet my mind is in a rage. No man has ever talked plainly to me about sexual acts. I've always been taught that men don't talk like that to ladies, especially not those they respect. "I'm not your queen," I hiss. "And you certainly aren't my king!"

"Ha-ha," he laughs. "Then why do you insist on calling me such? You have some serious hang-ups if you can't talk about the things your body obviously wants. It's just sex. And with me it will be incredible sex. That *is* what we both crave, is it not? I tried to ignore it, but I think we both know until we address it, we won't get any other work done."

I am outdone and start to speak louder than I planned to. "I call you 'king' because I respect you and your role. I admire the work you do for your people. A respect you clearly don't return judging by how you talk to me. I will never be your whore." I spit out the last word like a bullet and hit the target. His face changes quickly from amusement, to shock, and then finally pain. But what is he pained about? He isn't the one being propositioned like a concubine.

"But I am not interested in anything but a business relationship, Kofi Ajyei, and from now on, I'll make sure you understand that. Now, if you'll excuse me, I need some air."

He doesn't move or follow behind me as I walk out of the dining area. His servants act as if I am invisible. I find the first open door and stomp outside. I am seething with hurt. I can't exactly figure out why, though. I like the way he talks to me, and I did appreciate the much-needed release my body received from our make-out sessions over this past week. None of that was a lie. He also told me in the garden how much he admires my work. He respects me. I know that. I think what really gets to me is the honest answer to his earlier question about who feeds me. *No one.*

My body is not being fed at home. I'm lonely and broken-hearted over a breakup from three years ago, and that's pathetic. He's the first man I've allowed to touch me in years. I don't want him to know how pitiful my personal life really is.

Chapter Ten

ASCENSION

Ella

When the African sun starts to overtake me, I reenter the palace to cool off.

I am not ready to face Kofi yet. I made quite the scene. I decide to walk around the palace. Hopefully, the guards won't shoot me for touring the palace without him.

The more I walk around the palace, the larger it feels. It's beautiful. The hallways never seem to end; there are endless closed doors. I wonder what's behind them, but I dare not open one. That's a clear violation of privacy.

Soon, I feel lost. I start to regret going off on my own; the palace is empty and vast. It is full of secrets I will never be privy to. I start to get spooked. Then I feel him. His breath is on my ear and his hands are around my waist. My body presses against him too close but not close enough.

"Are you lost, Ella?" he whispers.

I want to explain. I want to tell him I was embarrassed at his earlier question and not disrespected. I want to apologize for going off half-cocked. I want to tell him that I didn't mean to snoop around. That I generally don't invade people's privacy. I don't normally traipse through strangers' homes. I want to plead my case so he won't think I'm crazy. I want him to make my body shudder and quake with his touch.

Before I can start my defense, my back is against a wall. His palms are on either side of my head, and he leans his strong, long body over mine. His body skims mine, not quite touching me but ready to do so whenever I say the word. He looks at me and his smoky eyes are liquid pools of dark lust. His stare sets my entire body aflame. I know then that there is no way I am leaving this palace without being thoroughly and splendidly sexed up and laid down. I feel my desire sweat from every pore on my body. It is so palpable it has its own scent.

He sighs and lets out a sharp breath before whispering onto my lips, "What do you want, Ella?"

"You," I pant.

He moves to my neck and speaks. "I'm here. You have me. What do you want me to do?"

"I want...I want..." I'm tongue-tied. I am so full of heat and filthy thoughts. Then, his body is gone, and he pushes away. I reach out for him and he eludes my grasp. He grabs my hands and begins to rub the inside of my palms. He is driving me mad.

"You have to tell me exactly what you want. Exactly how, where, and when to touch you. Where to lick, where to come. I want your verbal participation at every step of your pleasure."

I can't say it. I have never been sexually forward in my life. Marcus used to feel me out and lead the way. But this is different. This is real seduction. Kofi isn't asking me because he doesn't know—he's asking me because he wants to hear the words.

"I want you to worship my body like I'm your queen."

It's on.

He leans his strong body into mine, pushing me back against the wall. He lifts me and directs me to lift my arms above my head before devouring my mouth, one lip at a time. First, he nibbles and sucks my top lip before paying equal attention to my bottom lip. Then his tongue takes over and explores my mouth thoroughly while his hand begins to massage my left breast. He begins to pull and pinch my nipple until it is hard, straining against the strapless lace bra I have on. After he conquers that nipple, he moves to the next. My hands are all over him. I cannot get over how hard and tight his body is. He is so fit you can bounce a quarter off these abs. All I can think about is my mouth on him exploring every part of his six pack. If this is going to be the only time I get to touch him, I'm making the most of it.

I manage to remove his dashiki before tearing my mouth away from his. I lick a trail from behind his ear, down his neck to the top of his pecks down to his amazing stomach, taking my sweet time to get where I want to go.

"Damn, Ella! You're killing me, love." His endearment nearly unwinds me.

His hands are on the back of my head and neck as I lick down to his waistband. He isn't pushing or guiding me down; he's stroking me like I am his most precious treasure. That makes me want to ravage him. Lucky for me, royalty in West Africa don't wear a lot of hardware on their clothing. There are no belt buckles, buttons, or zippers to contend with. I simply unhook the eyelet at his waist and his linen pants fall to the floor. He is down to a pair of black boxer briefs that look like a second chocolate skin wrapped around the strongest pair of thighs and legs I've ever seen. I run my hands up the back of his legs and caress the back of his thighs while I hungrily drink his body in with my eyes. Finally, I settle on his large and pulsating bulge.

A craving overtakes me and I push my head forward, to graze my teeth over the cloth holding my prize. He tenses and lets out a sharp breath and some inaudible curse. I don't care. I want to see him, all of him. I hook my thumbs around the waistband and look up at him. His eyes are full of desire and longing. He's so vulnerable! I can get anything at this moment, his kingdom for my touch.

"May I, your majesty?" I ask seductively.

"Please do," he answers huskily, still stroking my hair and neck. I can tell he is fevered with lust.

I pull down his boxer briefs, removing the final barrier between me and his dick. It springs forth, huge and fully erect. It is beautiful. Chocolate, thick, and smooth. I reach out and began to slowly pump his base. His hand stills on my neck. When I look up, he is staring at me with a desperate look on his face. "Ella, are you sure you want this?" I stare at him, but I don't answer. Then I continue to pump until a bead of moisture comes to his tip; never taking my eyes off of his, I lick his tip clean of that tart delight before licking the entire length. I am filled with want and take him into my mouth, sucking base to tip and using my hands to help because there is no way I can fit all of him in my mouth. But I am going to try.

I let go and hold the back of his thighs, pushing his length to the back of my throat while he gently nudges my head forward. When I pull back to the tip, he pushes me back down his shaft, starting a rhythm that can only be described as fucking. After four or five pumps, he lets out a primal grunt and swiftly picks me up in his arms. He covers my mouth with his. He steps out of his pants and boxers and carries me to the door of the room we are directly outside of. He pushes open the door and I quickly realize it is a bedroom. He gently places me on the gigantic bed.

"Take your clothes off," he growls, "slowly, because I want to take in every incredible part of you."

I raise up on my knees and reach behind to untie the halter top of my dress. I slowly let the straps fall before shimmying out of the dress. I unhook my bra and let my full double D breasts bounce out. My nipples are at full attention. And so is the king. He doesn't say a word, but the heavy beat of his breathing and flinching of his jaw tells me everything I need to know. He is enjoying the show. I start to turn around on the bed.

"Ella, what are you wearing?" he rumbles in awe.

I look over my right shoulder with a coy smile. My black lace thong does him in, and he is over to me before I can completely turn around.

"I'm sorry, Ella—I need to have you right now, and it's going to be rough."

"Rough suits me just fine. Take me, your majesty."

He pushes me on my back and parts my legs with his knees. "Open those thighs for me." I hesitate; I am not used to being so bare to a lover. "Open wide, baby. Let me see that beautiful pussy. I want to see how wet it is for me."

I obey, feeling as open and exposed as I ever have. He takes me in with his eyes, and I hear a sound at the back of his throat. It is raw desire. He bends his head down and moves my thong over with his teeth, ripping the lace before grabbing my clit with his lips. He does not let go. He sucks and nibbles my bud until I don't even know my name anymore. Then his tongue follows, licking my folds from my backside to the base of my stomach, before returning to the assault on my clit again. Back and forth he goes with hard nibbles and soft licks until I almost burst at the seams. I call his name and my body becomes a waterfall.

Before I can come down from my climax, he flips me over. He hooks his arm around my waist, to pull me up in an all-fours position. He slaps my ass and kisses my back before I hear the familiar sound of a condom ripping. *Where did he get that from?*

"Are you ready, Ella?"

"Yes, please, Kofi, I need to feel you."

He thrusts into me so deeply that I can feel him on all sides of my walls. I've never felt so filled up before. I gasp, not knowing what to do with this new sensation that is overtaking me. He pulls all the way out to his tip and slams back into me again. I fall on my elbows from the sheer force and pace. Then his rhythm picks up and he starts talking me through it. Each slap of his thighs against my ass is a command: *You. Drive. Me. Insane. I. Have. To. Have. Your. Sweet. Pussy. Come. Right. Now. Come. Now!*

I am blind with pleasure. I have never been taken with such intensity.

He keeps his relentless pace. "Give it to me, baby. Come on, baby. I want you to come, Ella. Come all over this royal dick. Tell me you're going to come for your king. Tell me," he rumbles.

"I'm going to...oh...my...God...Kofi!" My body does what he commands, and he pulls my upper body up so that we are aligned from top to bottom as he finishes off inside me.

He joins my orgasm with a roar that sounds like...*a lion*. We sit there for a few minutes trying to catch our breath. He kisses my shoulders and my neck, whispering every sweet word he can in Twi, his native tongue. *Medɔ wo, Ella. M'akoma bɔ ma wo*. I don't know what he is saying, but I know I want to hear it.

When he finally disconnects from me, he lies on his back and draws me closer until I am curled beside him. My head rests on his chest and my leg drapes over his powerful thighs. We don't say anything—we just lie there letting the sun wash over us from the skylights above. At some point I doze off as Kofi strokes my hair, but not before I hear him say, "Now, you're mine."

Shit...I'm screwed...

Chapter Eleven

AFTERGLOW

Kofi

*M*ine. That's what Ella is now.

The feelings are sudden and all-consuming. There's no way I will allow her to leave Ghana now. I hope she knows just how caught-up she is, because I'm not letting her go. The way she gave herself over to me in the hallway was hot. I enjoyed the fight and the making up. She's feral when she gets mad. It makes my whole body stand at attention. I understand the anger is not really towards me. She shut down our earlier conversation about past relationships, but I can tell she's been hurt. That's a damn shame.

She's so sweet. Her body, her eyes, her wit; all of it twists me into knots. But how will I pull this off? This isn't like my other sexual encounters where I screw them and start the countdown to an ending. After the first sexual episode with a woman, I generally start to plan exactly how many events we will attend together and how many trinkets I will need to buy before I can let them down gently. Then I begin planning where we should be when I remind them I'm a king with no desire for a queen or girlfriend, for that matter. That's how I've always conducted my affairs.

Conversely, I'm lying here twitchy and semi-hard, desperately trying to see some kind of future with Ella. I want to lie like this for as many days as she will allow me to be this close to her. She made it clear there's no man in her life, which is a crime. Her sexy ass should be worshipped well and often. However, that's the past, and she's in good hands now. I'll give her the world as long as she wants to explore it with me.

I feel her shift slightly and I sit up on one elbow to support my head while I stare at her. She's tucked comfortably under the sheet with seemingly no cares from the outside world. She's so beautiful. Her toffee lips are taunting me for a kiss. She's sleeping so peacefully it would be a sin to wake her. But I want her again. My dick is a monster, and I can't get him to calm down. I'm already addicted to the way she sounds when I stroke her walls as they collapse around me. Besides, we should get going soon if we're going to make it to dinner and the night market before it closes.

I gently plant kisses all over the side of her face and neck until she stirs awake. She looks up at me with the sweetest smile this side of heaven.

"Hi, Kofi," she whispers while grazing my cheek with the back of her hand. If I wasn't fully erect before, I definitely am now. I smile and arch my eyebrow.

"Oh, so I'm Kofi now? What happened to your insistence on calling me 'your majesty'?" I chuckle.

She grabs a pillow and tries to cover her face in embarrassment, but I remove it and plant more kisses. She rolls her eyes and giggles. "Well, after you've seen all my tids and bits, I think the air of formality has lifted, don't you?"

"Tids and bits!" I exclaim. I gently pull the sheet down and climb over to straddle her, so I have unobstructed access to her beautiful breasts. I was happy to wake up from our nap and see that she was indeed still naked. My move over her is a welcome one; her caramel brown nipples stand and welcome me. She lets her eyes meet mine and follows me as I lean forward to slowly lick the left nipple to feel the hardness against my tongue. I nibble and suck the nipple into my mouth before I move to the right nipple and repeat the action. Ella gasps and her back arches.

"These are definitely more than tids," I say as I slide down her stomach, and my tongue catches the crevice between her thighs and center. I smell her headiness and lick there once on both sides before placing a final lick on the seam of her center fold. Lifting her thighs, I place each leg on either side of my head, resting her heels on my shoulders before I dive onto her clit. My mouth grabs it with a strong suction and her hands are instantly in my hair. I pause and look at her. "And this is definitely more than a bit."

I return to the sweet center and swirl my tongue around her little ball of nerves with the determination of a soldier at war for her pleasure. Alternately, I flick my tongue against her clit before leading a campaign of sucks, flicks, and swirls until she's up on her elbows greedily looking down as I eat her center for all it's worth.

Her breathing turns into pants before she huskily starts to speak. "What are doing to me?"

"Making you come. Hard," I answer against her trembling thigh before licking her center from top to bottom and running my fingers through the subsequent pools of wetness that form. I insert two fingers into her sex, winding them until I find the front of her wall. I press there and she reacts. Yeah, that's her spot. I almost come right over the damn sheets. "You're so hot, Ella—tell me you're hot for me. Tell me your hot, wet center is just for me." I start to move my tongue faster and it causes a guttural sound to start in the back of her throat. Oh yeah, she's there.. "Tell me now, tell me it's mine."

"It's yours, Kofi."

"What's mine? I want to hear it."

"My pussy, it's yours."

"Well, in that case, let me make my pussy come." I open my mouth wide and French kiss the inside of her center, coaxing out a small gush of wetness before my tongue presses hard against her clit. Her eyes roll to the back of her head and she chants my name like it's a prayer. She crashes fast all over my mouth. It's so amazingly hot. I take my hand and borrow some of her precious juice to lubricate my hand. I lean back on my knees to pump my throbbing dick.

She sits back up just in time to watch my hot release land all over her perfect body. With a grunt, I continue to milk my release. It's a load for the ages.

She continues to watch with her eyes wide with arousal.

Between grunts and hard breaths, I speak. "That's you, Ella. That's what you do to me."

Once I'm empty, we both fall back on the bed and clasp hands over my stomach. I kiss the back of her hand while we breathe in silence. A few minutes later, I rise and go to the restroom to prepare a warm wet cloth to clean her off. When I return she greets me with a smile. I gently wipe her off. I place the cloth on a nightstand and rejoin her to lie on the bed. We lay for a minute before I break the silence.

"You know, I can't believe we're in my grandparents' old bedroom."

She sits up and turns to me. "Really? That's where we are?"

I reach up and put my hands in her hair before moving to stroke the nape of her neck. "Um hmm. When the new palace was built, my grandparents were still alive. This was their room. You were walking down the guest living quarters wing; that's why there are so many doors. The master suite, my room, is on another wing closer to all of the palace action. There's nothing but bedrooms on this side of the palace."

She laughs. "Just my luck you'd find me near all the beds."

"Yes, it is lucky, and today I'm grateful. If there hadn't been a bed near, I would have taken you right against that wall. I think we both know we were at a point of no return." I feel her body stiffen and I sit up to meet her eyes. A look of panic has taken root.

I rub her back. "What's wrong, Ella? You look concerned. I can't have that."

"Do I? I didn't mean to. I was just thinking. What the hell are we doing? I mean, I'm here to recruit you as a client for my charter network. Yet, I'm lying in an antique bed after letting you take me in every way imaginable. And the worst of it is I just gave you the biggest speech earlier about how I'm not going to be your whore, but look..."

I pull her to my lap before she can finish and kiss her passionately. She tries to talk against the kiss for a second before melting into my mouth. I let her go before I really want to. I don't want to stir my body up again. Then I shift to gently place my hands on either side of her face.

"Ella, I don't ever want to hear you use the word 'whore' in relation to yourself ever again. Is that understood?" She looks down at her fingers. I remove a hand from her cheek and lift her chin, giving her what I hope to come across as a tender look. "Do you understand?"

"Yes, I understand. But—"

"There is no reality, on this side of heaven or the other, in which you are anything other than a queen. You are a beautiful woman, a brilliant businesswoman, and an exceptional school leader. You are also slowly stealing this king's heart. I will not have you talking about the woman I adore that way." She looks up at me and gives a slight smile.

"You think I'm brilliant?"

"Yes, and beautiful. Please don't forget beautiful."

"Oh, trust me, I will never forget that." Her expression has turned into one of joyful admiration. That's what I like to see. "So, Kofi, where do we go from here?"

That's the million-dollar question for which I have no answer. I have no plan. I finally got what I've wanted since the moment I laid eyes on her video weeks ago. I got all of her, but I'm not sure if there is enough of me to sustain Ella. She makes me happy and I definitely want her in my life, but how much will a relationship require? Can she make me a queen? That I don't know. If I'm honest with myself, right now I really am in no place to try and find out. Hopefully, like me, she won't overthink this. We can take where we go from here one day at a time.

I pull her into my chest and kiss the top of her head. "Well, first we're going to the marketplace so I can show you off and give you the surprise I planned for you."

She pushes up from my chest to look at me. "And then?"

Damn. She is overthinking this. Hopefully I can redirect her thoughts...for the moment, anyway. I need to reassure her that not knowing is OK. I lift her off my lap with a peck to the lips and roll off the bed. Then I reach for her hands and beckon her to come with me.

"Then we will go where you lead, Ella. When it comes to us, you're the queen and I'm your servant."

Chapter Twelve
GENEROSITY
Ella

nce we leave the bed, Kofi leads me to his master suite, where we shower and head out to the marketplace.

We shower separately—otherwise we would never leave the palace. But that doesn't stop him from looking while I shower. The way Kofi stares at me as I undress and step into the steaming hot shower makes me want to jump his bones. Nonetheless, it is already six p.m. and the marketplace closes at nine. Hot king or not, I'm a sucker for a good mall.

When we arrive, I quickly assess that the marketplace is the hub of Kumasi life. The food vendors line the entrance with all types of West African delicacies. Tonight, the marketplace is packed with shoppers and spectators alike. The sound from an African Hi-life band is everywhere. The West African food scents of stewed tomatoes, onions, and nutmeg waft from stall to stall. I now know jollof rice can be prepared and presented in at least a dozen different ways. One vendor we pass promises the best meat pies in Africa. The little piles of meat wrapped in fried dough smell divine. I point and pull Kofi toward the stall.

"Kofi, may I borrow two cedis? I have to have one of these pies. I forgot to convert my dollars to cedis at the airport. I can pay you back tomorrow after I stop by an exchange."

Kofi looks bewildered for exactly one second and then breaks out into a roar of laughter. It is one of those laughs that makes you want to laugh. He is genuinely amused.

"What?" I grab his arm. "Tell me, what is so funny?"

"Come, Ella." He approaches the owner of the stall. She is an older woman with her hair wrapped in a gorgeous kente wrap. I instantly prefer her wrap to the 20 Hermes scarves I've collected over the years. "Auntie!" Kofi shouts. "How are you…" Then Kofi begins to speak in Twi and the woman behind the stall joins him in his chuckle before kissing the back of his hand and giving him six meat pies on a plate. I stand behind him looking like a petulant child.

"OK, let me in on the joke. I'm beginning to feel like you're laughing at me and not with me," I say only half joking.

He arches his eyebrow in mischief. "But you aren't laughing at all, so it's definitely the former."

"Oh, it's like that!" I laugh and ask incredulously. I playfully snatch the pies away. "Well, fine then—keep your little jokes, but give me my food."

"Ahhh. I am just teasing you. I pay for nothing in the market-place; I've tried many times before, but the people are offended by my money." He lifts his hands in playful defense. "We were laughing because it's considered an honor to serve the king food. I learned a long time ago that giving aunties money was absurd."

He studies me for a minute before speaking again. "However, Ella, I have to ask: why would you ever pay a man back for food when he has the pleasure of spending time with you?" He pulls me close and whispers in my ear, "Not to mention in the palace I had the privilege of exploring the softest place on earth. You will never owe me another thing in life, least of all money for a meat pie."

I blush. "I see. I was trying to be polite. It's an old habit. My ex, Marcus, used to keep score of who spent what down to the penny. He truly believed in partnership being 50/50. If it was my turn to buy dinner and I left my wallet or something of that nature, he would make sure I paid him back. He was worse than a bill collector. It used to make me feel so uncomfortable."

Kofi crosses his massive arms across his broad chest. "Wait. You were in a relationship with this man?"

"Yes."

"You were his woman. He claimed you as such?"

"Well, not in the well-versed way you let me know I was yours today, but yes." I nod.

"And you and this man made love?" Kofi uncrosses his arms and places a hand on the small of my back. "Let's continue to walk a bit while we talk." He's attempting to make me comfortable enough to answer uncomfortable questions. It's working.

"Yes, we had sex."

He furrows his brow. "You didn't make love?"

"I don't think I've ever done that, actually."

He pauses and turns me to him. He looks at me with a sadness in the back of his eyes and determination in his voice. "I will address that tragedy later tonight."

"OH, OK," was all I could muster to say. He continues.

"Sounds like Marcus was a fool. Please promise me from this day forward you will demand better treatment from men. If for some reason an act of God occurs and I let you leave my orbit, you better make damn sure the man who replaces me never asks you for a damn thing but time. He is to take care of the rest. You're the queen, he's the servant. Got it?" His voice is so authoritative I dare not challenge his decree. Plus, why would I?

"Yes, your majesty."

"Oh, I'm a king again now?"

I give him a smile so big my cheeks are likely to break. "Yes, after that tongue lashing you most definitely are. However, you should know that when the act of God occurs, I doubt I'll ever be able to replace you." It's truth. This time together will inevitably end, and I doubt any man will live up to Kofi.

His face softens. "I want to kiss you passionately right now, but we are in the marketplace and I cannot. Do you understand why that can't happen?"

"Of course I do. Public displays of affection wouldn't be becoming of an Asantehene."

"Yes. That's right." He leans into my ear and whispers, "But I want to kiss you so deeply right now that you would not know where my mouth begins and yours ends. The type of kiss that leaves you wet and aching for my thick rod to push inside and relieve that pressure. Can you imagine that for me right now?"

"Yes," my voice hitches. "I believe I can."

"Good, let's eat these meat pies before they are cold. Auntie gave us two of every flavor she made today: chicken, beef, and fish."

We pause to eat the pies. They are delicious. Kofi then finds us some Malta Guinness to wash it down. I am wary of drinking the beverage at first; I hate the taste of beer. However, he assures me it's not beer and actually pretty sweet. I close my eyes and take a swig. He is right, I am a fan.

Kofi hands our trash to one of the many people that keep asking for the honor to throw it away. The royal treatment is equal parts off-putting and amazing. I don't know how to feel about it, and then I realize it's Kofi's life and title. How I feel about what he was born into really doesn't matter. I just need to focus on who he is outside of it all.

"Come, Ella—it's time for your surprise."

"Oh, yeah! I almost forgot. I'm excited to see what it is." He guides me down a long stretch of stalls before we land at one with a simple sign that reads, *Mawuli*. I pause, remembering that name from Maya. This is where she called in an order for my Akwasidae outfit. "Kofi, this is the shop that Maya sent my measurements to for the Akwasidae. It must be the best if Maya shops here when she's on the continent."

"Yes! Mawuli is my personal tailor. I had her prepare something you could wear for the Akwasidae also. It looks like you'll have two looks to wear that day. That actually works well."

"But how did you get my measurements?"

He chuckles. "I had Adom send them to me. He asked your friend Maya for your dress size."

"Oh, that's silly. He did not have to ask Maya—Adom knows all my sizes. He likes to buy me things to wear."

Kofi's jaw tightens and he starts to tense. "How does Adom know such an intimate detail about you? And he buys you things? Are you sure you never slept with him again?"

I roll my eyes. He just can't let my drunken night with Adom years ago go. I count to five before I respond, as not to bite his entire head off. The jealousy is kind of cute but way out of line. "As I stated before, Adom is my Morehouse brother and nothing else. We share a love of clothes and he often sees something I will like and purchases it. Furthermore, your question is asinine."

Kofi looks slightly chastened. "I apologize for the offense. I just don't want to think any man has been where I have been. I don't share."

"You know that's borderline misogynistic, right?"

"No, I don't. No man likes to share what is his, especially when it is a precious thing that he adores. I know it's unrealistic because, regrettably, I am not your first lover. However, Ella, I aim to be your last."

I am flabbergasted. What is this man saying? He keeps dropping hints of forever and exclusivity without really saying it. Maybe he's just a smooth talker that's a little sex drunk right now. I shouldn't read too much into it, but it's hard not to.

"Let's go in and see what Mawuli has prepared for me. Shall we?"

"Of course." Kofi leads me to the back of the shop, where a beautiful dark chocolate-shaded woman greets us with a brilliant smile. She wears her hair bone straight and jet black to her chin. When she speaks, her voice has a cherubic sound to it. She is all joy and warmth.

"Your majesty! Is this the beauty you were expecting from the states?" She envelops me in a hug and I instantly like her.

"Yes, this is Ella Jenkins. She is CEO and founder of Revolution Academies. We are looking to possibly bring her schools here to Kumasi for our children."

Mawuli lights up with a look of recognition. "OH, are you Maya's friend Ella?"

I nod emphatically. "Yes, I'm sorry. It seems you have made two garments for the same girl."

"Oh, no worries! Two garments will work well for Akwasidae. You can wear one during the day to the parades. Then you can wear the other for the banquet and dancing. I did not put together you were the same person because Maya was very clandestine about your visit." She looks over to Kofi. "Now I understand why."

Kofi lifts his finger to interject. "She should wear my requested design for the evening."

Mawuli nods in agreement. "Yes, I agree. Ella, why don't you undress in that room right over there, and I'll get the evening dress onto you for some tailoring first."

I look at Kofi and he nods in the direction of the room. His gaze tells me he wants to come back there with me and watch me strip. Of course he can't do that here.

When Mawuli brings the dress back, I gasp. It is shimmering gold lace with gold crystals dispersed throughout all of the fabric. The dress creates its own light. On the rack, I can see the lace pattern is an Ashanti tribal print overlaid on a silk bodice. It is stunning. Once I put it on, I can't believe how well it fits. It is a sparkling glove hitting every curve of my body just right. The dress is a mermaid style with a bit of a train in the back. The front has a high scoop neck, but the back dips so low you can almost see the slip of my ass. It is conservative in the front and full of sex in the back. It is perfect.

"Perfect," Mawuli says with a gasp. "You know, we won't let the king see this until the night of the event. You will be a beautiful surprise."

I laugh. "I agree."

Mawuli then brings in a kente print pantsuit with a train attached to the bottom of the pants. The pantsuit has a cigarette pant and halter top; it is very chic. "Now, this one we will show the king."

When I walk out, Kofi gives me a 'make your panties wet' stare before coming over to grab my hands. "You look like regality, Ella. You look like mine."

I turn to look at Mawuli. She blushes and nods. "He's right! You look like a queen! Your majesty, wait until the night of the Akwasidae —Ella looks like a million bucks in the dress you designed."

Kofi looks disappointed. "I can't see that one now. too?"

I playfully wag my finger at him. "No, that will be my surprise for you."

Kofi chuckles. "Very well, I look forward to it. We really should go now—it's getting late. I need to get my lady some dinner. Those meat pies will only hold her for so long."

"You're right—I *am* hungry again."

Once I am dressed, Kofi and I head out into the darkness of night-fall. It is nine and the vendors are closing their stalls. "Kofi, thank you for an unforgettable day. It really has been special."

Kofi looks down at me and grabs my hand before ducking into an alcove behind an empty stall. He quickly takes my lips into his and presses his strong body against mine. The kiss starts at my lips and mouth but ends in a trail down my neck to my breastbone before crashing back into my mouth again. I am spent.

Once we come up for air, Kofi places his forehead on mine. "The pleasure was all mine."

RELAXATION

Ella

Our drive back to Bonbiri is quiet.

Kofi keeps his hand over mine in the back seat of the car but remains silent. Every few minutes, he looks over to me and kisses the back of my knuckles with a half-smile before returning to his pensive look, staring out of the car window. I'm actually grateful for the silence. Between the conversation in the gardens, sex in the palace, and the gown Kofi designed for me at Mawuli's, I am officially overwhelmed. I need some time to think about what we're doing and why we're doing it. We're magnets and can't keep our bodies off of each other.

But it's more than that. When we talk, I'm talking to the other part of me that's been missing. I know this is crazy; I've known the man for nine days. Yet, it feels like it's the only nine days in my life that have made me truly and completely happy. That's scary.

We are moving fast, and I don't even know what we're moving toward. I have 21 more days in Ghana, and then I am returning back to my life and business in Atlanta. Kofi will continue to rule the Ashanti and live the playboy life he always has. I cannot take the fact of me being the object of his affection as anything other than a fun fling across the sea. Even though he talks like it is more. He stated he wouldn't let me willingly leave this orbit. Then, he made the heated promise to truly make love to me tonight. Those words signal more than a fling.

He seems sincere. But how can he be? I'm just a woman from Atlanta with a pretty face. There were others before me, and I'm sure there will be others after me. But somehow, he makes me feel like I'm the only woman he thinks about. He was even thinking about me before I arrived in Ghana—he admitted that in the gardens today. Nevertheless, I'm not making this more than it is. I need to slow it down and focus us back on the business of building schools in Kumasi. Whatever is happening between us is secondary to that and will take care of itself.

Each time I approach Kofi's home, it is more breathtaking than the last arrival. It really is a spectacular property. In the moonlight, it looks like a shimmering palace. The light bounces off his home's expansive glass surfaces. I can envision living here with him forever. But I won't imagine that right now. Right now, I will go in and eat some food and start to ask him about his plans for education.

"Kofi? Do you think we can eat dinner on one of your decks? It's a gorgeous night."

He looks at me and grins. "I was thinking we would eat in the river room."

I tilt my head to the side and purse my lips. "But that's my bedroom."

He laughs. "I know, Ella—I am seducing you. Lovers often have breakfast in bed, so why not dinner? Plus, we will already be in place for dessert."

This man is always making my panties wet. It is becoming a real problem. But I have to resist and remember first things first. But I don't want him to think I am opposed his suggestion. I definitely plan on having him for dessert later tonight. "Kofi, you can seduce me just as well under these gorgeous stars. Plus, I want to talk to you about my proposal. I think we will be able to focus more outside of the bedroom. Don't you?"

He sighs and chuckles while pressing his body flush against mine. "OK, we can talk business underneath the stars if you like. But I will ravish you before tonight turns into tomorrow. I crave you."

Yep. I'm pretty much soaked between my legs. My thighs clench together as he leans over to place a soft kiss behind my ear. It feels like a newly discovered place on my body that only he was able to find.

I look up at him and smile. "Thank you. I'm excited to show you my plans."

"Great, well, let's go inside." As is his custom, Kofi exits the car first to walk over and open my car door. I haven't touched a door handle in the past nine days. No man, whether it is Kofi, Senya, or even Chief Owusu's son, allows me the chance to open any door. I swear they don't make men like this in the states. Kofi makes me feel cherished and protected.

Kofi takes my hand and leads me out of the vehicle and up the path to the front door. When we enter the hallway, he takes my purse and gestures for me to walk ahead of him into the family room. Everything is clean and, in its place, the exact way it looked when I arrived nine days ago. It makes me wonder if it always looks like this. I know he has servants to keep his surroundings constantly clean, but I realize it looks more than clean. It looks unused.

"Kofi," I turn around and ask, "May I ask you a question?"

"Of course." He leads me to sit in a very comfortable-looking cognac leather sofa. The sofa is huge and can easily seat four or five people. As we both sink in, I note that the soft leather has a distressed look that still manages to look new. It's a beautiful piece of furniture. Once we settle, he places his hand on my knee and gives me his attention.

"Do you ever use this room? Or any other rooms- besides the kitchen and your bedroom? Everything here seems so undisturbed. Are you always alone?"

He chuckles and arches an eyebrow. "Is this your way of asking me if I have women over here much?"

I laugh too. "No, you already told me that you entertain women at your palace and not here. I don't know...the house seems lonely and not very lived in."

He nods. "Well, I do prefer to be alone at Bonbiri. That's why I built it. So, if you're asking me do I have dinner parties or family Christmas here, the answer is no. However, I do allow special women from Atlanta who light my body and soul on fire to take up residence as long as they like."

I blush, not knowing why I'm so embarrassed by his obvious infatuation with me. "I see. So what you're saying is...I'm all the dinner party you need?"

He leans over and kisses my lips with enough heat to set us both on fire. When he pulls himself away, he answers, "What I'm saying is, if we don't go and eat dinner soon, you will become the entire meal and not just dessert."

I caress his jaw with my right hand and trace his lips with my left. "Well, in that case, we better get you fed, then. You'll need your energy up for what I have planned. Will Akua serve us in the kitchen?"

He stands up and motions for me to take his hand and join him. "No, I've given her and most of the servants the night off. She cooked dinner and left it in the warmer for us. I can make us a salad and get our food plated. Why don't you go wash up and I'll meet you in the bedroom with our meal?"

I am relieved Akua retired for the night. Our daily morning meetings are tense, to say the least. Right now, all I want to do is shower, eat, and talk about the wonderful services Revolution Academies is prepared to bring to Kumasi. "OK. I will grab a quick shower and meet you upstairs on my balcony in 15 minutes. Does that work?"

He shrugs. "Or the bed. You know, I'm open."

I playfully hit his arm and scold, "Kofi, behave. Business, then pleasure!"

He kisses my forehead. "Perfect." I turn to go, and he watches at my ass as I climb the stairs. Knowing he's looking makes me put an extra swing in my hips as I slowly ascend. I hear him chuckle as he walks away into the kitchen.

Once upstairs, I decide to take a quick shower and change into something comfortable for dinner. The hot water feels good against my skin. The shower has a rain shower head and jets that hit your body all over. After such a long day walking in the heat, the water feels like a massage. Stepping out of the shower, I take off my shower cap to shake my curls out before I grab my silk robe and drape it over my damp body while I venture toward the closet to find something for dinner.

I must have stayed in the shower longer than I thought, because when I step out of the bathroom, Kofi is setting our food on the balcony. His eyes catch mine before I can escape into the closet. His eyes start at mine and then slowly work their way down my open robe. The heat radiates from my hardened nipples to the warm core between my legs. I can't tell if I am still damp from the shower or if Kofi's stare is responsible for the moisture pooling between my thighs.

Now he is coming inside the patio doors and moving toward me. Once he reaches me, he places a kiss on my forehead and lingers there for a second as his hands rub up and down my arms. He takes a small step back to take my body in again before he grabs the silk belt of my robe and ties it in a beautiful tight knot, covering my exposed body. His eyes never leave mine as he works the knot.

"Wear this to dinner. The berry silk looks amazing on you. Find a pair of heels that will compliment it and meet me outside," he commands.

I'm taken aback; I didn't expect that request. "But Kofi, we will be outside. Everyone will see me eating dinner in this robe."

He laughs. "Do you trust me, Ella?" I chew on my bottom lip but nod without any more hesitation. His voice drops an octave. "The servants are gone for the evening and each balcony has a tree canopy to ensure privacy."

I look out the door and realize he is right. No one can see past the beautiful trees obscuring my balcony. Plus, there is smoked glass to separate each bedroom's deck space. It feels like he planned for an evening like this when he designed the home. I'm pulled out of my thoughts when he leans in closer and says, "I hate having to ask you twice, so go on, find those heels."

"O-OK," I stammer. He kisses the back of my knuckles and walks back outside; I catch him untucking his shirt as he walks away. I can't believe how quickly I acquiesce to him. If any other man told me he didn't want to ask me things twice, I would balk. But Kofi makes me want to ensure he never has to ask me anything more than once ever again. I am more than happy to be at his service.

I grab a pair of strappy silver heels and head outside. He looks pleased with my choice and pulls out my chair. He set a beautiful table for dinner. There are candles and African violets. He pours me a glass of South African wine and takes a seat across from me as he starts to serve our food. I neglect my wine while I stare at his every move. He's serving dinner effortlessly. There is something extremely sexy about seeing this powerful man serve me.

"This is nice, Kofi. Thank you for preparing dinner and this table. You never cease to amaze me. What other skills are you hiding from me?"

He pauses from tossing our salad and gives me an electric look. "My talents are endless. I plan to acquaint you with more of them later tonight." He searches my reaction as he continues to toss the salad. I quickly grab my glass of wine to hide the heat I'm sure is flushing my face.

"I'd like that," is all I manage to get out.

"Good. But we need to eat. Plus, I promised you I'd talk business with you before we play." Kofi passes a bowl of stewed chicken and rice to me followed by some plantain and bread. I eat all of my food and a bit of his. It's delicious.

Kofi smirks. "I love a woman who's not afraid to eat."

"OH, well, I'm your lady, then. I didn't get these hips by eating like a rabbit."

"Your hips are phenomenal. Please never turn into a rabbit. As a matter of fact, I'm going to worship your hips and all adjacent parts tonight."

My breath catches on his promise. "I thought we were going to focus on business before play?"

Kofi looks disappointed. "Can I tell you something?"

"Sure." I lift my glass, asking for more wine. Kofi pours me a healthy glass.

"Promise not to get mad?"

I put my glass down and clear my throat. After shifting in my seat, I answer him. "No, I will not promise that. The fact you asked that is a sign that I will probably not be pleased with what you have to say. But I promise to hear you out."

"Very well." He places his napkin on his plate and gives me his most serious face. "I've already picked Revolution Academies as the choice for Kumasi's Education Grant. I flew you out here so you can see the people, meet me, and determine how you want to proceed, not to convince me that I should go with your organization. I knew you were the best the moment I saw your application with the UN. After I saw you and heard you speak, I selfishly decided I had to meet you person. I'm so drawn to you. I wanted to be near you."

I am not upset, even though I absolutely should be. He brought me to a foreign country under false pretenses. But now those pretenses feel even better than the original claim. I want him to need me. And I am also getting the contract, something he apparently decided before we had sex, before I even set foot in Ghana. That makes me feel much better about the direction our relationship has taken. "So, what does that mean? What exactly did you imagine me getting accomplished on this trip?"

"Well, before I got the privilege of meeting my crush in person, all I wanted you to accomplish is a solid plan for building schools here. I planned to take you to our churches and cultural events, which I still will do, to give you all the cultural knowledge you need.

Then, I wanted you to be so engrossed in the work and our people that you realize you need to stay here, at least a year, to ensure implementation goes well and that we achieve a true Revolution Academy at every site. I don't want a watered-down version; I want the real thing. We need what you have to offer."

He has done his research. I generally support my new academies' founding teams for a year. It is called the planning year. However, those academies are in the states. I can easily fly back and forth between the host city and Atlanta. This is an entirely different continent. He knows that and still expects the same level of service. I'm inclined to give it to him...I may need to. This is our first international endeavor, and I want it to succeed. I also want to explore whatever is starting between Kofi and me, for however long it can last.

I clear my throat. "I see. Well, now that you have more than met your crush and shared your original goal for my visit, what else is there for me to accomplish?"

He rises and walks over to take my hand in his while leaning his tall frame against the table. "I want you to accomplish the greatest orgasm of your life while I make love to you on the bed just across the threshold. Then after I've given you at least three more glorious orgasms, I want you to accomplish a deep rest. Then I will wake you up with my mouth between your legs and wish you a good morning before we accomplish a hot shower together. Then, Ella, over sweet fruits and baked pastries for breakfast, we will discuss everything you can accomplish in Kumasi before I take you into the village to meet my people, the people you will serve."

I lick my lips and stare at his. I'm ready to kiss him and start all of what he just said immediately. "How long did it take you to plan my additional accomplishments, King? They're very specific."

With a sinful grin, he takes my other hand, standing me up to face him. "Go and lie on the bed. Take everything off. We must get started now if we plan to meet all your goals."

I go without hesitation, making sure the king doesn't have to ask twice.

Chapter Fourteen

SUSPICION

Kofi

The morning comes quickly.

Too quick. I want her lying in my arms like this all day, her beautiful face against my chest, her perfect ass uncovered. She gets hot in the middle of the night and blankets are banished to the floor. A woman as magical as her requires the world. I never thought I'd be willing to give it. Now there is nothing I want to do more. I will move my entire kingdom to keep her open and vulnerable, waiting for me. Her king.

I never could see myself sleeping beside any of the women I've dated, let alone waking up with them and spending an entire day together after mind-blowing sex. Even during their 90-day period with the king, I never let them stay here with me. They were never invited to Bonbiri. They were wined, dined, and thoroughly banged at the palace, then sent home at first light. But Ella, she's different. I knew it the moment I laid eyes on her during that TED Talk. Now I have to figure out how I can give her what she needs and what my people need within the next 21 days. I need her to stay. But right now, I just need to touch her.

Just when I decide to wake her to fulfill my morning promise of my mouth between her thighs, I hear a loud vibration come from the nightstand. I remember hearing the noise throughout the night, but we were so thoroughly engaged with each other I blocked it out.

Thinking it's my phone, I reach over and grab the blasted distraction and realize it is not my phone at all. It is Ella's. She must have left it here yesterday while we were out...I don't remember seeing her with it at all.

With a quick glance, I see that she has 12 missed calls and over 20 missed texts all from the same person, Adom Annan. Why is my cousin calling and texting her so incessantly? What is going on? What could possibly warrant such harassment? Against all the principles of privacy that I hold dear, I consider looking at the texts. The *swipe up to open* message is beckoning me to.

I can't believe she doesn't lock her phone, then I remember the palace provided this phone the second day she was here. When Senya took her to pick up some clothes her friend Maya had sent. He also took her to replace the items lost on her flight and she tried to make some calls. That's when she realized her phone was not properly set up to work in Africa without enormous costs to her phone bill. After Senya supplied her with a royal phone she must have shared the number with Adom. Have they been communicating this entire time? I wonder what the jackal is telling her about me. I need to know.

I rationalize that since it is not really her personal phone, the invasion of privacy is minimal. I take one more look at her sleeping face and open the messages. The moment I swipe up, I regret the action. It feels wrong, but then I see the first message and regret turns to anger.

 Adom

> 7/13 6:00 pm: Hello Lady. Where should I meet you and Thomas for dinner? How about you both come to my home in McCarthy Hills. Thomas can give Senya the address.
>
> *Ella*

7/13 6:02 pm: Thank God you texted. Thomas is handsy as hell. Kofi tried to warn me. You always know exactly when to come and save my day. We will see you in an hour.

Adom has been in Accra this entire time! Why didn't she tell me? We had multiple conversations about Adom, and I assumed he was back in Atlanta. She didn't exactly lie, but she's withholding information. I'm not convinced these two are just friends. Adom hates coming to Ghana. He avoids his mother and family like the plague. He must have made the trip just for her. I scroll down to the unopened messages she missed the past 24 hours, and it does not help her case.

> **Adom**
> *7/20 10:22 am: Lady. I need to talk to you. It needs to be in person. Can you make up an excuse and ditch Kofi? I can send a driver wherever you are.*
> *7/20 1:02 pm: Lady. Why haven't you responded? I need to be with you when I tell you this news. Come to me as soon as possible.*
> *7/20 4:28 am: Ella, Love, where is my cousin keeping you? Surely, I outrank him in importance. You need to hear what I have to say more than anything else right now.*
> *7/20 7:34 pm: Ella call me now!*

The messages just continue like that all through the night. *Call me, come see me.* The last message simply said, *Fine, I'm coming.* Coming where? What the hell is going on, and why does he call her 'lady'? Is that some sort of dumb pet name? If she had not left her phone here, would she really have ditched me to go see him? I try to shake it out of my mind. The fact that she didn't even remember to take a phone or mention missing one yesterday tells me she was not expecting to hear from him. There has to be a logical explanation. I can't believe Ella has been stringing me along for a contract. What if she is? What if Adom has been here the whole time coaching her? What if he is just waiting for an OK from her that the contract is secure? I gave her that reassurance last night!

I need to wake her up and get some answers. Otherwise, my imagination will continue to run wild. I mark the messages I read *unread*; she doesn't need to know I went through her phone. *Great! Now I'm lying by omission.* I can't stew over that now. I will just simply ask her if she knows the last time Adom came to Ghana. I can be smooth. *I think.*

I place the phone back on the nightstand where I found it and turn to wake her when I hear a knock on the bedroom door. Who the hell is knocking on her door this early in the morning? My servants know better. The knock comes again, and I groan as I get up and throw on my pants from yesterday. Since I'm not in my room, I don't have access to a proper robe.

I make my way across the room and open the door. "Yes!" I don't hide my displeasure at the interruption. However, once I see it's Akua, I soften a bit. "Auntie, it's 6:30 in the morning. Why would you disturb Ella this early?" No matter how hard I try, I can't banish the annoyance in my voice.

She looks at me keenly. "Well, I certainly didn't expect to find you at her door, your majesty. I hope you slept well."

I hear the scolding she's giving me without her saying another word. She's saying, *didn't I warn you this would happen?* She's saying, *how will you ensure we have the schools we need if you're shagging the source?* She's saying, *how will this ever end well when you know you can't give this woman what she will ultimately want because of who you are?* She's saying, *you're going to ruin everything just like you did with your mother.* I know what she's saying, because I'm saying those things, too. However, right now I'm not interested in dealing with that reality. I want to get back to Ella and figure out what the hell is going on between her and Adom.

"Yes, Akua. I slept well. Ella is still sleeping. What do you need with her?"

She raises her hands in front of her and sighs, shaking her head with incredulity. "It's not what *I* need, your majesty. It's what her visitor downstairs wants."

I shut the door behind me and step out into the hallway with Akua. "Visitor? What visitor?"

She gives me a small smile. "Your cousin Adom is here. He says he must speak to Ella at once. I left him in the kitchen."

"I see." Though I speak those words calmly and I stand still, my center rocks off balance for a moment. So that's what he meant by *I'm coming.* Of course! We are blood, and if I knew where the woman I wanted to be with was, I would go there too. Only I would have arrived faster. There's no way I'm texting a nonresponsive woman for 18 hours straight. I always knew he was weak.

What does he want with Ella? Is he here to tell her about my mother and how I failed her? Is he here to break us apart and claim her himself? How would he know we're doing anything but planning schools unless she told him? I know he is possessive and protective of *his lady*—she said as much in the garden. Is she in love with him? Does he touch her?

Suddenly, I don't feel like performing my morning duty anymore. The idea of him anywhere near her makes me want to break something. I turn my attention back to Akua and place my hand on her shoulder. "Do not tell my cousin you spoke with me. Just let him know you made his presence known."

I dismiss Akua, open the bedroom door, and return to the bedside. I pull on my shirt and take one last look at Ella before I head downstairs to greet her guest.

*W*hen I enter the kitchen downstairs, Adom's eyes roll with impatience when he sees me. He is sitting on a stool at the island sipping a cup of my favorite mint tea. I can smell it steeping on the stove. Clearly, he was anticipating Ella. He stands and speaks first, offering his hand to me. I bypass it and lean against the island across from him.

He sighs. "Cousin. So good to see you...I'm surprised you are awake this early. You know, with royalty needing its beauty and power sleep." His eyes search behind and around me. "Where's Ella?"

I tighten my crossed arms against my chest. "Ella is sleeping. She had a busy day and a long night."

He does not take the bait. "Yes, well, I asked Akua to wake her up. I need to speak with her at once. How is it that I am speaking with you?"

I turn and walk to the stove to pour myself a cup of tea. "What is it that you so desperately need to speak with Ella about? I have not heard from you in years—now, suddenly, you are at my doorstep. How did you even find Bonbiri?" *I know the answer to that.*

He smirks. "Ella told me, of course. She tells me everything. She didn't tell me you were her keeper, though. I wonder if she knows?"

I slam my cup down. "No, cousin, apparently you think keeping her is your job," I say through gritted teeth.

He breaks into a grin. "Oh, it is. It has been for the past 15 years." He comes around the island and steps directly in front of me. "I don't take the safety of her person or heart lightly. You may be sleeping with her, but I protect her. She is one of the most important people in my life. If you hurt her, I will kill you. Now, where is she? I must speak with her."

I clench my fists at my sides. "So, you're not going to tell me what this pop-up visit is about?"

He crosses his arms. "No. It is none of your business." He

uncrosses his arms and leans with one hand on the island. "Now, will you please go and wake Ella? Or would you prefer I do it?"

I slam my fist against the island table, so close I almost hit his hand. I wish I had. "You will not go anywhere in my home. I will go and see if she wants to see you. Stay here."

He smirks and returns to his seat on the other side of the island and picks up his tea. I eyeball him until he is fully seated and leave him in the kitchen.

A king does not compete for a woman's affections. If he came all this way to get Ella, he can have her.

Chapter Fifteen

ABANDONMENT

Ella

"*E*lla, wake up."

I hear Kofi's strong voice and feel his soft hand sweep across my chin and down my neck. Last night was incredible. It was something I've never experienced before. I've had decent lovers in the past, but no one as attuned to my body's needs and hidden desires as Kofi. Plus, coming four times is quite fun. I want to come again.

"Good morning." I sit up and groggily greet my lover. "Didn't you promise me a morning wake-up call that included you between my thighs?"

Kofi half-smiles. "Indeed, I did."

"Well, sir, my thighs are over here. Come back to bed and properly rouse me. I'm practically still asleep."

He looks down at me like he's holding an emotion or thought back. Maybe both? Is he already regretting our last 24 hours? Does he want to pull back? He finally speaks. "Well, I would, but you have a guest waiting for you downstairs."

"A guest? Who would come see me at this hour?"

"Apparently, your good friend and my cousin, Adom." Kofi sits away from me at the foot of the bed. For the first time, I notice he is fully dressed. His entire posture and demeanor are distant. This is the exact opposite of how I expected my morning to start.

"Your cousin? Did you invite him?" Kofi abruptly stands and walks over to my side of the bed. He grabs my hand and motions for me to get out of bed.

"No, he came here expressly to see you at this hour. Of course, I had no idea he was even in Ghana." *Shit.* "Is there anything you need to tell me before you head downstairs to greet him?" I recognize the edge in his voice. He had it when we first crossed each other in the car ride from the airport 10 days ago.

"What could I possibly have to tell you, Kofi?" *Maybe that your cousin is in town to handle some shit with his mother and your jacked-up family. But I was sworn to secrecy.* I rise from the bed and walk toward the bathroom very aware of my nakedness and his eyes following my every move. "I'm just as surprised as you are that he's here." *Well, I am.*

He sniggers. "I find that very hard to believe."

I stop in my tracks and face my accuser down. Now I admit I didn't tell him that Adom was here. In the beginning, it did not matter. Adom is like a brother to me and I barely knew Kofi. He was just a business interest. I definitely would have told him now that things in our relationship have taken on a different face. I just haven't had the chance. But now, I feel he is accusing me of something else, and I don't appreciate it. "Are you calling me a liar?"

"No, I'm not calling you a liar. But I do think you're lying right now." In two strides, he's face to face with me. "Adom does not talk to me unless it's family business, which is rare. It has been years. He hasn't been to Ghana in over five years to my knowledge, and definitely never to Bonbiri. You're here a little over a week, and now he's showing up at my doorstep demanding an audience with you. What am I supposed to think?"

My face flushes with heat. No one questions my integrity, especially a man with no reason to do so. I close my eyes and take a deep breath. This is a misunderstanding, and I don't want to say anything I'll regret.

"You're supposed to think that you trust me and what I say." I drop my voice even lower into a soothing tone, not wanting to betray any hint of my chief emotions right now: anger and panic. "What reason would I have to lie to you?"

"I don't know, Ella. Why does any woman lie? I barely know you." His jaw is clenched, and his fists are balled at his sides. He continues. He looks to the nightstand and walks over. He grabs my phone and tosses it on the bed in my general direction. "The next time you seduce a man for 24 hours to secure a contract, make sure you take your phone. You may miss your real lover's messages!"

I shake my head in confusion. "What are you talking about?" I walk over and grab my phone, seeing all the missed calls and messages form Adom. Then it clicks. "Wait! Did you go through my phone?!" I yell. "Are you insane? How dare you! You should be ashamed of yourself."

Instead of shame, his face contorts into a blend of indignation and rage. "I should be ashamed?" He guffaws. "The only thing I'm ashamed of is thinking that you really were starting to have feelings for me. Tell me, Ella: Was anything you told me over the past 24 hours true? Did Adom also get the chance to make love to you on African soil? Maybe you have a fetish for African royal families. Or maybe he is he your fix in America and I'm your new fix here?"

I have no words. I back away farther away from him, barely recognizing the man seething in front of me. How can this possibly be the same man that brought me so much pleasure and security just hours before? It is happening again: betrayal. This is why I vowed to never let my guard down and completely give myself over to another man after Marcus broke my heart. They never live up to the hype. I feel the tears wanting to rush through my eyes, but I refuse to let him see me cry. I don't care who he is—he will not treat me this way.

I stiffen my posture and look him directly in the eye. "No, it seems

I've come to Ghana and developed a fix for assholes. But no worries, your majesty—that is one fix I will break right now. Now, if you would please leave so I can get dressed and greet my guest, I'd appreciate it."

He looks at me like he can see right through me and turns on his heel, leaving without a word. Leaving me naked and alone.

🗺

Once I dress in a simple black sundress and sandals, I start to head to the family room to greet Adom. I really have no idea what he's doing here. But knowing Adom, it's a good reason—he never interrupts my life unless it is absolutely necessary. Hopefully Kofi will be nowhere around.

As I head to the door, I hear my phone buzz and I remember that even though Kofi clearly has, I haven't checked my messages or missed calls since Kofi and I left for the palace yesterday. I can't believe he went through my phone. Thinking about it angers me all over again. I'm surprised it still has a charge. I look and see I have many missed text messages from Adom as well as about 20 missed calls. I start from the newest one and work my way up.

❝ **Adom**

7/20 9:01 pm: Ella it's an emergency; please give me a call.

7/20 10:32 pm: Ella I called Bonbiri. Akua said you and Kofi are still out in Kumasi. This is the only way I can reach you please respond.

Why did she tell him that? We were home by then. I know she had the night off, but she's too nosey not to know Kofi and I returned by then. What is her deal?

7/20 11:04 pm: Ella Akua won't give me much help in locating you. I never liked her. Call me!

7/21 1:52 am: Ella. It's an emergency you've got to call me.

7/21 3:30 am: Fine, I'm coming

The next one I read came less than an hour ago. Kofi must have had already greeted Adom downstairs and missed it. Had he read it, he would've known that he is a fool. It clearly states why he is here.

 Adom
7/21 7:02 am: Ella it's about Maya. It's an emergency. Prepare yourself before you come downstairs.

Maya? What's wrong with Maya? Now I'm panicked. If anything happened to her, I'll never forgive myself. She's like a sister to me. Maybe she needed me and I was too busy frolicking around with a dickhead king, living a stupid fantasy. But that can't be it—I don't have any missed calls from her. At this point, tears are starting flow. As I run down the hallway, I bump into Senya.

"Hey, hey, slow down. You'll fall!" He grabs my arms to stop my forward motion. "Trust me, I know." He chuckles and tries to crack a smile. After one good look at my face, he figures out that it is not a good time to joke. "What's wrong, Ella? What did that asshole do?"

He's clearly talking about Kofi. Hearing his confidante admit that he did something that would make him an asshole without so much as a blink of the eye doesn't bode well. But I have no time to contemplate Kofi at the moment.

"Plenty. But screw him!" I almost scream. "Have you seen his cousin Adom? He's here to meet me. I think there's something wrong with my best friend Maya back in the states." The waterworks really start to fall, and Senya grabs me in a side hug to escort me downstairs.

"Yeah, I just said hi to him. He's in the kitchen, of course; Akua's feeding him. I'll walk you, come on."

"Thank you." I sniffle.

Once we enter the kitchen, I see Adom immediately. He doesn't look like his normal, polished self. He's in a pair of gray sweats and a Morehouse T-shirt. He has a strong five o' clock shadow. His eyes

103

look like he hasn't slept in days. When he sees me, he immediately embraces me in a hug and brings me to the seat next to him. Senya hangs back at the kitchen entrance. Akua is at her normal spot, leaning against the stove glaring at me.

She speaks first. "Would you like some coffee or tea, Ms. Jenkins?"

"No, thank you." I barely look at her. I turn my attention to Adom. "Adom, what's going on? What's wrong with Maya?"

Adom's eyes well up and I hear him audibly gasp to keep them at bay. Adom Annan does not cry. At six-foot-seven and 220 pounds, he's a literal tower of strength and a monument to apathy.

"Adom!" I say forcefully while he just stares at me. "Tell me."

He starts to speak slowly, like he is trying to gauge my reaction to each phrase he speaks. "It's Maya. Ella, she was in a terrible car accident yesterday morning. Her BMW was hit head on while she was driving to the gym." He pauses to assess my reaction before he continues. "You are her emergency contact since she has no family. However, no one could reach you. Finally, they saw a text from me on her phone, one in which I called her sister and assumed I was her brother. I've been trying to get in touch with you ever since." He picks the teacup in front of him up and throws the rest of the hot contents into his mouth.

At first, I don't process anything he said. There's no way Maya can be hurt. She can't. Wait...he didn't tell me if she was dead or paralyzed or anything.

"Adom, is she...is she..." My voice cracks.

He leans over and grabs my arms quickly. "No, Ella, she's alive. But she has 10 broken bones and because of the pain, they've put her in a medically induced coma. The doctors have a positive prognosis, but it's going to take time. It's just...well, she's going to need around the clock care when she gets out. She broke both legs and bruised her hip."

After I know she's alive, I crash into sobs. My sweet friend needs me, and I'm thousands of miles away. "Adom, I've got to get back to

Atlanta. Get back to her. When is the next flight? Please tell me we can take your jet!"

"No, wait!" Akua says. "You can't leave; you haven't finalized the plans for the village schools." Then she turns to Adom in a flash of anger. "Why did you come here? There's nothing she can do for her friend right now while she's in a coma. I told you that when you arrived this morning!"

It takes everything in me not to smack the old lady for her apathy. We're talking about one of the closest people to me almost being killed, and she's talking about work. Wait a minute. If she knew why Adom was here, why didn't she just tell Kofi? That sneaky little wench! No matter—he should not have reacted the way he did; it showed his true colors. He also should have never touched my phone. I don't do irrationally jealous men, especially not one that calls me a liar.

"I'm not staying here when Maya is laid up in a hospital."

Her face turns to stone. "Yes, you are. Did you read the travel contract you signed to come here? All expenses paid as long as you fulfill your proposal and village visits. You will be in breach of contract if you jump up and leave. Plus, think about the work! That's what you came here for. Or was it just to sleep with a king?"

"How dare you..." Adom stops me mid-sentence. He turns his face to Akua.

"Akua! Enough! You've done enough, and I'll be sure to let Kofi know all you've done." Akua clucks her tongue and whooshes past us out of the kitchen.

Adom stands and runs his hands over his face. "Senya, I need to speak with Ella alone."

Senya nods. "Of course, just let me know if you need to go anywhere. I can take you. Kofi left for Kumasi early this morning, so I'm free. Also, I'm sure he will want to see you again before you leave."

So that's where he is. The coward didn't even stay after he showed his entire ass upstairs. Un-freaking believable.

Adom chuckles. "Trust me, Senya, he does not want to see me again."

I wonder if Senya knows they already spoke this morning. He must not. Judging by the way Kofi reacted upstairs, it probably was not a friendly reunion.

Senya stares at him before speaking. "It's different now, Adom— he no longer blames you for the past."

The past? What the hell is Senya talking about? But I can't focus on that right now.

Adom shrugs and turns back to me as Senya exits. "Ella, you need to stay here."

"What!" I look at him incredulously. "You're crazy."

"No, I'm not. Maya worked hard consulting on that UN grant application, and she wants you to build schools here more than anyone else. She'd be so disappointed if she knew you didn't get it accomplished and came back to Atlanta to just watch her sleep while she is looking her worst." He cracks a half-smile. I try to smile back.

"I know what you're saying, Adom, but I already have the contract. Kofi told me so last night."

"Yeah, but do you have a plan? Have you even been to the villages?"

I hang my head. "Only a few, not all. But Maya!"

"Ella..." He grabs both my hands and looks me in the eye. "My flight leaves for Atlanta in three hours.". I plan on sleeping on the plane, because I do not know when I will truly sleep again. I promise you I will be by her side every single day, every single moment. And if you answer your phone instead of gallivanting with my cousin, I can keep you updated by the hour."

"I don't know if you can exactly call it gallivanting." I smile.

Adom shakes his head. "Never mind the semantics—you've slept with him." I release a slow breath in response.

He nods knowingly. "And where did that get you? In a mess. I warned you, Ella! But I'm not here to scold; are you going to be OK to finish what you and Maya started?"

I slowly nod. "Yeah, but I can't stay here. Can you book me a room at the Westin in Accra? I can have Senya grab my things; I already packed."

"Are you sure you want to leave? This is a beautiful home. Or you can stay at my home in McCarthy Hills. My staff will see to your every need."

"Yes, I'm sure. Bonbiri has lost its luster. Plus, I might fight that old woman if I stay here a minute longer. And though I'm sure your house is the definition of over-the-top luxury, I don't feel comfortable staying in a house full of unknown servants without you."

He gives me a full laugh and pulls me into one of his rare bear hugs. He teases me and kisses my forehead. "OK, I'll have Senya get your things and you can tell me all about you and my arrogant cousin on our way to Accra."

"Thank you, Adom. And thank you so much for being such an amazing friend to both me and Maya. Having you tell me that news face to face was better anyways. I'm glad you couldn't reach me on my cell."

He releases me and leans back on the island. "I think you're right. And Ella, I will take care of Maya. I know we bicker a lot. But when I thought we may have lost her, it was never clearer to me how devoted I need to be to her right now. You take care of the Ashanti, and I will take care of our friend. I'm going to be there when she wakes up and help nurse her back to health. Don't worry."

I sigh. "OK, Adom. It's only three more weeks. I can close this deal and have a proposal written by then. I'm going to head to the car."

Adom calls Senya and has him grab my packed luggage while I wait in the same Range Rover that brought me to Bonbiri. Tears fall from my eyes for the first time for what my heart has lost.

Chapter Sixteen

CONTRITION

Kofi

I had to get the hell out of that house.

My house! This is exactly why I don't bring women to Bonbiri. When shit hits the fan, I like the security of a huge palace brimming with loyal servants to politely escort my overnight guests to a car waiting to take them home. I don't like having to hide from my overnight guest because her beautiful ass has bewitched my heart into holding her again even while she is lying to my face.

I can't believe she actually expects me to believe she has no idea why Adom came to see her this morning. My cousin doesn't seek me out for anything. I'm surprised he hasn't enlightened her about this fact, especially if he's sleeping with her back in Atlanta. Then she would know that any excuse other than *yes, your majesty, he's coming to see me because we are secret lovers* is futile.

I've forgiven him for killing my mother. Well, he didn't kill her, as years of therapy helped me admit. But I've forgiven him, nevertheless. It's not like I still hate him and his face. But he does not know that. We used to be extremely close. Then after my mother died, all that changed. We competed against each other for everything, but that was 15 years ago. From the way he talked to me this morning, he must think I still have patience to enter silly contests with him. I will not, especially not for a woman.

The playing field is different now. I'm king and he's in Atlanta making a shitload of money buying and selling businesses. It all worked out in the end, and thank God he's not living in Ghana. At least I don't think so. I was surprised to read in her texts that he has a home in McCarthy Hills, Accra's most exclusive neighborhood. I'm not surprised by the neighborhood—Adom has always been posh. I'm surprised he wanted a home here. Well, he can have whatever he wants, including Ella—just leave me out of it. I don't need the drama.

But damn! I already miss her. And the way she looked at me when I left her there, beautiful and naked at the bathroom door, wasn't a look of, *I just got caught.* She looked genuinely hurt. Maybe she was just sad she wouldn't have the pleasure I provide her body anymore now that the gig is up. I made love to her so properly last night that it is enough to last her the rest of her life. That's hard to give up. Thinking about it makes it hard for me to give it up, too.

I have to face her and Adom at some point, so it may as well be now. I've run about eight miles from the house into the nearest village. I decide to call Akua and have Senya bring the car because I'm too tired to run back. When I call, she picks up on the first ring. Was she waiting for me to call?

"Maakye," she greets in Twi.

"Maakye, Auntie. It's Kofi. Can you send Senya to pick me up? I ran to Tafo this morning."

She sighs heavily. "Senya is not here, your majesty. He has taken the American and Adom to Accra. She's staying there for the rest of her trip."

Her words hit like a dagger to my chest. Of course she left; I said some terrible things to her. But with him? How could she do that? She's not who I thought she was. I also can't believe Senya was complicit and took them to their lover's nest.

"Well, let her be with him. I don't have time for these games. Can you send Yao, then? He may become my right hand if Senya continues to show such disloyalty. I'm at Mama Yi's having breakfast."

Akua gasps. "Disloyalty. Anh-Anh. That's enough, Kofi. This is all my fault."

"Don't defend him, Auntie. You're always defending him! He's taken my enemy and lover away. How is that befitting of a king's right hand?" I yell. I regret losing my temper at the woman I think of as a mother.

"Your lover! Oh, my goodness. I knew that woman would be trouble the moment you brought her here. Now you listen to me, Kofi. Adom is not your enemy and Senya is not disloyal. You're going off half-cocked about things you know nothing about. I'll send Yao at once, and once you get here, I'll explain everything."

"Fine, you can present your defense of them. But I'm not inclined to hear it."

"Nante yie," she snaps her goodbye in Twi and hangs up.

When I arrive home, Akua is waiting in the den. She never sits in this room, so her presence startles me.

"Akua, why are you sitting here alone? Is there something you need? Do you feel OK?"

She clucks her tongue and dismisses my concern with a wave of her hand. "No, I am waiting for you. I wanted to talk to you about Adom and the American. I think you are handling this all wrong. Did you even listen to Adom and find out why he came?"

I shake my head. "Akua, I asked him and he refused to tell me. He thinks we are still two boys competing in the school yard." She tries to stand and interrupt, but I gesture for her to stay where she is. "Akua, I have no desire to talk about Ella and Adom right now. I've had a long night and an even longer morning; I just want to rest. You will have to wait until later to say I told you so."

She nods, knowing not to press me when I'm in this mood. "OK. Do you need me to bring you anything?"

I go over and kiss the top of her head. "No, I'm fine. I will find you a little later." She looks at me like she has a world of worry. I wonder what is on her mind. After today, I do not have the energy to find out.

🌍

*W*hen I awake, it is dark outside. I pull out my phone, secretly hoping Ella called to confess and apologize. I need the closure. Or maybe, I just need to know she's OK. Hungry, I walk downstairs toward the kitchen but hear Fela Kuti's Hi-life music playing from my study. The only one who plays Fela is Akua. What is she still doing up? It's almost 11 p.m.

"Auntie!" I yell as I walk down the stairs and to the den.

She peeks her head out of my study across the room. "I'm here in your office, your majesty. Waiting for you. Come!"

Akua only waits to talk to me in my study when it's serious. As I approach her, I see that her eyes are damp, but obstinate.

"OK, Akua, what is it that you so desperately have to tell me?" I go over to the stereo and turn off the music. This, along with his record collection, are the only things of my father's I kept after he died. It is over 40 years old, but still plays his records with quality sound. I take a seat behind my desk and motion for her to return to the couch she was undoubtedly waiting for me on. She looks up at me with a proud and defiant look. What is this about?

"Kofi. I know why Adom came this morning, and it isn't why you think."

I tense slightly and continue to listen. "Go on."

Akua starts to fidget and look down at her hands. She's nervous about something. She looks guilty. What has she been up to? "Auntie, if you have something to say to me, I'd advise you to get on with it. My patience is already worn thin from the events of this morning."

"Let me start by saying everything I did, I did for you. For the Ashanti! I just saw you making a fool of yourself over that woman..."

"Her name is Ella," I cut her off with a statement that sounds like a command.

"Yes, Ella," she repeats while looking at me, pleading. "Adom called several times yesterday, and I didn't know why at first. I didn't press to get ahold of you since I know how you feel about him. When he started asking for Ella, I demanded to know why, and he told me that Ella's best friend was in a serious life-threatening car accident."

Blood whooshes between my ears and I steady myself by grabbing ahold of the desk in front me. I swallow hard "Go on," I bite out.

"Neither of you were answering your phones well into the night and morning, so I figured you'd taken her back to the palace. I told him I didn't know where you were, not wanting to spread your personal affairs." She gives me a disapproving look, confirming she knew what we were doing in the palace. I'm sure she has spies there, too. She looks to me for affirmation that it is safe for her to continue. I offer none. Nevertheless, she continues.

"I finally told him if her friend is in that grave of danger, he should come here to tell her, because it would probably be too much to take over the phone. Also, since I could not confirm your whereabouts, I told him to come early in the morning. Of course, he hesitated to come here, given your past history. But I assured him it was the best way to get to Ella. It took some convincing, but he saw it my way." She stops and purses her lips, never letting her eyes leave mine. With that gesture, I know that's all she has to say about it.

This can't be. Ella's best friend, the one she calls sister, was in danger of dying 3,000 miles away and I accused her of sleeping with my cousin? Shit! Why the hell wouldn't Akua tell me this when she came to the door this morning?

"So, when you came to her door this morning, you knew why he was here but didn't tell me?" I try to hide the hurt in my voice.

"Yes! I'm sorry, Kofi. I just needed you to break out of whatever spell that woman—Ella—put on you, so you could focus on your duty. I didn't mean for it to go this far. I guess I didn't think it through."

"It wasn't a spell, Auntie. It was love. She was loving me and making me happy, and you ruined it with your needless meddling and prejudices." I stand up and slowly walk to the couch. I drop my body down on the couch beside her and cover my face with my hands. I cannot believe how easily I was tricked, and now I may have lost the only woman I have a true connection with over misplaced jealousy. After my private moment of internal agony and regret, I turn to Akua.

"You absolutely thought this through, and your plan worked perfectly. I'm beyond angry with what you have done, but I can't entirely blame you for what has happened. No, I have driven her away on my own, with harsh words and accusations that she does not deserve. It is I who did not trust in her."

I need to find Ella and make things right; I need to check to make sure she's OK after learning of Maya's accident. "Auntie, tell me where she is. I need to go to her. Is she staying with Adom? Or did you continue to twist the story with your deceptive words when I called you from the village this morning?"

Her tone remorseful, she answers, "Senya took her to the Westin in Accra, if she's even still here. Adom is returning to the states, and I'm unsure if she is going with him. I explicitly heard her ask if she could go with him this morning. I told her she could not leave before she fulfilled her travel contract and made a proposal for our schools. But Adom dismissed me, and I overheard her say she could no longer stay here. Senya told me Adom had his private plane waiting for a 11 a.m. departure this morning."

So, she ran away, too. Aren't we a pair? What if she really went back to Atlanta? I can't blame her if she did. Maya is unwell and a fit of irrational anger and jealousy took away the only reason she would stay here. If she left, not only has she taken my heart with her, but also any chance of having Revolution Academies in the villages. What have I done?

I have to figure out how I'm going to get her back to Bonbiri— back in my arms, back in my bed. I know it won't be easy. She no longer trusts me to take care of her heart. Also, if Ella figured out Akua's deceit, she definitely doesn't want to be around her, either.

However, that is one problem I can remedy very easily. I turn back to Akua.

"Auntie, I'm very disappointed in you. Your meddling has caused hurt to someone I've grown to care about deeply over this past week. I'm going to Accra to grovel at Ella's feet, and hopefully she will forgive me. You better pray that she does. In the meantime, I think you should retire to the palace for a while. At least until after Akwasidae."

She leaps up with defiance in her eyes.

"This is my home, and you're going to kick me out because of a lover's spat?"

I restrain my anger in reverence of her age. "No, Auntie, this is *my* home, and I'm reassigning you to a place where you can rest and not cause any more trouble. We will revisit your assignment at a later date. What you did was wrong, and no matter how much I love you, I can't let deceit go unpunished. Do you understand?"

She looks at me for a long time. She used to stare at me like this when I was a boy to get me to bend to her will. But I'm no longer a child—I'm a king without the first woman I thought could be my queen. If I have any chance of getting her back, I have to put Akua in her place.

"Anne," she verbally agrees in Twi. "I will gather my things and have Yao take me to Kumasi within the hour."

I kiss her cheek. "Auntie, do not ever deceive me like this again. If you do, I will buy you a small house in the village and hire a servant girl to take care of you there. I hope you heed my words, because I mean every one of them." She walks away from me, still proud and defiant. But I know better—she is hurt. I almost call her back, but I know that is not what needs to happen.

Instead, I pull out my cell phone and prepare to make a call that I don't want to make. If I'm going get Ella back, I'm going to have to go through the one man she trusts right now. I'm going to have to call Adom. Hopefully, she's not on his plane.

Chapter Seventeen

CONCESSION

Ella

"That's the fifth time Kofi has called me in two hours, Ella. I cannot misdirect him forever. There are only so many ways to tell a man like my cousin to get lost. The best way is directly, and that, my dear, must come from you."

Adom looks at me through the camera of his computer with his signature countenance of severity.

It's been one week since I left Kofi's secluded home, Bonbiri. I miss him, but I'm too furious to do anything about it. My new hotel suite opens up to an amazing view of Labadi Beach—it's no Bonbiri, but the views of the Gold Coast are breathtaking. Currently, I'm taking in the view from a lounge chair poolside as Adom and I Facetime.

He's been a saint, alternating between accepting and ignoring the many calls from Kofi over the past week. I have ignored twice as many, if not more. His constant calling is ridiculous. I don't know what he plans to say. After the way he talked to me, I'm not interested in anything but a business relationship. He already told me I've secured the contract to build Revolution Academy schools in Kumasi and surrounding villages. I can afford to ignore him one more day before I'm forced to interact with him during final village visits. With rigorous scheduling, I can complete those in the 13 days I have left here.

Yesterday, Adom called me to tell me that Maya was out of her coma and ready to talk. It felt good to hear her voice even if it was weak. She made me promise to stay and finish our school implementation plans. She still couldn't believe that Adom was with her when she woke up. It was unreal to her that he traveled home just to be by her side. It is so unlike him. I felt like his presence meant more to her than mine. I think I always knew her heart belonged to him. He is just too foolish to take care of it for her. I'm still not convinced he will ever be cured of his foolishness. He's too tightly wound to let go and love. However, time will tell. All that matters right now is that he's keeping her happy and safe.

I motion for the passing waiter to refill my mojito and move in closer to the screen to speak. "I know I can't dodge him forever, Adom. I simply have no motivation to deal with him until I absolutely have to. I can complete village visits and planning with him over the next two weeks before I leave. Right now, I want to spend my weekend enjoying the beach I was booked to stay at all along." A slight smile reluctantly comes to my lips when I think back to the clever way Kofi hijacked my lodging plans. Up until seven days ago, I was glad he did so. Seven days ago, I thought I might be falling in love.

Now, I know what I've always known: love is for fools. I told him the first night we met that my mama ain't raise no fool. I'm over it all. I lie back in my lounge chair and sip my drink to signal I'm done talking about Kofi. Adom responds by clearing his voice loudly. I turn to the screen.

"Adom, you are ruining my sun time. I want to return to Atlanta with a deep bronzed hue, if you don't mind."

He rolls his eyes. "You've got it all figured out, huh? You think you can just go back to your boring ass life with no drama after being with a king?" I sit up and shoot him a signature *have you lost your mind talking to me this way* look. He adjusts his tone and tries again. "Ella, I refuse to play buffer forever. Shit, for the first full day, the man didn't even know you were still in Ghana. I gladly gave you that revenge." Adom smirks. "He was a wreck until I finally confirmed you are indeed in Accra. But now the fun and games are over. Have you forgotten about Akwasidae tomorrow night? You're supposed to attend with him, remember!"

I sigh and start to put on my cover-up. The way Adom is stressing me out, I may as well go back to my room. "Of course, I remember. I'm just not going."

Adom laughs. "Oh, my dear, you are definitely going. It's the most important government and cultural function of the Ashanti." I attempt an interruption to remind him I no longer need their favor. Reading my thoughts, he moves to fill the screen and raise his hand to stop me from speaking. "And don't tell me it doesn't matter now, because it does! You have to keep the contract by keeping favor with the king, village chiefs, and parliament. Snubbing the event and the king will win you no support with the village chiefs you're trying to serve. You need those chiefs to partner with you, and their loyalty is to the Asantehene."

I search to find a hole in his reasoning, but there isn't one. I'm going to have to dress up in the sexy dress Kofi designed for me and attend Akwasidae with him. That's probably why he keeps calling; he knows I have to answer eventually. He's not silly enough to think I'd allow my heart to convince me to return his call after the stunt he pulled. However, he's keenly aware I still need him to get our business done.

"Fine, Adom. I'll keep my obligation, but he needs to keep his hands and thoughts to himself. I don't want him saying shit to me."

"Ella," he begins to scold. A nurse calls for Adom, and I see him stand and stretch. I'm sure his beautiful chocolate body is receiving more than one appreciative glance from the nurses station. Adom is a slave to the gym and clean eating. His six-foot-seven frame is muscular and strong without an ounce of fat. He's fine as hell and knows it. That's why I've never been interested—just drunk. We both decided a long time ago that our drunken night of fumbling sex at 19 is not worth ever mentioning.

He leans down so his face is back in the camera. "Kofi is a jealous, mistrusting asshole. I swear before he met you, he was well on his way to misanthrope status. Even as a young man in school, he was never a people person, women included. He attracted them and had sex with them with no idea how to handle them. So, he tightly controls that part of his life."

"Adom, you are definitely not doing your cousin any favors here, are you? You make him sound more terrible than I already believe him to be."

"I do not care to paint him any other way but the truth. I do not care how he comes across, as long as you know what you are dealing with. Kofi is not used to being out of control, especially when it comes to his love life. He is scared; I can tell from the way he's harassing both of our phones. Now that I think about it, he sounds like someone else I know." He smirks and wags his finger in my direction.

I laugh and stand, carrying my tablet with me as I move toward the lobby. "Whatever, you didn't hear the things he said to me. He was so unforgiving about something he knew absolutely nothing about."

Adom nods. "Yes, that sounds like him." A sadness hits Adom's eyes and I remember something Senya said in the kitchen seven days ago when Adom told me the tragic news about Maya. *It's different now, Adom; he no longer blames you for the past.* Adom has never gone into detail about his broken relationship with Kofi, and clearly Kofi didn't want to talk about it during our time in the garden. What happened?

"Adom, why don't you and Kofi get along? Senya said something at Bonbiri about him no longer blaming you for the past?" Another guest opens the hotel door for me as I continue speaking to Adom.

"He just blames me for the death of his mother. But just as with you a week ago, it's misplaced anger and blame. He's always been swift to judge and lash out. Even as a 12-year-old."

There's something Adom isn't telling me. He's usually a masterful storyteller, so this succinct and evasive answer is odd. I wait until I am inside the elevator to my room before I push further.

"How did his mother die? How could he ever blame you? You both were children."

Adom gives me a cautious look. "Ella, that's a story for another day and a lot more alcohol. Why don't you ask Kofi about his mother's death? As desperate as he is to speak with you, he will more than likely tell you anything you want to know. For now, just know that I lost more than my favorite aunt that day."

"Hmmm. A family secret! I won't pry. I just thought it might help me understand him more."

"I thought you said you were done with him. Why do you need to understand him? You don't fool me at all, Ella Jenkins. You've foolishly fallen for him."

I roll my eyes as I step out onto my floor. "No, not at all. It's always good to know what makes your business partners tick." I don't say that with enough conviction to even convince myself. I'm a fool. "Plus, I hate to think you two can't mend your relationship."

"Pfft," Adom replies. "That's up to him. I've extended the olive branch as far as I'm willing to." Adom waves goodbye and starts to log off. "I have to go check in on Maya and see what the nurses are doing. I'm sure whatever it is, it is wrong. I will check back in with you tomorrow."

I tell him thank you for everything and log off of Facetime. Once inside my room, I open my phone and call the number I've avoided for seven days. I need to hear his voice more than I need to hear what he has to say. It only rings once before he answers.

Chapter Eighteen

RESENTMENT

Ella

"Ella?" he answers hesitantly. "Are you...OK? Is Maya OK?"

Hell no, nothing is OK.

His voice over the phone betrays his fear. It sounds like he is scared to face the call he has been waiting on. Adom tells me daily how desperate he is to hear from me. In this case, his trepidation is wise. I want to keep this call as short as possible.

"I'm fine." I sit perfectly still on my hotel bed and release the breath I've been holding since I picked up the phone and called Kofi. Before I called, I showered and put on linen pajama shorts and a camisole to cool off. I poured a glass of Riesling and dialed his number. Now, I wonder if I am even ready for this call.

There is a long stretch of silence after my statement. I hope he is not waiting for me to elaborate. That's all I can say to him right now. This is not a social call, and the familiar feelings of anger and betrayal begin to rise at the back of my throat. I start to remember the way he treated me. I realize I am the one who called him, but I really don't have a plan. Maybe I should just hang up and try again tomorrow. The moment I decide to hang up, he speaks.

"I'm pleased you called." The timbre of his voice almost destroys my resolve. I want to say *come over and touch me until I forgive you.* But I don't say that.

Instead, I sit in my anger. "This call is not to please you. If you knew the things I want to say to you, you would know it is not..."

He sighs in disappointment. "I see. Well, why don't you tell me some of those things."

I release a quick breath. "Pfft! You don't mean that."

He gives a deep sigh. "I never say things I don't mean. If I'm asking you to tell me, then I am truly inclined to hear whatever is on your mind. Now, please share your thoughts."

Is that exasperation I hear? Apparently, the king is not used to apologizing and facing his faults on someone else's terms. I bite the inside of my cheek in an effort not to curse his entitled ass out.

"Fine. First off, I think you are a world-class jerk for demanding I leave my life and responsibilities in Atlanta and come to Ghana, knowing you were going with my organization from the start. I would have come to Ghana eventually to help implement on an agreed-upon timeline. If I were in Atlanta the past couple of weeks, maybe my best friend would not be lying up in a hospital fighting for every piece of her life back." I feel the tears wanting to break, but I hold them steady.

I pause to get myself together, and he takes this as a hesitation. "Please go on," he says.

With pleasure. "Next, you take every chance you can to cross lines and seduce me. Not that I'm complaining, it was wonderful. But I opened up to you in the garden at the museum that day and showed you my scars. You know I am cautious about relationships and love; to trust you with my body and thoughts over the past two weeks took a lot. However, you did not extend that same trust to me. I told you Adom and I are just friends on numerous occasions. You simply would not let go of the fact that we slept together once, when we were practically kids. You continued to ask about it until finally, your imagination made you do the unthinkable by going through my phone and accusing me of some very vile things." I pause. I have more to say, but he needs to say something in response that sounds like a real apology or I'm shutting up. I don't have time to explain to him why he is an asshole if he is not willing to address the behavior. He speaks immediately, like he was waiting for me to take a breath.

"What about Adom? You didn't tell me he was even in the country. We talked about him on several separate occasions, and you didn't think to mention he was here and that you were in constant communication with him? I told you our relationship was strained and that yes, I am jealous. I never lied to you, but when it came to Adom, you lied to me, by omission."

What is it with him and this Adom hang-up? It's tiring.

"Kofi, the only reason I did not tell you Adom was in Ghana was because he asked me not to. I'm sure you know more about his reasoning for you not to know than I do. But he is my friend. Once you and I figured out what our relationship status was heading toward, I would have told you despite his request. You just didn't give me the chance. You let your jealousy consume you. I don't need this kind of drama. Not believing what I said and leaving me was the worst thing you could have done. I trusted you. No man has had my heart or body the way you have these past two weeks since Marcus. I thought you were safe to have those parts of me, but apparently you are not the man I thought you were." I spit the last part out with as much venom as I can muster.

He breathes into the phone. It sounds pensive. "I've listened and clearly you're still mad about what transpired."

Is he serious? Of course, I'm still mad!

"Why wouldn't I still be mad? What reason would I have to set my anger aside?"

Silence. I can't believe it. The Asantehene is speechless. Then he continues, "You're right, I haven't apologized."

"Pfft. Your apology won't stop me from being mad."

"Well, nevertheless, I was an ass and I deeply beg your pardon. I should have believed you. And Ella, I'm really sorry to hear about

Maya. I know she's very important to you. I should have been there for you."

Thoughts of Maya bring back my anger and an unexpected sadness. My tears silently fall. "Yes, I needed you. I wanted to come to you and explain everything, but Senya told Adom and I you left for Kumasi that morning. That let me know that you didn't just display a flash of anger, you meant what you said. You didn't even want to be in the same house with me. You ran away."

I breathe through the familiar heavy pause before he speaks. I actually appreciate him weighing what I say before he answers. I feel like he is listening. "You are correct. I was a coward." *Whoa, I can't believe he admitted that.* "But I promise you, if you allow me, I will make it right. I don't know how I will, but if it takes the rest of my life, I will return to your good graces. I also must thank Adom for coming to be with you. He is a good friend."

I smile. "He's the best. At the moment, he is the only man I can depend on and trust." I know that is a low blow. But he needs to feel the weight of the pain he has caused me over the past week.

His breaths become a bit heavier. It sounds like desperation. "That is not true! No matter what your anger has convinced you of, you are still my heart's only desire, and I'm still your servant." The timbre of his voice drops to something purely carnal when he says, "servant." I don't know how long I can keep my irate demeanor up.

"As a matter of fact," he continues, "It is you that rules me. You are the queen of my mind, body, and soul. I will do anything you command to have you smile at me again."

Damn, he's good. I pause to gather my heart, body, and thoughts back together. "I'm a queen now? Wait a minute, queens can order executions, right?"

He laughs a full, hearty laugh. "Is my offense really worthy of death?"

I reluctantly break into a smile I hope he cannot hear. "No, not yet. But in my experience, assholes never commit just one offense. I need to be prepared for your next transgression."

A pause. "You should stop dealing with assholes, then. Kings learn from their mistakes and do not mind working to get back into the good graces of their queen." His voice is clear and lacks any hint of hesitation.

I match his tone. "My good graces are not open to you at the moment. But we do have the Akwasidae tomorrow, and I'm mature enough to be civil and keep our commitment."

He drops his voice. "Ella, by the time I finish the apology tour I have planned for your heart and body, you will be more than civil."

I ignore the clench between my thighs. "Kofi, we are attending as business associates and nothing more. Is that clear?"

"Crystal clear. Now, what time should I send a car to the Westin to pick you up? Will seven work? I've also booked the very best hairstylists, makeup artists, and stylists to help you prepare for the evening. You will be pampered to no end."

Damn! He's really good.

"Seven is fine."

He releases a breath. "OK, I'll let you rest. Would you like to visit the village Tafo in the morning? Unless you have other plans?"

Oh, hell no. He thinks it's that easy to go back to the way things were. I'm not going anywhere with him but this damn ball. But then again, this seven-day hiatus has really put my community mapping behind schedule. I need to start getting to know more of his people. My tour with Thomas Owusu was a waste of time. I'll make him sweat.

"I'll have to think about it. I already have plans for tomorrow."

"Oh, I see." I can tell from his tone that he is taken aback. "Well, please let me know as soon as possible."

"I will."

He lets out a deep sigh, clearly grateful he survived this call. "Perfect. I look forward to your response. Good night, Ella."

"Good night."

Chapter Nineteen

REUNION

Kofi

"Kofi, why are you here again?

Ella is not going to like this one bit. Especially since you didn't tell her you were coming with me to pick her up."

"She will forgive me, Senya. I just know it." Senya is pretending he doesn't hear me, but I see him stealing glances at me from the rearview mirror. Senya is not just my chief of staff—he serves as my bodyguard, driver, best friend, and general overall right hand. Partly because I don't like or trust anyone else. But also, because we grew up like brothers. He was orphaned at the age of six when his mother was mysteriously murdered. His village abandoned him because he never had a father. When he showed up at the palace kitchen doors begging for food, Akua took him in and raised him as her own. My mother would not have much to do with him, but she encouraged me to treat him like a brother. It was odd, but I loved having a constant playmate and confidante.

Consequently, Senya is also at times my therapist and the first one to call me on my shit. The look he's giving me now is screaming BULLSHIT, but he won't say it. Not because I'm his king. It is because he, more than anyone else, knows once I've decided something, it's done. I've decided surprising Ella by picking her up for our day in the village instead of sending a car is the best way to get her to start forgiving my egregious transgression of not believing her. The element of surprise is all I have.

She didn't even agree to come with me until six a.m. this morning over an email. I can't blame her for the move. If she treated me the way I treated her eight days ago, I don't know if I would have the grace to agree to go anywhere with her.

Senya clears his throat to get my attention. "Yes, Senya. What is it you have to say?" I smooth the white linen pants I'm wearing to ward off wrinkles, preparing for his rebuke.

"I was just going to say I don't know why you think this is a good idea. The last time you changed logistical plans on Ella Jenkins, she almost got back on a plane to Atlanta. I don't think your fit body, accent, or charm will work this time. She's had all three and is still mad at you."

He has a point, but I don't care. I'm committed to this plan, so I may as well see it through. "Sure, she'll bristle at first, but I will wear her down." I throw a wink at him through the mirror and he shrugs in disgust.

"Well, please don't wear her down in the royal limo. I knew I should have taken the armored Range Rover out."

I chuckle. "Don't worry, Senya; that's what partitions are for."

"Yes, and I will definitely raise it as soon as she enters the car. Not because you will seduce her, but because I am sure she will curse you out properly in person. Better yet, I will summon one of the royal drivers from Accra so he can escort you two. I will take a motorbike back; I feel like taking a ride."

I nod in agreement. What if she really starts to yell at me when she sees me? I need to prepare myself now to withstand the attack. No matter what, I cannot mess this up. If she needs to scream obscenities at me, I will take it. I'm hoping she will be screaming at me for different reasons by the time we reach the village of Tafo.

I spend the final hour of the 90-minute drive preparing how I will greet Ella when I see her. It's been eight days since I last held her, and it feels like an eternity. It will take great strength not to kiss her on-site. I should prepare for her rejection, but in my heart that scenario does not exist. When we arrive at the hotel, Ella is waiting on a bench in the beautiful kente pant outfit her friend Maya had Mawuli make for her. She looks like a vision. Her hair is down and framing her face; her curls seem bigger than ever. I love the her afro; it makes her look fun and serious at the same time. No Black woman would ever wear an afro like that unless she was very confident in who she is. That's sexy.

As we pull up to the curb, suddenly I'm nervous and very grateful for tinted windows. I'm not sure how she will react when she notices I'm here. Then the car stops.

"All right, your majesty—there she is. Go get her. I've already alerted the royal guard that you need a driver. One should be here within three minutes; we're a little early."

I take a deep breath and exit the car. She sees me instantly and rises. If she's shocked to see me, her face doesn't show it. She looks relaxed. Like she was expecting me. Her eyes take me in slowly from top to bottom, and I do the same with her. Her gaze pauses at my kente cloth-clad chest before moving to my lips. Maybe she wants this as badly as I do. I approach with outstretched hands.

"Ella, you look lovely today. Mawuli outdid herself." She steps closer to me.

"King, you saw me in this at the shop. You already knew how lovely I would look." I chuckle and step closer to her.

"Ah! But I think she's tightened cloth where she needed to tighten. Your body is now one with this kente. How will I ever separate the two later?" She steps even closer; our noses are almost touching.

"Who says you'll get the chance?" *OK, Kofi...let's slow this down a bit.* I take her hand and kiss the back of her knuckles.

"I hope you're not terribly disappointed I came to retrieve you myself."

She laughs a full laugh as she tucks her hands away behind her back. "Your majesty, I expected as much. You have too much to lose to leave me to Senya. Shall we?" She points to the limo, and I notice my new driver has arrived. When I open the door, she notices Senya is missing. "Where is Senya?"

I guide her into the car and follow. I give her space by sitting on the bench opposite hers. "He wanted to grab a motorbike from the palace and ride back into Kumasi. Plus, I think he was concerned about the outcome of our reunion...wanted to avoid the potential fighting and all that." Her face lights up in amusement and I decide to take the moment to truly apologize to her. First, I roll up the partition.

"Ella, I was scared you loved Adom the same way I want you to love me. I apologize for all the foolish things I said. Will you please forgive me?" *I, a king, am begging but I don't care.* "I can't promise I won't get jealous, because I am possessive over what is mine. But I do promise I will never doubt you again. This past week has been pure hell. It's only been eight days, but now that I know what it is to have you in my life, I'm not prepared to ever have you out of it."

She looks at me intently, trying to weigh the veracity of my words. It seems like a lifetime before she exhales and replies.

"What does that mean, Kofi? What do you want from me?"

I move to her bench and our knees touch. It's electric.

"Ella, I think I'm falling in love with you. I've never felt this way about anyone. I think about you all the time and how you can be a part of my life in a more permanent way."

"I can't be a permanent fixture in your life, Kofi. You're a king. And I'm definitely not an Ashanti queen. I'm not an Ashanti anything. I'm a Black woman from Atlanta that has found her heart in an impossible situation."

"You're exactly the woman I need by my side." I take a chance and take her hand. She does not pull away. "You make me feel like there's a little piece of the world God designed just for me. You are made just for me."

Then, I take the ultimate leap of faith and stroke her hair, signaling a kiss. She hesitates, but then leans into my hand. I take her mouth with all the zeal I can muster under the uncertain circumstances. The kiss is tentative, but a start. She immediately pulls away and her face contorts into deep thought.

We say nothing else to each other. I am grateful she allows me to hold her hand while she gently sleeps. The nap is a welcome reprieve. It stops me from my natural inclination to influence compliance when I cannot command it. I want to push her; I want to know if she too is falling in love with me. I want to know if she forgives me and if she will stay in Ghana longer than the initial 30 days. Will she stay with me? Before I can think of a way to broach the subjects, I too fall asleep.

When I awake, I look out the window and see we have arrived in Tafo. The time went quickly. As tense as it still feels in this limo, our arrival is probably for the best.

VISITATION

Ella

$\mathcal{I}$ awake from my car nap to red dirt roads and dilapidated tin-roofed buildings passing by our car windows.

Tafo in many ways is exactly what I pictured it to be. The absence of paved roads and sound structures was expected. However, I'm surprised to see the number of businesses lining the streets. There are drugstores, restaurants, and braiding salons. I assumed the villagers went into Kumasi for all of their business needs. Conversely, this is a small town with its own thriving economy. The Owusus' Tarkwa was vastly different.

Then there's the children. The children are everywhere and nowhere at nine a.m. on a Saturday morning. Most don't wear shoes and play aimlessly on the side of the road. I look over at Kofi, and he's sound asleep and his soft snores are cute. I want to move closer to him, but my mind refuses to allow my heart to concede. I reach over and gently shake him awake. "I think we've arrived, your majesty." He shifts in his seat and smiles as if he were dreaming. He turns to look at me and takes a deep breath. The intensity of his stare leaves me breathless. His eyes break away and he looks out the window. He nods, pleased with what he sees.

"Yes, this is Tafo. Tell me, Ella—what are your first impressions of our largest village?"

I answer him eagerly. It is time to get down to business. "I see need and enterprise in equal supply. I can tell this is a village that is self-reliant and works hard to keep it that way."

Kofi turns from the window and lays his hand on my shoulder with a smile. "You're very perceptive; you sound like a future queen. That is exactly what Tafo is, an enterprising village that needs a new spark. That spark is you and the public schools you will bring the next generation."

I give him a hesitant nod. "That's a tall order. It's the tallest order I've ever had to fill. How will I convince your community that they should allow and welcome Revolution Academies into their village?" *How will I convince myself I am capable to be queen?*

He gives me a serious look. "By becoming a part of it."

I shake my head in disappointment. "I usually do. I generally stay three to six months in the communities I'm supporting. But I do not know if I can do that here. It's another country."

Kofi takes me by surprise and drops to his knees on the floor of the limo. He gently places his palms on my thighs and looks up at me with a steady gaze. His eyes are bigger and more intoxicating than ever. For a moment, I'm convinced he's about to ask me to be his wife and stay with him forever. But of course, he's not. He needs a queen. Not an independent American that opens schools easier than her heart. Still, his eyes are imploring me to do something unspoken.

"Ella, you can do this. You've done it in disadvantaged cities across the U.S." He grabs my hands to offer a reassuring squeeze. "What makes Tafo, Tarkwa, or Aboso any different?"

I tear away from his gaze and start twisting the Cartier love bracelet around my wrist. "Kofi, you must know poverty in the states does not look like this." I gesture to the passing landscape before meeting his eyes again. "America at its core is a welfare state with a stronger infrastructure. It camouflages poverty well."

I search for a better explanation, but there is no clear explanation for the effects of racism versus colonialism on communities. Plus, that's too heavy of a conversation to have right now. "I don't know. I just think education is clearly the game-changer here. And everyone from the students to village leaders and the king knows it."

He nods, finally understanding. "I think what you're trying to convey is the level of accountability is the highest you've had to manage. Since our community is all on one page, anyone can take you to task. The people you serve will have a great sense of investment in your proposal and its implementation."

I raise my hands in agreement. "Yes! I don't want to let them down."

Kofi grabs my hands and gives a warm look. "You won't let anyone down. I've seen your work. I think every school you've opened and every community you've transformed up to this point was preparation for this moment." He abruptly knocks on the partition. "Driver?"

The driver rolls the partition down, revealing a much older man behind the wheel. He looks to be a slight man not a day younger than 80. "Yes, your majesty?"

"You may let us out here and pick us up in the same spot two hours from now." Kofi pats my thigh and rises from the floor to take the seat opposite mine. He starts to smooth his clothes and look in the mirror of the window glass to check his reflection. The king is making an appearance. The transformation from pleading lover to dignitary is quick and appreciated. I need him to provide unbiased feedback as I attempt to influence members of his community to trust the Revolution Academy vision.

I take another look out the window and realize our first stop is a very old church. At least it looks old. The wood frame and bell in the small steeple are reminiscent of an episode of *Little House on the Prairie*. There is a large cemetery that surrounds the sides and back of the church. I determine it is probably the main church in town.

"Kofi, do you worship here?"

Kofi looks out the window with a tinge of sadness. "It is my mother's family church. When I do have the privilege of attending church, this is where I come." He looks over at me to explain. "It's not as often as I'd like, but I have to stay neutral on religious matters. I have to lead everyone and alienate no one."

I chuckle lightly. "I know all about that. My mother was a Baptist and my father a Catholic. To avoid war, we just became Baptists. Then they became Baptist pastors. I think my father still misses parts of his Catholic faith."

"It's a bit more complicated here. Religion is such a sensitive issue. No matter where I visit, another faction might feel slighted. So, I am careful to keep my visits anywhere sparse."

"Smart man." I grab my bag and gather my items. "If your visits can be so divisive, why are we here?"

He opens the door and steps out into the blinding African sun. He places the sunglasses he never leaves home without on his eyes before leaning down back into the limo to offer his hand to me. I climb out and instantly regret forgetting my shades. I turn to him and place my hand over my eyes. He smirks and takes his shades off and places them on my eyes. "There, that's better." He strokes a tendril of hair from my face and I nearly melt. *But I don't.*

"We're here, Ella, because this is the place to be." He takes my hand and starts to walk me to the entrance. "It is the most populous church in Tafo, and the pastor and I are close."

As we approach, I see a sign outside the church reads *Tafo Presbyterian Assembly est. 1689.* I gasp, realizing the congregation is over 400 years old. I take out my cell phone to snap a picture. "Wow, Kofi, this building has real historical significance."

"Why do you say that?"

"It's over 400 years old!"

He pauses at the door of the church and breaks out into his hearty laugh. "Oh, my Ella, you're in Africa. Everything is old! This village alone is 1,000 years old and broken up into two sections, Old Tafo and Tafo. If we go by your definition, everything you see today will have historical significance. I forget how young your country is."

I laugh, too. "Yeah, it's crazy to think this church is older than America by quite a bit."

We continue inside the church and I touch each and every pew. I think of all the services and community meetings held here. Did they meet here to combat the slave trade? Did they strategize in this very room about how to keep the villagers safe from their would-be captors? A booming voice interrupts my musings.

"Asantehene! What a pleasant surprise." A portly man in a clergy attire comes from a room at the back of the church and grabs Kofi in a fatherly hug. Kofi looks genuinely happy to see him. "You should have told me you were coming to visit; I would have held a full service just for you." He laughs, patting Kofi on the back.

"No, sir, I only came to introduce the woman who will bring public education to the village." He motions for me to join their reunion. Once I'm close enough, he places his hand in mine and squeezes. "This is Ella Jenkins, CEO of Revolution Academies." The reverend looks at our joined hands and calculates something quickly in his head before smiling. "Ella, this is the Reverend Paul Asante, also known as my uncle."

"Your uncle!" I reach out to grab his hand in a shake. Instead, he grabs me in a hug equivalent to the one he gave Kofi moments before. When I'm released, I smile. "It's very nice to meet you, reverend. Now, are you really his uncle? Or is that another term of endearment?"

He tilts his head and gives me a curious look.

I offer a laugh. "Because I found out the hard way that Akua is not really his aunt!"

Kofi's uncle places his hand on my shoulder and laughs with me, while escorting me to the nearest pew to sit down with him. "I assure you, I am his dear late mother's only brother, and I am pleased to meet you." He grabs and vigorously shakes both my hands. "We have been waiting for you. Our young people need schooling they can afford so they can have hope. I can preach hope all I want from that pulpit..." He pauses to look up at his lectern.

"But if I can't offer a tangible plan to help to change their lives, it falls on deaf ears."

Kofi walks around to stand in the row in front of us. He looks at me though he's speaking to his uncle. "Well, that is what Ella is, uncle; she is hope."

Kofi's uncle looks up at him as he stares at me and claps his hands together once in joy. "Praise God, praise God! Ella, you let me know any way the church can help you in this endeavor."

I respond immediately. "Do you think you could host one or two community meetings where I can present the school's proposal and get feedback?"

He leans forward and squeezes my hand. "Of course I can!" He leans closer to me and whispers, "And if you need my help in another endeavor..." He takes a quick and furtive glance up at Kofi before winking at me. "Just let me know. I think you're here to change more than our community. Maybe a king's heart?" I blush.

Kofi interrupts by clearing his throat. "Well, uncle, if you are done flirting with my CEO, I'd like to show her the gardens out back."

Kofi's uncle stands. "Of course. I will be in here if you need anything."

Kofi offers his hand and I stand. I shake Kofi's uncle's hand. "See you later, reverend, and thank you!"

"You are very welcome, dear." He releases my hand and walks back toward the office he appeared from. After he disappears, I hear him yell, "You two enjoy the village today. Akwasidae is always fun."

Kofi and I walk out the church into the cemetery and gardens. It is beautiful.

"Come." Kofi holds his hand out. "I want to show you something very important to me."

We walk for a few minutes deep into the forest, passing fewer and fewer headstones until we are covered with tree canopies and walking through brush. Kofi's pace is two steps ahead of mine and determined. It slows once we approach a grand white and bronze sepulcher. The grandeur and size look out of place among the humble surroundings of the forest. Yet, Kofi looks at it like it's where it has always been. Instinctively, he walks to it and rubs his hands along the marble, embracing it in some way. I keep my distance, feeling that I need to be invited into his moment. After a few moments, I speak up.

"Where are we, Kofi?"

He snaps out of his trance and turns to me. "Come."

I walk to him and read the front of the structure: *In loving memory of Akosua Asante Ajyei. Queen of the Ashanti. Mother to All. May the ancestors watch all that she loves.* I stand reading the inscription over and over again with my arms hugging my chest. I shift from one leg to the other knowing this must be his mother's grave but needing him to confirm he brought me face to face with the one subject he does not speak about. "Is this where your mother rests?"

"Yes." The pain in his eyes confirms it although her death was over 25 years ago. The weight of it hangs on him like it was only yesterday. "This forest was her favorite place, and Tafo is her hometown. My father insisted she be buried in a place she loved." He turns back to me. "She hated the palace and the city. She thought it was isolating and pretentious. She was out here any chance she got."

I reach out to touch his arm. "Kofi, what happened to your mother? How did she die?"

Kofi rolls his shoulders back and takes a cleansing breath. He turns and I see a single tear threaten to unleash more, but he doesn't allow it. I wipe it away and he looks me in the eye before gently grabbing my wrist. A beat passes, and he brings my hand to his lips before sitting down in front of his mother's grave. He reaches up for me and I allow him to pull me down into his lap. He buries his nose into my hair and breathes in the confidence he needs to tell his story.

"I'll start from the beginning."

Chapter Twenty-One

REMEMBERANCE

Kofi

"My mother was a beautiful woman and set apart to be queen at an early age.

We can trace our lineage back 14 generations, and her father, my grandfather, was Tafo's 18th chief. The seat of Asantehene may only be passed to men, and that man may choose any wife that shows she can uphold the honor and customs of the Ashanti to stand by him. Of course, this can easily be many Ashanti women. However, due to our own form of aristocracy and classism, power is only exchanged through a few families and villages: the Asantes of Tafo, the Ajyeis of Tarkwa, and the Apeagyeis of Aboso. Each of these villages has a chief that makes up part of the council that appoints and advises the king. Are you following me so far?"

Ella looks up at me and nods. I run my finger down her jaw and continue. "If the chief has a daughter, he prepares her for the honor. My grandfather had two daughters to choose from, but my mother was the obvious choice. Not only was she beautiful, but she was pliable. My grandfather was an unethical tyrant. He would do anything to win favor and money, and that made him a hard man. My mother's mother died when she was very young, so she and her younger sister, Afia, grew up with just my grandfather and his regime. They both became very good at handling powerfully moody men. My mother especially knew how to turn the head of a king. However, she was never able to capture my grandfather or father's heart.

"My parents married right away, as soon as they both turned 18. It was a good marriage for about five years, and then my father became Asantehene when his father suddenly died." I start to shift and rub my jaw. Ella places her hand on my thigh to calm me down.

"I came the year after he was crowned, and my mother doted upon me. However, she almost died having me, and it was determined she could not have any more children. My father was disappointed...he wanted a house full of children, as does any king. You know African virility and all that jazz."

Ella snickers at my comment. "It's powerful stuff, huh?"

I squeeze her shoulder and chuckle—that would have been borderline offensive coming from anyone else. But from Ella, I take it as an attempt to lighten the moment. "Yes, ma'am. We make babies without even touching a woman."

Ella turns around in my lap and smiles. It calms me and she continues her joke. "Lucky for me, my birth control has never lost a battle."

I smile back and rub her cheek before she turns back around and lies against my chest.

"So, after your mother had you, what happened?"

I take a deep breath. "My father pulled away. He started taking a mistress. The council advised him to take her as another wife and not have concubines; however, my father never entertained the idea of ordaining a second wife, a custom that many had abandoned. However, as king, he argued it was his right to have lovers and not answer to anyone. He wanted to do business in the West and knew that Western culture did not approve of polygamy. The council was not pleased and ordered his discretion. He obliged. We never knew who his mistress was. If she could not be legitimized as a wife, she would remain nameless. If anyone did know, they dared not speak of it."

Ella shifts in my lap to straddle my hips and face me. "Hmm. I'm sure his wife's father being a member of the council didn't help his cause."

I shake my head. "No, it did not. But my father doubled down and started spending more time with his mistress than my mother. My mother knew and did not fight a war she would not win. However, I saw it slowly eat away at her for years."

"That's so sad. She stayed knowing he didn't respect or love her?"

I swallow hard and my jaw clenches. "This is not America, Ella, and unfortunately, she loved him. Where was she to go? Back to her father's home? The one saving grace was she had no idea who the mistress was. Besides the council's edict, I believe my father did not flaunt it as a twisted way of sparing her. We lived like this for 11 years." I shift again and rub my face with my hands. I hate talking about this, but she needs to know.

Encouraging me to continue, she takes my hand and kisses each finger. I am surprised and pleased. She then lays her head on my chest. I continue.

"One day, there was a knock at the door. It was Adom."

"Your cousin?" she asks for confirmation.

"Yes, my cousin. My mother's sister's son and only nephew. He asked Akua to see my mother, and she invited him to have lunch with us outside. Little did I know, it would be the worst lunch of my life. He dropped a bomb of information on us that neither of us ever expected. His words were like a jagged knife in my mother's back. I watched helplessly as his words slowly destroyed her."

Ella sits up. "What words?"

"He told us that he was my father's son. I didn't want to believe him, but the more he spoke, the more I realized it was truth. He told us that for years, my father came to visit his mother nearly every night. Adom started investigating, listening in on conversations, asking more questions among the servants. Finally, he confronted his mother, and she gave in and confirmed the decade-long affair and that Adom was indeed, a son of the king. My mother nearly crumbled there at the table—a double betrayal crushed her soul.

"Learning what her sister and husband had done put her into a partial catatonic state. I was the only one who could see her...she turned everyone away except for her most trusted maid. She also forbade me, for the first time ever, to spend time with Senya. From that point on, it felt like it was her and I against the world."

My chest starts to tighten, and my lips stop moving as I remember that last year of my mother's life. "I was an 11-year old boy without my two best friends, and she was a shell. I remember the conversations she would spontaneously burst into about killing my father or herself. She always asked for me to walk her down to her beloved river. I would walk her there and back every day, watching to make sure she was safe. Just trying desperately to make her life worth living again. I wanted her to know that my love was enough. I convinced myself I was enough to make her want to live again." I feel Ella wiping tears from my eyes, stopping them before they fall and alternately squeezing me in a hug. I don't know why, but her face wills me to continue.

"Then, one day, my father had tickets to a local football game and I really wanted to go. He was taking Senya and me. I think I was more interested in spending time with Senya than him. Akua assured me she would keep an eye on my mother. My mother begged me not to go, but my father insisted I could not live my life in her room. I needed to start doing the things young men do again. I remember when I stopped by her room to say goodbye and she turned away from me. I remember I was so angry at her and called her selfish. Then I left." I catch the sob in my throat long enough to finish the story. Long enough to lay myself and all my pain bare to Ella.

"When we returned from the game, Akua met us at the door. She whispered to my father, but I heard her say my mother was missing. She got dressed and said something about going to the river. Then I ran. I ran all the way to the river; I'd never run so fast in my life." Ella is holding and rocking me. She's the only thing keeping me from lying face down and crying to God in front of this grave as I did for many nights as a child.

"First, I saw her clothes. Then I saw the notes laid on the path to the river like a footpath, each one held by a stone. There was one for her sister, one for my father, and one for me. Then as I got to the riverbank, I saw her body floating. All I could think was, *God! I have to cover my mother; she's naked and no one should see the queen, my mother, like this.*" I push Ella away and stand up to pace and breathe. "Half the village was close behind me once word started to spread, but I managed to pull her out of the river and cover her."

Ella is crying and looking up at me. I can tell she's crying for the little boy that had to find his mother floating in the river, not for the man I am now. She doesn't pity me like I feared she would. Instead, it's clear she shares my pain. She stands up and stills my pacing with an embrace. "I'm so sorry, Kofi," she whispers in my ear.

"You know the worst part? My father actually mourned her. He was never with another woman as far as I know, and he built this God-awful shrine to her in her favorite woods. I was never truly his son after that. I could not love him after what he did to my mother. We lived like strangers until he finally agreed to send me away to London for secondary schooling."

"I understand," she soothes.

"I blamed Adom for years. I felt if he would have kept his mouth shut, she would have never known. I know that's crazy, but I was young. He was hurting just like I was. My father never acknowledged him as his son—therefore, neither did anyone else. Although everyone knew the truth, they basically shunned him. I'm not proud of it, but I felt I had to do the same. I would not betray my mother by treating him like a brother. I'd already let her down."

"Adom coped by endlessly competing with me. I guess it was his way to get my father's attention and to prove he was good enough to be my brother. In retrospect, he was as hurt and torn apart as I was.

Both of our lives changed the day my mother took that walk to the river. I should have never left for that stupid football game that day."

Ella places both hands on my upper arms and pushes back to look me in the eyes. "No, you were a child. Your mother was sick, Kofi; you couldn't have known."

"That's not entirely true. I did know. She would talk about it all the time, but I never thought she would do it. I thought she loved me too much to. But I was wrong. Love isn't powerful enough to save someone that's determined to be lost."

Ella sniffles and wipes her eyes. She tried to hold it together while I told my story, but this last revelation was too much for her to bear. Now she knows why I have never given myself completely over to love. I'm terrified to let the one I love down. I'm scared to lose them when I'm not enough to keep them. She tries to compose herself, but her voice breaks

"All I know is she must have loved you very much to want you with her. I think she was just hurting so bad that she didn't know what to do with the pain."

I rub my hands in her hair to soothe her. I love her more for sharing some of my pain. She doesn't have to care, but she does. "I know you're right. After my father died 15 years later, I became Asantehene and got a therapist. My therapist helped me sort all of my feelings out and I finally read the note my mother left me. I never had the strength to do it before."

Ella continues to rub my arms, waiting for me to decide if I want to share the contents of it.

"It said: *My dear Kofi. Be a good king. Love a good queen. And always save a place for me by the river.* I've done two out of three, but I don't know if I'll ever subject another woman I love to royal service. It destroyed my mother."

Ella doesn't comment—she just looks at me, waiting. She's waiting for me to lead us out of this physical and emotional place of pain.

CRAVING A KING

"Thank you for bringing me here, Kofi. But why do it if it brings you so much pain?"

"Because I want you to know everything about me. I want you to know all that makes me. Ella, I'm falling in love with you, and I don't want you to ever doubt my feelings for you. If I act crazy sometimes, it's because the last woman I gave my all to left me and it took me years to recover. That's why I've kept relationships really light over the years."

I grab her and hold her body flush against mine, placing my forehead to hers. "You stole my heart immediately, and I don't want anyone else but you. I haven't figured out exactly what that means yet. But please know that I think on it day and night. I'm beyond sorry I let my bullshit cloud my judgment of you and me. I will never allow that to happen again. I adore you."

She places her arms around my neck. "I know you do. You mean the world to me Kofi."

I press my lips to hers and she parts them like the sea, inviting me to lay my burdens down. I kiss her like my life and happiness depend on it. When our passion breaks, I take her hand and lead us out of the wilderness.

Chapter Twenty-Two

FORBEARANCE

Kofi

The rest of our visit in Tafo is lighter than our visit to my mother's grave, but just as important.

Her entire demeanor has changed. She is more relaxed. She understands me now more than anyone else in the world. The understanding makes a difference.

I show Ella the cocoa factory that used to employ 1,500 of Tafo's residents. Currently, it employs only 200. The cocoa industry in the Kumasi region used to thrive, but the community could not keep up with the technological advances in manufacturing. Even now, there are vacancies at the factory, but not enough trained human capital in the village to fill them. We need a more educated populace to bring the factory to its former glory. That's where Revolution Academies will help. I'm determined, with Ella's help, to make Tafo the center of cocoa production in West Africa once again by providing a trained and educated workforce.

We also visit the homes of some residents so she can get a sense of where the students we serve will be coming from each morning. Without fail, they are coming from poverty, but they are also coming from an abundance of love and pride. Ella promises me that Revolution Academies will focus on the latter.

Before we head home, Ella gets the chance to watch me in the Akwasidae parade—me being celebrated in the streets of Tafo is something to see. I am loved by my people, and they count on me for so much. I start to think of how I will fit Ella into this world. All of my talk of love and being together is little more than a fantasy without a plan. The reality is that I have a heavy job to do, and no one expects a foreign woman to come in and help me do it. However, I know that if it is not Ella by my side, then I will continue to go at it alone. Who else in the world is strong, beautiful, and intelligent enough to be my bride and the significant other of the next Asantehene? *No one.*

When our day is over, our driver retrieves us from the front of the church where we started our day. As soon as we are alone, I ask the driver to raise the partition and Ella shocks me by taking me into a deep kiss.

We are not tentative with this kiss; we are all tongues, lips, and moans, trying to take in more of each other with each movement. When she finally breaks away, I continue to nip her jaw and neck.

"Kofi," she pants. "How can this work? I live in Atlanta, and you're here."

I stop kissing her face for a moment and look her in her eyes. What else can a king with no answers do but act as if he does. "Shhhh. Let's just sit in the fact that I want you and you want me. We will figure the rest out later. Right now, I would really like to taste you. Lucky for us, I have time to do it before we reach Accra. Is that OK with you?"

She looks at me and nods.

I smile. I have lots of experience with receiving pleasure royal vehicles. Today will be the first time I give it. I'm eager to make my baby come. "Lie back and open those pretty thighs for me."

Ella complies with my request, and I lower myself to the floor on my knees. I place my head right at the center of her sex and smell the sweetness that will soon drip down my chin. I take two fingers and begin to rub her clit through the thin cotton of her pants, creating the friction she's missed. She swallows hard while looking at me before rolling her head back to the chair rest.

"Yes baby, you're already purring for me." I lick the cotton up and down, providing pressure to her sweet nub. I look at the imprint the wetness from my tongue leaves on her sweet pussy. She must not be wearing panties. I start to circle her clit with a firm press. "Naughty girl, you didn't wear panties today, did you?" She moans.

"Unzip your top for me and slide it off." She sits up and not only removes her top, but also removes her pretty red lace bra also. Her breasts bound forward and I reach up to catch her left breast in my mouth. I take the caramel nipple between my teeth before latching on for dear life. I look up at her and my cheeks hollow as I greedily take her breast in. I use my other hand to continue rubbing the moist mound between her legs. I move to the right nipple and repeat my oral onslaught while increasing my speed between her legs. Her moans of pleasure are tempered with hard breaths.

"Please, Kofi, I'm so ready." I feel the start of a tremble and know she's about to burst.

I remove my fingers to lean down and take a quick nibble at her kente-covered sex.

"So ready for what, baby?"

"Your mouth, I need you to taste me."

I lift my head and give her a knowing smirk. "Then let's strip you of these pants and make your pussy roar." I carefully unzip and peel the perfectly tailored pants off her full ass and thighs. In any other circumstance, I would not be this gentle with her clothing. But I don't want her having to walk back into her hotel with no panties and ripped pants. Once I have the pants totally off, I give her center fold a strong lick before my next command.

"I want you to turn around and place your hands against the partition and spread your legs wide for me." She looks at me nervously and gives a quick glance at the dark partition to where our driver is sitting.

"What if he sees me?"

"Trust me. He can't see or hear anything. He also has no idea who you are. He's only one of our many drivers from the royal guard."

She gives me a light laugh. "Yes, I guess you're right. It's not like Senya is driving us around knowing I am about to have my tits pressed against this glass."

I send a silent prayer of thanks up to Senya. He was a genius for suggesting I switch drivers out. Now Ella can relax. "All right, queen." I drop my voice. "You know I don't take to having to ask you to do things twice." She gives me a carnal look that makes me harder than a gold bar. She's turned on. The queen likes to be bossed. I can accommodate that desire with ease. "Arch your back a bit and get that ass up in the air for me."

She obliges and I shift over to press her back down to provide the perfect arch for my tongue's entry. Then I turn around to sit on the floor of the limo, so that my back is to her. I lift my legs and rest them on the seat across from us. I use my hands to grab her hips for leverage.

"Spread wider for me, baby, and sink down. I want you to sit on my face." She lowers her body until I'm face to face with her sex. It is still swollen and throbbing from my earlier assault. I lift my chin and graze it with my teeth before dragging my mouth over her center and flicking her clit. Then I forsake her clit for a while and focus on every other inch of her sex. I lick up and down, back and forth, in punishing circles and massage her ass over my head as I go. She drips like a faucet into my mouth and I can't get enough.

"Touch yourself for me, baby. I want to watch you get yourself off." When I see her perfectly manicured pink nails move over her clit in circles, I groan in appreciation. "Baby, that shit's so hot." I drag three fingers through her wet folds and then taste the juices before inserting a finger inside her tight core.

"Kofi!" she yelps. "Do it again."

I do, this time adding another finger and then a third, pleasuring her at a relentless pace. Her hand starts circling her clit harder and faster while I look and take her to pure ecstasy with my hand. "Come, Ella. Come now!" I command.

Without hesitation, that drip becomes a gush and my face is soaking wet. Ella screams out her release and I hope the poor guy driving us truly can't hear her.

Once she finishes her release, I gently smack her ass on both cheeks to let her know I'm coming up. I take a seat next to her and help her get settled back into the seat. I turn to my right and pull out a pack of scented wipes and clean her off before cleaning her sweet essence from my face. Then I help her place that perfect ass back into her pants. She leans her head back and closes her eyes to catch her breath.

"How are you feeling, love?" I ask her as I place her hand on my chest.

"Taken care of." Her statement warms my heart, because that's what I want to do—take care of her.

"Does this mean you forgive me? I hate that I hurt you, Ella."

She turns to me so I can fully see her face. "Yes, I forgive you. But if you ever do that shit again, not trusting me and leaving with harsh words, I will leave you and never return. I don't forgive the same sin twice."

I swallow hard and nod. Her tone is serious and unwavering.

Satisfied, she looks down at my bulging hard-on and arches her eyebrow. "How are you feeling? Can I, um, help you with that?" She places her hand over my bulge and begins to massage.

I chuckle and gently lift her hand to my mouth to place a kiss. "Don't pay him any mind...he will calm down in a second. Today is about you; I don't want anything in return right now."

She looks at me and pokes her bottom lip out into a pout. "But I really want to."

"And you will, but Ella, the way I want to take your mouth and body will not work in this car. I need space, time, and you completely naked. I plan on placing my mouth on every inch of your body in an apology before entering you again."

Her eyes get wide. "Ah! The apology tour...yes, I'm looking forward to that."

"So am I. We kick off the tour at Bonbiri tonight...that is, if you want to return. I will send for your dress and stylists. There is time for this change of plans."

Ella gives me a smile. "Good, I'm game for tonight."

I knock on the partition and instruct the driver to change his route and take us to Bonbiri.

"Good, rest your eyes before we arrive home."

She gives a grateful look. "I am rather worn out." She stretches out on the seat, laying her head in my lap. I lay one arm over her while I stroke her hair before nodding off into a sweet slumber myself.

Chapter Twenty-Three

ANTICIPATION

Ella

The nap with Kofi during the ride to Bonbiri recharges me. When we arrive, I enter his home ready to prepare for the Akwasidae Ball. Kofi brings me to his family room, and we spoon on his large couch before we have to part and get dressed. He kisses the back of my ear and entwines his fingers with mine.

"Are you hungry? I can send Senya out to get something if you like."

I shake my head. "No, I'm OK. Why would Senya go out? I thought Akua made all your meals here."

Kofi's body flinches against mine. "I sent her to the palace to serve for a while. I think it's best."

I know why Kofi sent her away. She was deceitful and was the behind-the-scenes architect of our fight over Adom. No matter how relieved I am that I don't have to deal with her snide comments or disapproving looks tonight, I can't help but feel responsible for a family rift. Akua has taken care of Kofi his entire life. He's known me all of a week. When I leave, he will need her. I wiggle out of his grasp and sit on the edge of the couch. I don't face him.

"Kofi, please don't send her away on account of me. She is so

important to you. I'm sure her behavior was motivated by her love for you and not spite for me, even though I'm pretty sure she hates me."

Kofi sits up on his elbow and reaches out to caress my hips and back. "Look at me."

I turn around and he sits up, shifting beside me on the couch. "Whether Akua hates you or not is of no consequence to me or my decision. Please do not feel guilty. My choice to send Akua to the palace was a royal staffing decision. It wasn't personal. She should not have lied. In my eyes, omission is lying. She is supposed to serve the king and protect the seat. Allowing my emotions to be incorrectly influenced was a failure to do her job. That is all."

I know he's lying to himself. Akua hurt him. I'd also like to believe that he cares about her hurting me, even though I just said the opposite. However, his stiff posture and disappointed eyes let me know this isn't the time to discuss it. There is probably no point. Like earlier with me and Adom, his mind is made up. I stand and stretch.

"Well, I'm going to go and take a shower and start to get dressed for the evening. We only have two hours before it's time to leave."

Kofi stands also and takes my hand. "OK, your dress and anything else you may need is set up in your room. Mawuli had just finished steaming it when I called from the car. It was still in Kumasi and on its way out the door to you in Accra. We caught it just in time. Your hairstylist and makeup artist initially went to the Westin to help you dress—they will be here in an hour."

I look at him and shake my head. "Kofi, you didn't have to do that. I am capable of doing my hair and makeup. You have enough to coordinate without adding my beauty needs to the list."

He steps forward and grabs me by my waist. I'm pulled into him and I don't know if it's his strong arms pulling me or an invisible gravitational pull I'm drawn into. His body feels like home. He kisses the inside of my ear and my body reacts. He starts to whisper, "I will take care of all your needs if you allow me." He drops his right hand between my thighs and runs his hand over my damp center. "Why don't we start with this obvious need between your legs?"

I laugh and try to gently push away. He keeps me close. "Kofi, we don't have time. But tonight, you can fill every need my body has. Trust me, there are many," I pant.

He rubs his face in my massive mess of curls before growling. "I want you so bad. I could bend you over this couch and take you like the ravenous lion I am right now." He takes my hand and pushes it over the hard bulge that has grown between his legs. "He's so ready for you, baby. Let me fill you up."

My breathing speeds up and I reach up, kissing him in an attempt to control it. We stay connected for a moment before I pull away. It is literally one of the hardest things I've ever had to do. *How does this man manage to make me want him so much?* "Later," I promise. "For now, I need to shower and prepare for the team you've hired to transform me tonight."

Kofi sighs and takes my face in his hands. "Baby, it's not a transformation. You're perfect. It's just a luxury for you to play with. You deserve to be pampered." He grabs my hand. "Come, let's both go and get started."

Hand in hand, we head upstairs. Kofi drops me at my room with a chaste kiss to my forehead. I'm grateful because I don't think I have the power to walk away from my body's desire again. Once in the river room, I am greeted with a rack of lingerie. The silk La Perla pieces are delicate and sexy as hell. The card attached to the first teddy on the rack has my name scrawled in script on the envelope. I open it and read Kofi's sweet note: *All of this is yours. Just don't get too attached; I plan to rip every piece of it off of you at some point. Love, Kofi.* I smile at the note. When did he have time to do this?

As I enter the closet to drop my bag and strip for my shower, I see the gorgeous dress he commissioned for me hanging up and glittering from every angle. Beneath the dress is a cache of designer heels for me to choose from. Then I notice a new vanity that wasn't in the closet when I left Bonbiri three days ago. On the vanity are various expensive French perfumes and an expensive clutch shaped like a crown. This man is pure class.

I decide I can't wait until after the ball—I need to feel him now. It must be all the pretty shoes. I take a look at my phone and confirm I have 45 minutes before the stylists arrive. I leave my room and knock on his bedroom door. He doesn't answer, but I hear the shower running and decide to go in. I strip my clothes off piece by piece as I make my way to his bathroom. I'm completely naked by the time I see his towering chocolate frame in the shower. His back is away from me and my eyes follow his strong shoulders and broad back to the perfect ass. It's tight and being held in place by two very muscular thighs. I imagine my tongue tracing every hill and valley that creates his body's landscape.

I approach the shower and open the door slowly. He turns and grabs me like he was expecting me. Immediately, picks me up in his arms and I wrap my legs around his waist.. We kiss and he eases my legs from around his body. As my feet touch the wet title floor of the shower, he kneels before me, parts my knees, and dips his head between my thighs to lick my slick, sweet center. He gives me one, then two, and a third strong lick before biting down on my throbbing clit. My head rolls back against the shower wall in perfect pleasure, and you can hear my moans over the rushing shower water.

He gently backs me into the shower glass door and lines his massive manhood to my opening. He knocks into me with a grunt that is pure need. He kisses my neck and places his arms around my waist to keep my body in place. He pulls all the way out and then fills me up again in long slow strokes until I'm bursting all over him. Once my shakes of pleasure start, he slams into me with reckless abandon, chasing his release with singular focus.

"God, Ella, I'm going to come." He tries to slow his pace, but it's no use. "Come with me," he growls before he places his mouth around my right nipple. He sucks and tugs at my breast while he continues to ride his wave of ecstasy. His grunts become pleads for me to come with him, and I can't refuse a king. We come. Hard. Together.

Kofi sets me down to stand and turns to shut the shower off.

"Wait here," he commands before walking to the large bathtub on the opposite side of the bathroom. He fills it with water and oils before coming to the shower and taking my hand. He leads me to the edge of the tub before releasing my hand and stepping into the steaming hot water. We don't have much time but I'm happy to sit with him as long as we can. Plus, standing under the shower gave me a bit of a chill. He takes a seat against the back of the tub and reaches for me to join him. He pulls me down and sits me on his lap before kissing and bathing every inch of me. After a few minutes, we hear the knock on the door telling us my beauty team has arrived.

"Let's just skip the ball," he muses. "We can stay here, and I will make you jollof rice and feed you until you're satisfied. Then we can do some dancing of our own...naked."

I chuckle and stand to get out of the tub. I don't face him until I'm completely out of the water. If I looked at him while I was still in his lap, I might have agreed to his alternate evening plans. "As good as that sounds, I think you'd be noticed if you were missing from the biggest Ashanti event of the year." I cock my head to the side and look at him with mirth. "I don't want to be known as the American that kidnapped the king."

He laughs as he exits the tub. "Very well, then. As long as you know I will skip the ball for you. Just say the word." He opens a linen closet and comes out with a fluffy robe. He beckons me to come closer and he wraps me in it before kissing the top of my head. "Here, go greet your team. I will meet you downstairs in an hour." He kisses me like he doesn't want me to go. "I'll miss you until then."

I walk out of his room knowing yet again that I'm completely caught up. My heart is in the hands of a king.

Chapter Twenty-Four

FESTIVITIES

Kofi

I do not usually wear a tuxedo to official events.

Whether I'm meeting with Western dignitaries or other African nation heads, I'm generally in my official regalia of kente cloth. The regalia is to be worn alone with nothing else except royal neck and head ornaments. However, tonight is different. This black Tom Ford suit is the perfect complement to the Akwasidae festival ball tonight. The ball has only been around for five years. I instituted it as my own twist on the state dinner Western nations have. We host it in Accra instead of Kumasi, and it has become the hottest ticket in West Africa over the years.

I take a look at my six-foot-four frame in the perfectly tailored tuxedo and appreciate what I see staring back at me from the mirror. While prior Asantehenes were generally older and portly, I take pride in my athletic physique. I work hard in the gym to keep my 33-inch waist. I add kente to my attire by draping the colorful cloth over my right shoulder, and I'm ready. Now I must wait for Ella.

I know she will be exquisite in the gown I commissioned for her. I look forward to dancing the night away with her. I wish we could enter together, but that would not be proper. No matter how much I love Ella, my duty is to the Ashanti. I can't spring an American beauty on my arm at them tonight. Plus, it's for her own good. The British and Ghanaian tabloids will have a field day if they catch us arriving together. They will twist something good into something dirty. I can imagine the headlines: *The King's New American Toy*. Maybe they'll add the twist about her leading a school network: *Are We Adding Schools in Kumasi or is the King Adding to his Harem?* Nope. It's best if we just take separate cars. Now all I have to do is tell her.

"Your majesty, we will need to leave in 10 minutes to arrive in Accra on time. Is Ella ready?"

Senya approaches in a navy blue tuxedo with kente lapels. It's a nice touch. "She will be down shortly," I say. "However, we will need your second to drive her. We won't be arriving together."

Senya puts his hands in his pockets and rocks on his heels before shooting me a perplexing look. "I thought you two would have made up by now. Is there still trouble in paradise?"

I chuckle as I head over to the bar to pour us a drink while we wait. "No trouble. Quite the opposite, actually. What would you like to drink?" I think about my day with Ella. I bore my soul to her at my mother's grave and made passionate love to her in the shower. We are indeed happy in paradise.

Senya walks over to where I am. "I'll just take club soda. I'm driving, remember?" I nod and pour his drink. He takes a strong sip. "So, are you going to tell me why we are taking two cars or not?"

"I had not particularly planned on telling you. But if you must know, I want to avoid the press spectacle that will ensue if I arrive with her on my arm. We don't need the harassment."

Senya gives me a skeptical look. "Or maybe you just don't want to be asked questions about your personal life and your unfortunate betrothal to Abena Owusu?"

I shoot Senya a dirty look. "The two things aren't mutually exclusive. With the press comes unwarranted questions and foolish conjectures such as that ridiculous betrothal agreement."

Senya leans against the bar and crosses his arms. His mouth spreads into a mischievous grin. "Ridiculous, is it? Have you told Ella about it?"

"No, I have not, and I don't expect you to, either," I bark at Senya.

I want to punch Senya in the face for even bringing Abena Owusu up at all. I only have to think about her once a year, and that is during Akwasidae. She comes down from London and shows her face to please her family. But the betrothal contract my father made with the chief of Tarkwa between his daughter and I is a non-factor to me. I'm not marrying anyone I was promised to at the age of five. Plus, I know Abena has no desire to leave her high-profile job as an official royal photographer to serve as a royal wife in Kumasi. We say hi to each other once a year and we do an obligatory whirl around the dance floor. Then we bid adieu until the next year. Why should this year be any different? I definitely do not want Ella worried about it.

Senya finishes his club soda in one gulp before setting his glass down. He holds his hands up in surrender. "You know I won't say anything, but she's bound to find out. Look, I know you really like this woman. I've never seen you like this before. If you really want her in your life, I'd advise you to be honest with her upfront. You don't want her to think you're hiding anything. I know a bit about American women, and they don't take deceit and hidden fiancées very well." He lets out a laugh.

I punch his arm and reluctantly laugh with him. "So now you know American women? Nonsense!" But I know he's right. I will have to find a moment to explain everything to Ella.

"Please share the joke, gentlemen. I want to laugh." I hear her voice and turn around. I'm not prepared for the beauty standing at the door of my study. Ella is always beautiful, but right now she's exquisite. The wild tumbling curls I love are straightened to a sleek black sheet hanging to the middle of her back. Her makeup is flawless in a natural way. Her lips have been painted a deep burgundy and her skin is shimmering with flecks of gold dust, matching the illumination from her dress. The dress fits her like it was made for her body. No one else will ever be able to wear the champagne-colored work of art. The African-printed lace and silk look like a second skin. Suddenly, she twirls to give us a 360-degree view of the sheath, and I see her exposed back. The fabric drapes right above her ass. She looks like a queen with her high neck in the front and the dream lover of any who dare try to win her affections in the back.

"You like?" She notices me salivating into my drink and winks, enjoying her effect on me.

I pour her a glass of champagne and walk to her. "You are breathtaking, Ella." I push an imaginary strand of hair from her face. "I miss your curls, but you made the right decision to straighten them for this dress."

She breaks out in a wide grin. "I know, right? At first, I was all like, *No, I love my afro—I always represent.* But when I looked at the back of this dress, I knew hair needed to tease my back. The team was fast and lovely to work with. Thank you, Kofi."

I grab her free hand and lace my fingers through hers before kissing the back of her knuckles. "The pleasure is clearly all mine." I lean in to whisper the rest of my thoughts. "I get to look at your hair tease the path to your ass all night. The ass I'm going to tap later tonight."

Her cheeks warm at my promise. "I'm looking forward to that, your majesty."

I recognize the tone of her *your majesty*. She wants to be commanded tonight. I will not disappoint.

"Ahem!" Senya interrupts our interlude. "Ella, you look amazing. Kofi, we must go. Who will ride with me, you or Ella?"

Damn. Senya has no finesse. I wanted to gently explain our travel arrangements to Ella. I look to Ella's face flickering with confusion and I rub the back of her hand.

I clear my throat into my fist and push gently away. "Yes, love, I thought we should take separate cars so we don't bait the press. I hope that's all right."

She relaxes a little, but not enough for me. "As long as it's not because you're ashamed of the American tagging along," she teases.

I grab her and pull her into a kiss. Screw her lipstick—she'll have to reapply it. I possess her completely and press my hardened bulge into her thigh, wanting her to feel what is only hers. When I pull away, I'm pretty positive she's wet. When I let her go to speak she is just the way I like her-breathless and longing.

"Quite the opposite. I'll be beating the admirers off with a stick. I'd much rather claim you openly when I arrive to avoid all of that. But honestly, Ella, you don't want your name splashed all over the British and Ghanaian press." Senya shoots me a look, but I ignore him.

She nods. "I agree. You will have dinner with me and at least one dance, right?"

"Oh, yes! The press is not allowed inside."

She smiles and kisses my cheek. "OK, may I have Senya, then? Arriving with him will calm my nerves." My jealousy flares for a second. I don't want Ella on anyone's arm but mine. But this is my fault. I guess Senya is the next best thing.

"Of course. Senya, please escort Ella in the limo. I will follow." I kiss Ella goodbye and whisper to her one more thing before she departs.

"Think of what we did the last time I rode with you in that limo with my face between your thighs. I want you nice and wet when you arrive to the ball."

*D*uring my ride to the ball, I decide to tell Ella all about the betrothal between Abena Owusu and myself during drinks before dinner. It can be the topic of our conversation. I will explain everything to her and hopefully she won't hold it against me. I long planned to get that agreement annulled, but I stalled. I admit I used it as an insurance policy in case I never fell in love and found my queen. Now, everything is different. I can't love Ella and marry someone else. It has to be her. First, I have to get her to stay.

Once I arrive, my walk down the gold carpet is uneventful. I enter and am greeted by everyone as I pass through. I finally spot Ella waiting at the bar chatting with Thomas Owusu. I forgot she met him when she first arrived in Ghana. I was under the impression she did not like him very much for being so forward. I guess drinks before dinner with my lady is out of the question. I will let them chat. I refuse to let irrational jealousy get the best of me tonight.

In the other hand, I always hated Thomas Owusu. In boarding school, he used to insist that we call him by his English name and not his Ashanti one. He is an entitled prick that always wants what others have. Hopefully Ella hasn't said too much about our connection. The fact that he's Abena's brother doesn't help matters at all. I notice her laughing at one of his stupid jokes and my blood boils. I quickly take out my phone and text her. That's a good alternative to what I really want to do.

Me:

What's so funny
She replies right away.

Ella:

This guy. He's a fool. Handsome. But a fool no less.
I smirk.

Me:

So, you think him handsome? Are you thinking of leaving your king for a peasant?

Ella:

I thought you told me there were no such things as peasants in your kingdom.
I chuckle. I did say that. She listens.

Me:

True. Ditch him and go to the restroom. Touch yourself until your panties are wet. Then bring them to me at our table.

Ella:

You're so bad. What table?

Me:

Number one of course. Hurry!

I make my way to our table. I stay on the lookout for Abena—hopefully, I won't see her until after dinner. By then, I will have told Ella.

I sit and wait for Ella before allowing the table to be served. After thirty minutes, I start to worry. I could have made her wet in two minutes. I will never again send someone else to do the king's work.

Just as I pull out my phone to send her a text, something catches my eye. Blinking twice, I register the fact that my auntie, Akua, is walking next to Abena, triumphant smiles on their faces as they leave the restroom. *Shit.*

Chapter Twenty-Five

TROUBLE

Ella

*E*ngaged! Kofi is engaged.

The entire time he's talked about loving me, needing me, and wanting me to stay, he's had a fiancée. I was over the moon a few minutes ago. Now, I'm outside with wet tears running down my perfectly made-up face. A face made up for him. I saw his face when I exited the restroom and gave him a death glare before walking out. No doubt, he is not far behind me.

Moments earlier, I walked into the restroom to follow the hot command from his majesty. I could hardly wait to make myself come to his words. I walked in the stall, lifted my dress, and quickly put my French-manicured fingers to work on my silk-clad mound. I made soft strokes up and down the length of my center to his previous words, *I will take care of all your needs if you allow me. I can start with this obvious need between your legs.* Quick firm circles to my bud remembering the heat in his voice, *He's so ready for you, baby. Let me fill you up.* A quick gasp and I was undone. My panties were soaked. Mission accomplished. I removed my panties and tucked them into the crown serving as my purse for the evening.

I left the stall to wash my hands and touch up my lipstick when I looked into the mirror and spotted Akua and a very tall woman the color of dark brown sugar at the entrance. They headed to the sinks behind me deep in a lively conversation. I didn't think Akua would be at the ball—not because she's a servant, but because she's 82 years old. Not in the mood to be insulted by one of Akua's back-handed compliments, I dried my hands and attempted to leave unnoticed. No such luck.

"Ms. Jenkins!" she announced with misplaced glee. I turned around with a tight smile. "Don't you look exquisite. Is this the dress Kofi designed for you? Mawuli does wonderful work. She can transform anyone into a beauty." *Bitch.*

The woman beside her cocked her head slightly to the side and took stock of me from head to toe. Somehow, I felt that was the purpose of Akua's small talk and jab—to allow this woman time to take me completely in. The woman was pretty in a false way. She wore jet black hair that obviously wasn't hers in a slick high ponytail that went to her ass. Her lashes were long and fake. She had perfectly arched eyebrows that announced hazel eyes below. Her slim frame wore a short kente-printed silk dress with towering red Louboutin heels. The four-inch heels were excessive, as she was clearly at least five-foot-ten without them. She clutched her Chanel purse like a weapon. Everything about her screamed, *look at me!*

"Akua! How lovely to see you," I lied. "I hear you are serving at the palace right now. I missed you at Bonbiri today." I pray the fake concern I plastered on my face said, *Yes, I'm there and you aren't. He chose me.*

Akua straightened her body. "Yes, well, I do help out at Manhyia from time to time." She painted her smile back on before turning to the woman beside her. "Allow me to introduce you to someone. This is Abena Owusu, an old family friend."

Abena gave me another once-over before extending her hand. I shook it. "Nice to meet you. I read a lot about Revolution Academies while Kofi was trying to decide which network to bring to Kumasi. I'm glad he chose you. I told him he should."

She told him he should! Who was this woman? Kofi is not the type of leader to discuss Ashanti business with random family friends. She must be more to him. But how much more? I shook off the surprise I'm sure was apparent on my face. "Ah, well, I guess I should thank you for the endorsement. How long have you known Kofi?"

She smiled. "Our whole lives. We've been devoted to each other since birth."

The smile I returned was a vicious dare. "Interesting...I've met most of the important people in Kofi's life since I've been here, but he hasn't mentioned you."

Abena did not miss a beat. She poked out her chest and radiated a superior stare. "That's probably because I serve the royal family in London as chief photographer. We don't get to see each other much, but that will all change once we fulfill our contract."

"Contract?" I openly mused.

Akua came forward and touched my arm. "Well yes, dear, surely you know of Kofi's betrothal contract to the daughter of Tarkwa's chief?" She flourished her free hand in the direction of Abena. "Abena is Kofi's intended. The future Ashanti queen."

The wind was knocked from me for a second, and I gently stumbled back before casually catching myself on the nearby wall.

"Are you OK, dear?" Akua fussed.

I glared at her before gathering my stride. "Yes, I think I need some air. If you will excuse me."

Akua looked satisfied. "Of course dear, we will see you at dinner. We are seated at your table. Are you sure I can't get you anything?"

"No, I'm fine. I will join the table shortly."

I left the bathroom and made a beeline for the door. Now I'm sitting outside on a bench in the lovely gardens I spotted behind the convention center. I can't remember the last time I needed a good cry. Actually, I can. Marcus! That coward revealed he was in love with someone else two weeks before our wedding. My heart broke into a million pieces. It has taken three years of therapy, self-love, and no sex to put Humpty Dumpty back together again. I was in a good place. My business is thriving. I'm in the best shape of my life. I'm taking my brand global. The tears are falling because I threw all that stability away for a king that has been promised to a queen I knew nothing about. All while he's been treating me as his queen. He lied. The betrayal is biting. What am I doing here? I never should have come. I've been wrapped up in a fairytale that is indeed fiction. It's time to get real.

I hear his steps approach before he speaks. "Ella..." He sounds less sure. Good—he should be afraid. He should be *very* afraid. I don't bother to look up. I throw my arm out, silently telling him to save it. He sighs. "Ella, I'm not leaving until you allow me to explain. Now, look at me. You know I don't like to—" I cut him off by snapping my head up.

"You don't like to ask twice." I mock him. "Well, I couldn't care less. You no longer get to dictate how I respond to you. That ended the moment I found out you were hiding a fiancée."

He sighs, closes his eyes, and wipes his hand over his face. When he looks back at me, there is regret in his eyes. "Ella, I did not hide Abena."

Somehow his answer causes even more hurt. I want him to at the very least deny her claims. I want him to say she is lying. That of course he doesn't have a fiancée, how could he? He loves me. Instead, he denies that he hid her.

"I'm sorry, but you sure didn't mention her before screwing me all along the Gold Coast."

He smirks and crosses his arms across his broad chest. "We haven't screwed up and down the Gold Coast. We've never even left Ghana. But if you give me a chance to explain, I can remedy that."

I stand up, incredulous. "You know what I mean! And if you think you will ever touch me again, you are sadly mistaken."

He stares at me as I pace and clenches his jaw. "I will. I will touch you again when you calm down and let me explain who Abena is."

I glare at him and loudly whisper, "Screw you!"

I try to turn away, but he grabs my arm and turns me to him in the blink of an eye. He pushes against my body and speaks so closely our lips touch in tenuous, fluttering kisses. "I will not hold you against your will, but you will listen to me. We owe each other that. Afterward, you may do whatever you like."

I don't owe him anything but a card of congratulations on his engagement. However, I stop fighting and relax in his arms. Not because I want to, but because I know at this point resistance is futile. I nod my head and he lets me go.

I maintain fierce eye contact with him as I walk a few steps backward onto the bench I was sitting on. I wrap my arms around myself and he takes it as a sign that I'm cold. He removes his kente and wraps it around me. I never got a chance to tell him exactly how handsome he is tonight. The tuxedo fits his hard body like a glove. The kente cloth screams king in the best way. Right now, I wish I didn't know just how amazing the body underneath the expensive fabric is.

He joins me on the bench and faces me. I face forward. "I should have told you about the betrothal. I'm sorry." I don't move a muscle. I don't nod. I don't protest. I remain looking off into the distance, waiting for the moment I can run back to my hotel and lie in my bed to cry and plot my escape from Kofi Ajyei.

He places his hand over mine as it lies in my lap before he continues. "She's not my fiancée in a traditional sense. I have not announced an engagement, and all we have is a 32-year-old contract my father drew up with the Tarkwa chief when I was five. I never have and never will have any intention to marry Abena Owusu. I loathe her and her nitwit brother Thomas."

I turn toward the hint of jealousy in his voice that is familiar and hot and raise my eyebrows. "Yes, Ella, the same man you allowed to take you around Kumasi your second day here and share drinks with you tonight is Abena's brother. I saw that was him talking with you at the bar. That's why I texted you. You two were the first thing I saw when I arrived."

I say nothing. I'm definitely not explaining harmless flirting to a man that's been hiding an entire engagement from me. "I see Abena once a year at this festival, and we speak and have one dance to appease our families. I don't even have the woman's phone number."

I shift on the bench to fully face him. "But in the restroom, Akua and Abena acted as if you two were close."

Kofi shakes his head and chuckles. "Akua is up to her mischief again. Ella, Akua believes in old betrothal contracts and tribal customs. I respect them, but I don't live my life by them."

I fight the fact I'm starting to understand his point of view. I want to stay angry. Anger is safe. I can walk away angry. I can't walk away knowing he never meant to deceive me. "Kofi, if that were the case, why didn't you just tell me?"

He cocks his head to the side. "The truth?"

I close my eyes in annoyance. "Do you think lying right now would help your case?"

He sighs. "Honestly, Ella, I didn't even think about the woman until today. It is like a little alarm clock that goes off every year." He moves closer to me and places his hands on either side of my face. "The only difference this year is that I'm in love with another woman. That has never been the case before." He drops his hands from my face. "So, I came up with the stupid idea that I didn't have to address it. We would arrive separately and avoid the press and any hardcore tribalistic guests. Then we would go back to our regularly scheduled programming."

He stands and looks down at me. "Senya told me that wouldn't work when we were having drinks in the study earlier. I agreed. I promise I was going to tell you at dinner and introduce you to her so you would know who she is. Akua got to you first."

I look up at him and uncross my arms. "You should have told me. A king once told me omission is a lie." I throw those words about Adom and I back at him and he smiles.

"Yes, I should have." He pulls me from the bench in an embrace. "I'm sorry, Ella. This is all new to me. You are so unexpected. I never anticipated having an 'us.' I'm still learning to share every part of myself."

Tears return to my face because I know I forgive him, which means I am still at his mercy. I have to trust him. That's hard. "Well, what do we do now? Can't you get the contract annulled?"

He steps back and grins at me. "Absolutely. I already told my lawyer to meet me in Tarkwa tomorrow. I'm fixing this immediately. My heart is promised to you."

I run back to his arms and he rewards the gesture with a kiss. We melt into each other's arms and hang on for dear life. We are learning more and more with each passing day how precious and precarious what we have is. He finishes the kiss by peppering my face and neck with soft pecks. When he's satisfied, he looks in my eyes with a bewildered look.

"What is it, Kofi?"

"You said Abena and Akua talked like we were close. They talked like the betrothal was a serious engagement?"

"They took pleasure in rubbing that in. She even stated that she was the one that convinced you to pick me as your school vendor."

Kofi steps from my embrace completely and rubs his jaw. "That's odd. Abena did send an email stating that Revolution Academies is always in the press for the good work you guys do. She forwarded a couple of press clippings and that was it. I didn't even reply. Now that I think of it, I thought it was odd she emailed me at all. Abena has her lovers and she has never tried to lay any claim to me. Why change now?"

"Akua's influence?" I half ask and half accuse.

He nods slowly. "Partly sure. But no, there has to be another reason. Abena is willful. Even as a child she was not easily controlled. Something is off." He starts to look off in thought before returning his attention to me. "But never mind that now."

He grabs my hands and places his signature kisses on my knuckles. "It's late—we've been out here for a while. What do you say I call a royal service car and we leave the foolishness of tonight behind? We can spend the evening at the beach and maybe put that hotel room you have here in Accra to good use."

I break out into a full grin. "Really? But, how can we? Won't you be missed?"

He laughs. "Yes, but I'm the Asantehene. The party ends when I leave, and I am leaving with you. However, we should have dinner first."

I give him a pained look. "But Akua and Abena are sitting at our table!"

"Great. Let them look at you and I in all our splendid love and devotion. They need to know that their little trick did not work. I will call a car to be ready to whisk us away in exactly one hour." He pulls out his phone and sends off a text to request the car.

"In that case..." I return to the bench, get my crown clutch, and remove the panties I wet all over for him earlier. "These, sir, belong to you." I hand the panties to him. "I expect you will follow up on some of the promises you made me earlier. You know, about bending me over and filling me up?"

He closes his eyes and takes a deep inhale of the silk scraps that were between my thighs two hours ago. He turns to me with a look that I can only describe as sex before lifting me and tossing me over his shoulder. He pats my ass and stalks toward the entrance of the ball.

"Don't you worry about a thing, queen. Tonight, I am at your service."

Chapter Twenty-Six

EXTORTION

Kofi

*L*eaving Ella in bed this morning takes an act of God. She's so beautiful and inviting in the morning. I count myself blessed that she loves morning sex as much as I do. The first thing I want to do in the morning is touch her. I want to be inside her. After last night on the beach, I feel a part of her. We walked the beach for hours before stripping and frolicking in the water together. Thank God it was late and dark. It was risky, but no one caught us. I felt so free with her in the water. Afterward, we went back to her suite and made love until we physically could not move anymore. It was incredible.

I came too close to losing her last night. That stunt Akua and Abena pulled almost cost me my queen. However, I ensured dinner at the table with them last night was more awkward for them than Ella. I took every moment to kiss and caress Ella at the table. I introduced her loudly to everyone as my lady, and I held her so closely that she was damn near sitting on my lap. I never recognized the presence of Akua nor Abena. Akua could not take it and abruptly left after the first course. Abena stood her ground and shot daggers at us the entire meal.

This morning, I'm on my way to Tarkwa to meet with Chief Kwabena Owusu and get this ancient betrothal contract annulled. I can at least remove this roadblock from standing between Ella and my future together.

When I call the chief, he is too calm for my liking. Generally, the village chiefs are openly curious or at least a bit anxious when the Asantehene asks for an audience. However, Kwabena Owusu doesn't sound pleased to hear from me. He sounds prepared.

Under normal circumstances, I don't drive myself anywhere, but today I want to take this meeting alone. I fight with Senya to allow me to go without a full security detail. I manage to win the right to drive the armored Range Rover with two guards, one being Senya, on bike not far behind. I guess this is as close to privacy as I will ever get.

The chief of Tarkwa's home is all sparkle and elegance when I arrive. Unlike Bonbiri, his home sits in the center of town made entirely of white stone and marble that gleam in the sunlight. It's actually fitting. For centuries, Tarkwa was the center of the gold mining trade. It still has prominence, but much like Tafo's cocoa industry, it is a shell of what it once was. Nevertheless, Tarkwa's chief has kept his familial line's sparkle through questionable tactics that are rumored to include bribes and offshore accounts.

When I approach the Owusus' gate, it opens to welcome me in. After I park, I approach the doors and a butler lets me into an overly decorated foyer. The intentional display of wealth annoys me. Everything is gilded in gold: mirrors, plant stands, even doorknobs. I turn to the butler. "I'm here to speak with chief Owusu," I demand. The butler bows and mutters, "your majesty" before disappearing down the marble-floored hallway.

While he's gone, I take the opportunity to look around. Pictures of the chief's family crowd the foyer walls. You can tell where his heart and pride lie after just a few moments in his home. *I wonder what a few minutes in my home says about me.* I continue to walk the length of the foyer and spot a photo of Abena in tribal dress. Even a portrait designed to show the Ghanaian beauty in her most natural state comes off as fake.

Nothing about Abena or her brother Thomas was ever real. We all went to the same boarding schools together in London. Thomas is a devilishly smart bastard. He would take a blind man's walking stick if he could attach a profit to the action. His sister is better, but not great. Abena never had time for mere mortals in school. She spent all of her time trying to climb the social ladders in London. She respects Western values and governance over ours. I'm sure that's why she never comes home. Looking around at the symbols of Kwabena Owusu's pride, I know her deliberate absence must break his heart.

Why am I still waiting in a damn foyer? I don't wait to be seen. This is a deliberate power move, but for what? I turn to leave before I hear Thomas' booming voice. "Your Majesty!" He strides quickly to me and grabs the top of my shoulders in a half-hearted embrace. "We are sorry to keep you waiting—we were finishing breakfast on the patio. Please come, we will have drinks in father's study."

I step back from Thomas and fold my arms over my chest, leveling a tight stare at the fool standing before me. "*We?* I am here to meet with your father about a tribal matter. This is not a social call, Thomas." I bristle past him toward the center of the house and hopefully the study, knowing he will follow me.

I hear his steps shuffling behind me. He catches up and extends his hand to show me the way. "I know the meeting was just with you and Father, but these days he has Abena and I join all of his business meetings." Business meeting? When did this meeting become about business? "After you, your majesty." Thomas ushers me into the study and I'm greeted by a standing Chief Owusu and his daughter, Abena.

I nod to both and Abena returns to her seat on the white leather couch nearest to her father. Chief Owusu sits on a chair that can only be described as a throne. Thomas sits next to his sister. I select the armchair opposite the chief, with a massive glass coffee table dividing us. I sit up and cross my legs, staring at Chief Owusu like he owes me an explanation. He starts to fidget on his throne.

"Well, your majesty, please tell me to what do I owe this honor? I was certainly surprised to hear from you. More so, I was surprised to know you were coming here and not summoning me to you."

I nod my head in agreement. "Yes, I guess that is odd for official or political visits. This, however, is more of a familial visit and one of a private manner. I don't have anything against your children—I just don't think what I have to talk to you about will concern them in any real way. It's a personal request."

At that, Abena crosses her legs and narrows her eyes in my direction. "How can you say that?" she squeaks in her birdlike voice. "When I have it on good authority that you're here to nullify the contract that binds you to me in marriage?"

I clear my throat. "That may be, however, no matter what you think, I have no intention of marrying you. And if we're both honest, you've never shown the slightest inclination that you even care. However, if you feel the need to stay, please do." My exasperation is palpable. Her eyes continue to shoot daggers at me. I turn away from her and address her father.

"Chief, I know the betrothal agreement has been in place for nearly 30 years now. I also know that you and my parents developed and signed this contract when Abena and I were no more than five years old." I glance at Abena, hoping her stare has softened. It has not. I continue on. "I think Abena will agree with me in saying that we have no desire to be married to each other. Furthermore, I do not think Abena desires to be an Ashanti queen. She clearly is an accomplished woman in her own right."

Abena licks her lips before tossing her obnoxiously long ponytail behind her. She stands up and walks to stand behind her father's chair. The annoying click-clack of her very tall stilettos almost makes me burst with annoyance. "Let's be clear, King," she starts. I'm surprised to hear malevolence in her voice. She places her hand on her father's shoulder. "King or not, you don't get to speak for me. You do not have the authority to voice what I want. As a matter of fact, we've never talked about the betrothal, so how would you know what I want to do or who I love?"

"Love!" I shout incredulously before a belly laugh erupts. "Abena, are you now saying that you are entertaining the thought of being in love with me? You know nothing about me and have never shown one inkling of concern about my person or reign." I drop my voice to a royal octave. "Whatever game it is you're playing must cease." Her father pats her hand, signaling for her to not react to my words.

Chief Owusu shifts in his chair and adjusts his kente cloth to show more of his knees before edging closer to the edge of his chair. "Asantehene, I respect your position. However, I must ask you to excuse any perceived insolence from Abena. This is her life we are discussing. Abena is not talking of games—" He gestures wildly with his hands. "—she's talking about a promise and a contract. Now, if you don't want to respect the promise, that is your choice. However, you are legally bound to respect the contract."

I stand and move closer and stand in front of the chief in 2.5 seconds. He responds by scrambling to his feet. "Are you threatening me, Chief Owusu? You're confronting the Asantehene with legal action?" He sweats and makes an indiscriminate noise, the makings of a doomed protest. I can tell his emotions are a runaway train. "Take care with your next words, Chief," I seethe. "I'd hate this to turn into a different meeting all together because of misplaced words and emotion."

Thomas stands and moves to a desk in the corner of the room. He returns to his father and I staring each other down with a packet of printed paper. "Asantehene. I think you should read this before anything else transpires." He offers the papers to me and I reluctantly accept them. "Father," he cajoles. "Why don't we all have a seat while Kofi reads the contract. That way, we can all talk from the same starting point." We both nod and retreat to our seats.

"Your majesty, would you like some palm wine while you read?"

Thomas places a smug smile on his lips. He would make quite the politician if he put his mind to doing so. He knows I cannot refuse palm wine with an elder without being disrespectful. It would be all over the village in a week. I give him a tight smile.

"Yes. That will do." The wine is poured and brought to me within seconds. I start to sip and read. The contract reads as a common betrothal agreement at first, but then the language turns. There is talk about stocks, the exchange of funds, and investment portfolios. Clauses that allude to an adjustable interest loan and the acquittal of debt. It slowly becomes clear that what I'm reading belongs in a bank, not a wedding chapel.

"What is this?" I look around at the Owusus. Thomas is now sporting a slick grin! His father is the one that speaks. "In its most basic form, it is a contract that allowed your father to borrow eight million dollars from me to clear personal debts he incurred. Your father, as I'm sure you know, was a good man. However, you may not know that he gambled. A lot."

I shake my head and slam the contract onto the table. "You're lying, and you will pay for your words."

The chief does not flinch. "I wish I was, but the entire debt is documented. This is very real. Your father refused to use any of the Ashanti treasury to take care of his family and lifestyle. He was too honest for that. So, he came to me to pay for your private schools, cars, and land to build forest homes on. In exchange, he promised you would marry my daughter. If not, all the money would come due immediately with interest. So, you see, if you don't honor the betrothal, your family will owe mine a little over 92 million U.S. dollars. Thomas did the math for me this morning." He chuckles. "I'm not so great with numbers myself."

I sit in shock for as long as I can stand it. I'm never comfortable being put in a weaker position. I stand and turn to Abena. "You knew about this? You were OK with being treated as property in a banking transition?"

She averts her eyes from mine and looks to her father. "I'm OK with taking care of my family. An Owusu will one day be Asante-hene through my womb. That is my family's right according to this contract, and I tend to hold you to it."

So, there it is. It's all about money and power. She doesn't care for me one iota. I always knew that, but the money aspect of it makes it worse. How can she stomach marrying a man she doesn't love? No matter, she will never have the chance.

I move to the center of the study to address the room. "This has been most enlightening. And though I admire your devotion to your family, Abena, I could never marry a woman I do not love. I hope that one day you realize you deserve to have the same attitude. Unlike my father, I am not a gambler nor am I bad with money. As you know, I'm worth ten times the total of this loan with interest and will gladly pay the balance to be done with it all."

Suddenly, a booming laugh cuts through the room. It's Thomas. He knocks back a glass of brown liquid before continuing. "Your majesty, do we look strapped for money?" He gestures all around the room. "We don't need or want your money. We want an Owusu on the throne. And he will be, or everyone will know what a gambling drunkard your father was." He dares to stalk over to me and sneer. "Everyone will know how weak Ajyei blood really is. We've always known."

I see red and slam Thomas to the floor by his neck. Abena screams something about me being a maniac. But I don't give a damn. I place my knee in his chest and land the perfect punch that breaks his nose. Before I can go in for another, I am pulled back by a strong set of hands. I turn to fight my new foe when I look and see it's a familiar presence. Senya. When did he get here? "Let's go, your majesty. That's enough!" He attempts to pull me from the sniveling Thomas, but I refuse.

"Get off of me, Senya. That's an order!" He ignores me and nods to his second to grab my other arm and assist him. The second hesitates, and Senya chides him to not be a punk. They manage to get me off of him and stand me up.

Once Thomas rises with the help of his father and sister, holding his now-bloody nose, he decides to make idle threats. "You're lucky you're the king, or that would have gone a lot differently," he shouts, pointing at me.

I shake my right hand to loosen it from the pain of breaking the fool's nose. I look him dead in the eye so he does not mistake my words. "You shouldn't have held back. I just beat your ass as Kofi, not as the Ashanti king. That was personal." I turn to look at the chief. "Owusu. I am not marrying your daughter. You can spread all the gossip you like. I will have my bankers wire your money first thing in the morning." I turn to walk away, but he shouts after me.

"Wait! Have you no honor?" he shouts. "You don't fulfill your family's promise to mine and assault family in my own home. Yes! All will hear of it. I hope that little American wench you're lying with is worth the legacy of your reign, Kofi Ajyei." His robust body shakes in anger as he continues. "Any king that can be brought down by a whore is not worth the golden stool he sits upon!"

I pause. "That will be the last time you will ever speak to me or about Ella Jenkins that way. If I ever hear of it again, I will have your chieftaincy within the hour of your disrespectful words. Count it a blessing that you're an old man. Otherwise, I would afford you the same courtesy I just gave your son." He says nothing in return and stands trembling. Good—he's not a total fool.

I gather the copy of the contract and stalk for the door, Senya and his one-man security team following behind me as we leave the Owusu home. Once I reach my car, Senya takes my keys. "I will drive you—you need to rest. I will collect my motorcycle tomorrow." I nod and slink in the back of the Range Rover.

I lie down in the car wondering if I can live up to all the hype I just created. Will I really let my father's legacy be tainted? Will I allow more family secrets to overtake the press as they did when my mother died 25 years ago? How will our regime survive such a scandal? Even though my father never touched Ashanti or government funds, people will assume he did as a gambler. There will be council meetings, inquests, and endless drama.

Loving Ella and wanting to be free to marry her is acceptable for Kofi, the man. However, it's unacceptable for the 20th Asantehene of the Ashanti Nation to be free in love. Maybe it's time I returned to the service of being king.

Chapter Twenty-Seven

AFTERMATH

Ella

I miss Kofi this morning, but I am glad to have some time alone.

I realize since I've been in Ghana, I've neglected a lot of my stateside responsibilities. I'm using today to check on my various school network offices across the United States. Most importantly, now that all my work is done, I get to talk to Maya.

When I call, Adom is at her side. He's been there every day since he returned from Ghana. Maya tries to sound annoyed about it, but I know that's not the case. After just nine days since her accident, she shares good news that she may get the all-clear to start physical therapy soon. They started calling her the *miracle model* on her hospital wing. The healing process will be long, but it's already going well. "My goal is to be walking in heels again by Christmas," Maya chirps. I laugh.

"Maya, Christmas is five months away...how in the world do you think you'll be able to walk in your four- and five-inch heels?" She giggles back.

"Oh, ye of little faith! You know I get anything done that I put my mind to." She is absolutely right. The girl never met a goal or project plan she didn't like. We spend the next three hours on the phone laughing and joking. Our last hour is exclusively dedicated to Kofi. I give her all the juicy details and she is more than happy to play the part of the squealing, excited best friend. "I told you! That man had a plan for you before you even got there. Look at you now, laid up in the forest with that African god. I can hardly stand it I'm so jealous!"

"What do you have to be jealous about? You have your own African hunk waiting on you hand and foot. Adom is completely infatuated with you. I think he always has been." Maya sighs in relief and appreciation.

"Yeah, he's been great, Ella. But let's not get it twisted—he's no Asantehene. Plus, he's so damn bossy. I always knew Adom had a diagnosis of obsessive-compulsive disorder—he told me that back in college. However, it is a totally different matter when I am the subject of his obsession. The nurses that wanted to fawn all over him now avoid him like the plague. He makes sure that they give me the exact dosages of pain meds at the exact times only. He's so worried I'll end up with an opioid dependence."

I laugh—that sounds exactly like something Adom would obsess over. Maya continues, "If I have pain outside of that, he prays or reads and sings to me in his native language, Twi, to calm me down before he will allow me to call for more meds. The crazy thing is, it works! He's crazy clean, and actually cleans up after the house-keeping staff. He refuses to let me wear the hospital gowns, stating they are made of synthetics. Ella, the man had pure cotton and silk hospital gowns commissioned and made for me within 24 hours after he arrived! He's too much!"

I laugh with Maya until tears stream down. I realize how much I miss my friend. We talk a bit more before she nods off to sleep.

To pass the time until Kofi returns, I decide to cook us some dinner. Since Akua's been gone, we've mostly eaten out. I manage to make chicken shawarma with rice. As I pull the warmed naan out the oven, I hear Kofi's footsteps come toward the kitchen.

"It smells good in here." He hugs me from behind to nuzzle my neck and stroke my still straightened hair. "You know I miss the kinky curls. I like to bury my face in them and smell that citrus oil you wear."

I laugh and turn around in his arms. "I don't want to waste the blowout your amazing beauty team gave me. We will have to live with the straight hair for at least a week. Do you think you'll survive?"

He strokes my cheek and looks at me like he missed me. Maybe today was a long day without us for him, too. "I will. Now, let's eat! I'm starving. I've barely eaten today."

"Really?" One thing I've learned about Ghanaian culture over the past few weeks is that hospitality is key. You can't go to anyone's home without them offering you a meal. To think the Asantehene went to a chief's home and was not fed is odd. "Your guests didn't feed you today?"

A look of anger flashes across Kofi's face before he carefully tucks it back behind his eyes to face me with a smile. "No, we were so busy discussing matters, food never even came up. I'm sure there was something prepared. We just never got around to it."

My stomach turns. His visit sounds tenuous at best. But I won't pry. He will tell me all when he's ready. I press against his chest and squeeze for a tight hug before inviting him to sit and be served. "Come, let me feed my hungry king." I attempt to move out of his arms, but he gently holds on.

Kofi's eyes spark with desire. "I'd much rather you let me eat you first. You know, as an appetizer."

"Kofi! You're so naughty. I'm not getting away, am I?"

He smiles and shakes his head. "No. And let's be honest, do you even want to get away?"

I smile and shake my head. "Nope. Where would you like your appetizer served, your majesty?"

He growls and tangles his hands in my hair to pull my head back and devours me in a kiss. The kiss is long, needy, and hot as hell. He traces my lips with his tongue before pushing inside and claiming every inch of my mouth. I get the chance to bite his bottom lip as he exits one last time, and he yelps. He looks at me like he could eat me. "You little minx!"

In a moment, I'm off my feet and carried to the island. Kofi lays me back on the cold marble and immediately begins to pull the cut-off shorts I'm wearing completely off. He plays with the scrap of damp silk fabric covering my sex before nibbling at the inside of my thighs. He uses his free hand to free my breasts from my tank top, while his fingers continue the campaign across my clit. He takes my right breast into his mouth and sucks and licks every inch of it. When he comes up for air, he looks at me and then at his fingers winding me up below. "Open," he commands. I gladly spread wide.

The next 20 minutes is a blur of screams, orgasms, and declarations to God. He possesses me fully, and the craving I've had for him all day is partially filled. I know I will have to feel him inside me before today turns into tomorrow, but it can wait. Right now, his head is laying on my exposed stomach while he mindlessly strokes my outer thighs. He doesn't say a word. I think he would never move from this spot on the kitchen island if I didn't. Every few minutes, he turns his head and lands a soft kiss on the center of my belly. After another 10 minutes, I'm concerned. More so because I'm spread eagle in the kitchen. The servants are discreet but not blind.

"Kofi, we should get up. This marble is a bit unforgiving on my back."

He stumbles upright and rubs the back of his neck. He looks like he just woke from a dream. "Of course, baby, I apologize." He forces a weak smile. "You feel so good, I was in the zone, you know?"

I sit up on my elbows and eye him curiously. "Yeah, I know." I offer my hand for him to help me jump down from the island. I quickly dress and gather him in an embrace. "What happened, Kofi? Clearly something is on your mind. Could it be the meeting with Chief Owusu didn't go as you planned today?"

He steps back and sighs. "No, not at all. But let's talk about it over a nice bottle of wine. I have a bottle of the 2015 South African

Constantia you enjoyed at the palace. You get the food and I'll meet you on the balcony of the river room."

I place my hands on my hips and give him a sly look. "The last time I let you talk me into dinner on my bedroom balcony, I ended up eating naked in a robe."

He smirks. "Yes, and you were the sweetest dessert." He raises his right hand to mock a scouting promise. "I vow to let you eat dinner and tell you all about my day before I pleasure your sweet body into the middle of next week. Will that suffice?"

I laugh. "Yes. And I'm keeping my clothes on!"

He shakes his head and feigns a frown. "That's no fun!" He walks over and pats my ass on his way to the wine cellar. He pauses to whisper in my ear, "No worries, I'll peel your clothes off with my teeth later."

I smile knowing he will absolutely make good on that promise. I have to reheat the food since our dalliance delayed dinner. While I wait, I throw together a quick salad to go with our meal. Ten minutes later, I'm heading upstairs. When I arrive to the balcony, Kofi is standing and looking over his property. His mind is clearly somewhere else. "Kofi, come, sweetheart. Let's eat."

FLIGHT

Ella

$\mathcal{D}$ inner starts quietly.

Kofi eats two plates of the spicy chicken and rice along with three glasses of wine. When he's finally full, he speaks. "Where did a nice girl from Atlanta learn to make shawarma this good?"

I laugh. "Nice girls do travel, you know! I actually learned during my study abroad in Istanbul during college."

He arches his eyebrows in surprise. "I didn't know you studied in Turkey. It's one of my favorite places to visit."

I nod and take a sip of wine. "I've been like eight times. I just love the architecture and the food. Not to mention the shopping; the Grand Bazaar is everything!"

He laughs heartily before pouring another glass of wine. "Yes, I'm afraid our Kumasi market can't compare to Istanbul's four-mile odyssey into retail." He looks at me as he takes a new sip and rests his eyes at my mouth. "You're so beautiful, Ella. One day I will take you to Istanbul in the most luxurious manner possible. No expense will be spared. We will search every nook and cranny of the city to find treasures that compliment your loveliness."

My heart skips a beat in response to his gesture. "Thank you," I respond. "But before you can whisk me around the world, we've got to solve whatever problem you've brought back with you from Tarkwa. The worry is all over your face."

He sighs. "Today was a disaster."

"A disaster?"

He nods. "An absolute catastrophe. It ended with me breaking Thomas Owusu's nose all over their precious white carpet."

I'm shocked. "You fought Thomas Owusu! What happened? Why was he even there?"

He rolls his eyes. "Exactly. I asked for a private meeting, but instead I was greeted by the entire Owusu clan. Abena included."

I tense at her name. That woman's very presence screams *bitch*. "What did she want?"

I ask even though I'm pretty sure I can guess. Women like her only want one of three things: money, power, or control. Sometimes all at the same time. He takes the next 30 minutes to recount the entire experience to me. His commentary is both colorful and thorough. He even reveals the gambling trouble his father had that created the need for such an agreement. This is a detail he could have chosen to omit. The fact that he shared it makes me feel closer to him. I share the sadness in his voice and witness the vulnerability in his eyes when he's done. The man is hurting. So am I.

I shift in my chair and take another sip of wine. Kofi stands and looks out into the sky from the balcony railing. I know he's trying to sort how he feels about it all, but I can't help but wonder about him and I. I must ask. "What does this mean for us?"

He turns around to face me. "I don't know. I've been thinking about us since the moment I saw the contract for myself. All I know is that I love you. I will figure this out. I just need some time to figure out what us will look like in the meantime."

This is not the answer I'm looking for. At this point in my life, I need him to know. Especially with the life changes he asked me to make less than 24 hours ago. *OK, Ella, calm down. Don't freak out.*

Ask objective questions. You're in the information-gathering stage. "Does that mean you are not marrying Abena?"

He leans back, places his elbows on the railing, and sighs. "It means I want to marry you."

Whoa, was that a proposal? I decide not to question it and let him continue.

"I'm trying to figure out how to get what I want without jeopardizing the crown and my family's legacy. If the terms of this contract get out along with my father's transgressions, it will cause some unrest. The Owusus know it will tarnish our entire reign. Between the council hearings and the press, it will be a nightmare."

I nod. "Kofi, that's extortion. Can't you bring them in front of the council for that? You're the king."

He simpers and shakes his head. "It doesn't quite work that way. I mean, I absolutely can. But I don't think that will win me any favors with the council. I'm also the speaker of the house in parliament, and reelection is coming next year. I can't afford a scandal."

The more he talks, the more I'm starting to feel animosity bubble up in my chest. I hate the Owusus, Abena, elections, and the council. This can't be healthy. I think we both may need some space to figure out how to deal with this and the past three weeks. I stand from the table and walk over to Kofi.

"Maybe it's good I'm heading back to Atlanta in a little less than two weeks. It sounds like you have a lot of thinking and big decisions to make. I don't want to be a distraction."

I walk over to him and he reaches out to grab my hands. "Ella, that's the last thing I want. I meant what I said last night. I want you to stay here with me. I asked for a year, but I will gladly take a lifetime. I just need time to figure out how to make everyone and myself happy at the same time. There has to be a way to fix this." His eyes look desperate. He's searching my face for assurances I'm not prepared to offer.

"Kofi, let's say you find a way for us to stay together. What does that mean for me? I mean besides moving to Ghana, what happens when we decide to marry? If I'm queen, what will my duties be? Will I be able to keep my company? My work is extremely important to me, and I don't think I could give that up for anyone or anything. I've already neglected my other commitments and clients enough since I've been here."

He squeezes my hands. "Of course. You will be able to continue the work of spreading free public education throughout Kumasi, Ghana, and even greater West Africa. Ella, with your talents, I believe the entire continent will benefit from the platform you will achieve as my wife. As far as your business, it will have to shift. You can't be a UN contractor or independent education consultant if you are a government official. As my wife and queen, that is what you would become. So, it is not giving up the work, just the autonomy to run an independent organization."

I release my hands from his and wrap my arms around my body. My head shakes in disbelief. "But Kofi, Revolution Academies has been my life for the past six years. I opened my first school a year out of law school at 26. When Marcus left me three years ago, a part of his reasoning was my business. He wanted me to practice corporate law like him, and I refused. After he left me, I was determined to make my work count and my business work, and it has. Now you're asking me to give all that up. Why is the woman always the one that has to sacrifice? Why can't we move to Atlanta and be bicoastal? I mean, surely we will have to travel quite a bit in our duties."

He walks behind me and wraps his arms around me. "I'm not saying we can't. I'm just saying I need some time to find out and share with you exactly what we can and can't do. I've never explored this avenue of my royal life before. I never had to until I fell in love with you. Can you give me some time to figure this all out, and in the meantime stay with me for however long it takes?"

My tears start to fall. Time is the one thing that I don't have to give. My flight back to Atlanta leaves in a little under two weeks. In that short amount of time, I'm hosting eight community meetings to promote the school network in the villages. Plus, I have a plethora of work waiting for me back in the states as well as engagements and business meetings. Not to mention my best friend is recovering from the biggest hit to her physical health she will ever see in her lifetime.

I don't have time to wait for Kofi to research if I'm worth the sacrifices he might have to make. I need to know now what his intentions are, because if I'm staying in Ghana, I'm only staying as his future queen and an international CEO of Revolution Academies. I don't know at what point it got that real, but with all the personal freedoms I will lose, those are the only two things worth gaining. It's not about the title. It's about being Kofi's everything. I have to know he will fight for the things that I need. I have to know no matter who is coming for me, whether it's the council or his messy auntie, that he will stop them before they get to my door. I have to come first. Without that assurance, I cannot stay.

"Kofi, we have time. Let's see what we can come up with in the next two weeks. But I do think it's best if I fly home at the end of my thirty days. I can always fly back when all this has worked itself out. If I'm going to come back to Ghana for good, there are loose ends I will need to tie up in Atlanta. There are also assurances I need that you still have to figure out how to provide. No matter what, our love is real and real love doesn't break just because it's tested." I try to sound convincing. Instead, it sounds like goodbye.

He gives me a soft smile before pulling me into his hold. "I'm never letting you go, Ella. No matter how far away you go, I will come get you. You're the only woman I love. Duty is just getting in the way right now. But please don't give up on me. Don't give up on us."

I try to hide my sniffle. "I love you, too. I just have too much in jeopardy to uproot everything I've built for uncertainty. I need more than that right now."

I feel him stiffen and nod. He's resigned. The king will not beg. I wouldn't want him to.

He rubs his nose in my hair and mumbles, "No more talk about this tonight. It's time that I fulfill the promise I made to you earlier." He looks up. "I've got to peel these clothes off for the night of love-making ahead of us. The way I'm feeling right now, I want to be with you in every imaginable way I can, while I can."

I reach up and kiss his lips to signal my yes. He picks me up and carries me inside to remind me no matter where I go, he's home.

Chapter Twenty-Nine

RESTORATION

Kofi

*I*t has been three days since Ella returned to Atlanta.

My home feels empty, and so does my heart. I sleep in the river room and I refuse to let my staff launder Ella's linens. Her pillowcase holds her citrus scent. Some days it feels like I'll never have her in my arms again. Other days it feels like I will turn the world upside down just to kiss her lips. Senya has had to stop me twice from plotting less than honorable ways to make the Owusus and this stupid contract go away.

I regret not being more open with my vulnerabilities and feelings when I left her at the airport. I was hurt. I could not believe she was really leaving my world. Instead of saying something I would regret at the airport, I said nothing and gave her a chaste kiss to the forehead. I should have grabbed onto her, promised whatever she needed to hear to stay, and held on for dear life.

I'm also angry. I'm angry at my mother for leaving me to practically raise myself once she gave up on life and decided I was not enough to make her stay a part of this world. I am angry at my father for not being the man he always insisted I be. I'm angry at the Owusus for their schemes. I'm angry at Ella for leaving me and

Ghana behind. Most of all, I'm angry at myself for allowing her to. I know what assurances she needed to stay, but I cannot deliver them. I cannot promise her that I will forsake all others and the crown to ensure her physical, emotional, and mental needs are met. I hate her for asking that of me. I'm not her ex-boyfriend stringing her along only to choose my career over her. I am a king trying to keep her at my side, to share my work and our lives together. To lead is to sacrifice. I wish I had worked harder to make her understand.

Today, I am at my palace meeting with yet another set of royal legal advisors. None of them understand the predicament. If I'm willing to pay the debt with interest, then there is no breach of contract. If only it were that simple. I dismiss them and place my head in my hands. It's hopeless. Either I marry Abena and lose Ella along with my happiness forever, or I marry Ella and fight the slander that will come against our family's royal reign. Once I solve this problem, the matter of what Ella's reign will look like is going to slap me in my face. I'm rubbing my hands across my head when I hear my office door slam shut. I snap up to see Senya's imposing frame walking toward me.

"Kofi. Enough! It's time to fix this," he scolds.

Irritated, I reply, "What the jackal do you think I'm trying to do? You think I'm here 12 hours a day meeting with lawyers and poring over this contract for my health?"

He shakes his head. "No, I think you're doing it to avoid the truth."

"What truth?" I snap.

"That you have to go to the council for this. You need Akua."

I push my chair away from my desk in disgust and stand up to leave. This is nonsense. Senya blocks my path. "I know that you don't want to mess with the tribal customs or regulations, but I think it is your only answer. The fancy lawyers can't help you deal with this, and the Owusus know that. You are the strongest tie to the community, and they know that as well. I think you need to ask Akua for help. Even though she's been a thorn in your side since Ella arrived, if there is a loophole that will allow for your happiness and protect your family's reign, she will find it."

I know he's right. But I'm still angry at Akua for the way she treated Ella. I also suspect that she kept the true nature of that contract away from me for all these years. I seriously doubt there was anything going on in our house that Akua was not privy to. How can I trust her?

Then again, how can I not? She has been in our family for over 60 years and mothered me when I was motherless. Before coming to serve our house, she was a young woman in the village, sought after by every powerful man to be in their bed. She refused to be anyone's mistress or second wife, no matter how powerful they were. When she came to my grandmother's royal door with her stew to sell, she never looked back.

I turn my attention back to Senya. "I don't know if Akua and I are at a place where we can talk again. Plus, no matter how much she loves me, I doubt she will lift one hand to help me marry my *American*." I use air quotes to emphasize the title she's given Ella.

Senya laughs. "She's stubborn. But she's also loyal to the house of Ajyei. There is no way she would allow herself to justify not helping you save your family's legacy. Look, she would kill me if she knew I told you this, but she has cried to me every night since the gala. Over two weeks of her lamenting her decisions! I promise you, she really thought she was protecting you. She thought the safest route for the Ajyei name and your reign was Abena. I think she knows better now." Senya walks over to my desk and places his hand on my shoulder. "She is an old woman that thinks of you as her son. You need to swallow your pride and make this truce happen. I mean, you're already here at the palace. Just go to her."

I sigh and lean on the back of my office chair. "All right. But you're coming with me!" I point at Senya. "We both know you're her favorite."

He grins. "Of course. Let's go!"

Senya and I leave and head to the residential side of the palace.

192

On our way to Akua's palace quarters, I pass the royal bedroom and my heart aches at the memories I made when I was there last. That was the first time Ella and I made love. I should feign going to the restroom just so I can check and see if any remnants of her sweet scent and spirit are left behind. Instead, I mentally send her a kiss and head to Akua's room.

When we arrive, I make Senya knock. "She needs to see your face first. She might slam the door on me! Like I said, you're her favorite."

Senya balks. "No way. I agreed to come for moral support. I'm not going to be the one to wake her up." Before Senya can continue whining, the door opens. Akua appears with one of her infamous disapproving looks.

"Both of you should be whipped for waking a woman my age at this hour. At this moment, neither one of you is my favorite."

I look at Akua and smile. I move in and kiss her on her cheek. "Old woman, if you were really sleep, you would not have been eavesdropping at the door. Admit it, you were waiting for us." I shoot Senya a knowing look. He steps back and raises both hands in the air to convey his innocence.

She ushers both of us into her sitting room and chuckles. "I may have heard of a possible visit. But I never reveal my sources." She sends Senya a sly look. "However, I told this source to ensure the visit happened before my first sleep." I chuckle at Akua's reference. Senya and I gave her sleep shifts because she would sleep for a couple of hours and then wake again. She literally has three shifts of sleep. It made it impossible to sneak around or get anything past her when we were younger.

Senya rolls his eyes. "I tried, Auntie. But you know how stubborn he is. It took an hour to convince him to come here." Just as I suspected, Akua knows all. She knows the predicament I'm in. The woman has always made it her business to know and manage my business. Akua fixes her stare on me.

"Kofi, you know I will help you." Tears start to prick her eyes.

193

"I'm saddened you did not come to me earlier. You're like my son. I don't want you hurting or worrying about anything."

I exhale the breath that I've been holding for the past couple of days. "Akua, if you knew about the contract, why didn't you tell me the details of it sooner? I hated finding out from the Owusus. It was embarrassing, and I was so unprepared for the revelation about my father. I...I...was out of control."

She chuckles and passes me a cup of tea. "Yes, I heard about Thomas' nose. I have a feeling you've wanted to do that for the better part of your childhood, so maybe it wasn't all bad, huh?" She gives me a sly smile.

I return the smile. "It felt great. But Akua, how can you keep something like that from me?"

Akua sits back and sighs. "You know I advised your father to never enter such a contract. Your mother knew nothing about it. If she knew he was gambling and making silly investments, she never showed it."

I interrupt her. "I think she knew. She used to allude to Father's faults, always mumbling it wasn't just his mistress that caused him to fall from God's grace."

Akua nods. "Your mother fiercely loved your father from the first moment she laid eyes on him. Much like you and Ella. Like you, she gave her entire heart over to him. In the end, he broke it. I've always known that you were like your mother, and I think I just didn't want you hurt. That's why I opposed Ella so much. She's a lovely woman. But she's not from here. I didn't know if she would be able to love you properly as king. She is clearly a fiercely independent woman, and serving as queen is a huge sacrifice to ask someone of her stature."

I smooth my hands over my thighs. "Yes, I know. She's in Atlanta now, and I feel like I'm about to die daily. I also know that if I were truly all in with her, if I promised her my love and devotion no matter what, she would be here. You see, Akua, the only way Ella can give me her all is if I give her mine."

194

She nods. "Yes, I know that now. I apologize for meddling. I never thought you were even looking for love. I always assumed you would marry Abena out of convenience and duty once you figured you really did need an heir. I think she expected the same thing. That's why she lives her life the way she does. She treats you like an insurance policy. Once I saw that, I was sad that I ever placed myself between you and the woman who truly loves you. Ella was a shock to us all. We never saw her coming."

She leans forward and grabs my hand to squeeze. "But Kofi, I'm so glad she did. You are happy. You deserve that."

I shake my head. "I was happy. Until this. Now the woman I love is halfway across the world. I have no idea how to fix this mess so I can bring her back. Akua, she's not coming back for less than a promise to love and protect her and her interests forever. I can't say I blame her. Honestly, at first, this fight was more about my right to choose my queen, flexing my autonomy as king, then about making the decision to make Ella my queen. I think she knew that even if I did not. That is why she had to leave. She needed me to determine what I was really fighting for on my own terms. Now, the answer is overwhelmingly clear to me."

Akua nods in agreement. "Smart girl. Well, lucky for you, Akua still has some tricks up her sleeve."

Senya jumps in his seat and shouts, "Yes!" before settling back down. "I told you she could fix this. You should listen to me more, Kofi. You would worry less."

I roll my eyes and Senya and I focus back on Akua. "Akua, what will I have to do?"

Akua yawns. "Nothing at all. Just be at the council meeting I've called for tomorrow at noon. It will be here at the palace."

I raise my eyebrows and give Akua a wary look. "And how, pray tell, did you manage to call a council meeting? You're not an official member of the council."

"Oh! I didn't. You did." She winks at me and rises from her chair. "Now, if you two will please excuse me, I need to get started on my first sleep of the night. Kofi, just be in the throne conference room at noon, and I will take care of the rest. Trust me."

I stand and look at her. "I will."

She claps her hands together. "Wonderful, now please leave."

Senya joins me in a laugh as we head to the door to exit. I leave her room feeling like an entire weight has been lifted from my chest. If Akua says she'll handle it, then it's done.

Chapter Thirty

COUNCIL

Kofi

s I enter the throne room along with Akua, all six chiefs are waiting for me.

No one looks directly at me, but the shifting of large bodies in small chairs makes it clear my presence is felt. I deduce Chief Kwabena Owusu ensured everyone knew about my conduct in his compound during my visit a little over two weeks ago. I take my seat at the head of the conference room table, forcing everyone to turn and acknowledge me. Akua and I decided it would be best for me to address the council and my intentions before I give her the floor. When I have everyone's attention, I begin.

"Hello, council," I start, "it's good to see each chief here today. This meeting is called to address an unjust contract plaguing my family. A contract drawn up from one of our very own members." I shoot a look that could kill to Chief Owusu. He is obviously less confident in his pretense without his boisterous son. I continue, knowing no one will dare stop the Asantehene from speaking. "I'm sure the rumors have spread that I've become involved with an American. Those are true; however, I've fallen in love with her."

The room starts to erupt in low grumbles and sparks of conversation between neighbors. "I assure you, I do not make the choice of whom I love and want to spend the rest of my life with lightly, especially not as lightly as my father and Chief Owusu did 30 years ago. Ella is good, kind, and she loves our people. She wants to lead our public education efforts at my side. That's where she belongs. You all know I have had much pain in my life. For the first time, your king knows joy. I'm asking you to nullify the contract that binds me to Abena Owusu. I have agreed to pay the debt, and anything beyond that is extortion." I shoot another deadly look at Chief Owusu. Unsurprisingly, he averts his gaze. *Coward.* "Wise elders, I also ask you to accept Ella as one of us." It is quiet for a full minute before Chief Apeagyei of Aboso breaks the silence.

"So, are you telling us you mean to make her queen?"

I pause and think before I answer. "Yes, Chief, if she will have me."

The room gasps. Chief Aboso continues, "I'm not sure if we can even allow that. She is not Ashanti. Isn't she an American businesswoman here to build our schools?"

Chief Owusu takes this opportunity to pounce. "Yes, and we all know our king has corrupted many of our villages' girls into willing bed partners that I'm sure he's claimed to love." He turns his sweating face to me. "No offense to your majesty, of course. I'm just stating facts for the sake of our discussion." I do not acknowledge his fake apology. Instead, I continue to drill a hole in his confidence with my posture. "Looking at his behavior inside the bedroom and out of it, no Ashanti women are good enough for our throne. Yet he spends four weeks with an American we know nothing about, and suddenly he is in love. It is witchcraft, I tell you. Why else would our benevolent king break a promise to the daughter of one of his most loyal chiefs?!"

The room starts to verbally sway and agree before Akua stands up and addresses the room. "If I may shed some light on the issue," she begins, "I think it will help you all wrap your minds around all of this."

Owusu rises from his chair to object. "You are not a member of council; you may not address us without expressed invitation. Who even invited you to this meeting—why are you here?"

At that, I snap at Owusu, "Sit down now, you oversized jackal." He trembles his huge jaws in defiance but sits, nonetheless. I continue to address only him. "Did you not see her arrive with me, your king! Obviously, she was invited. Now you will sit here with the rest of the council and hear what my guest has to say, or you can leave, and we will discuss it without you. Now, which do you prefer?"

He stares back with curled lips. He knows he cannot verbally challenge me without reprimand. "I will stay, your majesty."

"Good." I turn to Akua. "You may address the room."

She nods at me with a smile and continues. "Our king is the victim of a flawed but benevolent father and a greedy Chief Owusu. Kofi's father never handled the Ashanti treasury. Most of you don't know that. However, Chief Adu does." Akua turns her warm eyes to the eldest of our council chiefs. Chief Adu is 92 years old and has led the village of Suame for 65 years. Without a word, he nods at Akua to go on. "This was set in place a year after Kofi's birth and four years before Owusu's sinful contract. He never wanted it to be said that he used Ashanti government funds inappropriately; therefore, he imposed his own oversight."

Owusu interrupts Akua. "But what does any of that have to do with today's proceedings? Guest of the king or not, you are wasting our time."

Akua shoots him a deadly look. "You try to extort our king by holding him to a marriage that he does not want even when he agrees to pay you the sum of the loan with interest. You do this because you know he will not want his father's name tarnished. However, what you do not know is that even though his father was a gambler, he was a good and smart king. He put in measures to assure his reign will always be above financial reproach, while you still operate the very casinos our king lost his personal fortune to. I wonder what we will see if we open those books!"

Owusu's eyes open wide and I swear the man turns beet red even though his skin is the color of a dark chocolate bar.

"Yes," Akua continues. "You think no one knows that much of your wealth comes from the gambling houses in Accra. Well I know, because your wife, God rest her soul, used to cry about it at church every week to the elders. I served in those prayer rooms. I know more than you think. And if it weren't for you trying to extort our king now, I would have let that secret along with all the others I know go to the grave."

It gets so quiet you could hear a giraffe piss in the savannah. Owusu drops his head in shame before he laments. "I meant no harm." He starts to weep. "I just wanted my family to be taken care of. The gold mines were drying out, and I had to find a way to turn a profit. The casinos were the perfect investment. When I started to hear that King Kwame was frequenting the establishment, I tried to stop him. But he would not listen, and he was so arrogant. So, when I found out he was losing so much so fast, I decided to present the loan and betrothal to him as an insurance policy. That way, if any of you hypocrites found out how Tarkwa was really keeping its coffers full, you would not blackball my daughter from having a chance to be queen while Kwame would have the money he needed to live a king's lifestyle. I never thought Kofi would really fall in love. No king really gives his heart away."

Akua lifts her chin. "My king does." The rest of the council mumble in agreement.

Akua continues. "Kofi will pay his family's monetary debt. Nothing in our tribal laws state he has to marry an Ashanti woman, only that his wife must be a woman of noble character and not a harm to the Ashanti Nation. She must honor and protect our customs." The chiefs nod in agreement, essentially admitting they cannot choose my wife nor enforce the asinine betrothal contract to Abena Owusu.

Akua sits and continues to speak. "The council will speak no more of this, because you know King Kwame did not mishandle any government funds. This will never leave this room." She turns to Owusu. "Finally, no one will shame Owusu or speak of his business again, or I will come to your next council meeting and share some of the things I learned about each of you in those prayer rooms. Is that clear?"

"Anne," everyone agrees. Akua turns and grabs my hand. "Your majesty, the floor is yours."

I kiss the back of her hand and address the council. "This meeting is adjourned. I have a plane to catch."

Chapter Thirty-One

PURSUIT

Ella

"Don't you have anywhere else to be besides hovering over me?"

Maya screeches as I try to force a homemade pedicure onto her. She let me know she has people to do that, but I insist she allow me. I've been back in Atlanta for a little less than a week now. I miss Kofi terribly, but I know I made the right decision to leave. He needs space to figure out exactly what he's willing to sacrifice to have me at his side. After my last relationship, nothing short of everything will do.

In the meantime, I try to wait on Maya hand and foot to take my mind off my sadness. I came back to my best friend living in Adom's mansion in Cascade. The doctor was ready to release Maya to a rehabilitation center one week ago, but Adom would not hear of it. He hired the best private physical and occupational therapists money can buy and converted a room in his home to Maya's new sanctuary. He only started going back to work two days ago, once he realized I basically had nothing to do with my time but mope. I think both of them resent me for infringing on whatever is budding between them. I'm sorry but not sorry; they are both my best friends and owe me for all the times I helped them get their lives back together after a breakup. I just can't face my lovely empty home right now. It no longer feels like home. Bonbiri is where I belong.

I look up at her and huff. "Oh, I apologize for trying to be a good friend. Your toes look horrible. You never let them go like this."

She sits herself up further on the mass of pillows I continuously fluff for her. "Bitch, I was in a major car accident and spent almost two weeks in a hospital." She looks down at the undone toes poking out of my Gucci slides and shakes her head. "What's your excuse?"

I throw the nail polish bottle at her and laugh. "Why I got to be a bitch, though?"

She breaks a smile. "Because you are smothering the hell out of me. I finally got Adom to leave me the hell alone, and then here you come. If you and Adom don't get y'all hovering asses the hell on. Oh my God! I'm going to scream." Uh-oh, when Dr. Maya Taylor starts a cursing, she's at her wit's end. Maybe I should give her a little space. She eyes my pensive look and takes pity on me. "Ella, why don't you just call Kofi and put us all out of the misery you are determined to expose us to? I mean, clearly you are hung up on the man. This is ridiculous. You haven't even been to the office!"

I take a seat on the edge of her bed and finger her duvet. The purple and gold silk are a nice touch. Adom knows Maya well. The whole room is decorated precisely to her tastes. "I know. It's just that work reminds me of him. It reminds me of the work starting in Ghana right now without me. You know, I sent our best operations director to jumpstart building in Tafo."

She arches her eyebrow. "You sent Dara?"

"Hell no! I sent Brandon."

She points her finger at me. "You ain't fooling me. You know Dara is much better at brand new construction than Brandon. You just didn't want her fast ass near your man."

I laugh because it's true. "Well, she does work fast. I don't need anything else about Kofi to obsess over. Maya, why hasn't he called?

It's been five days!" I feel the tears start to well up. I've cried no less than three times every day since I've touched back down in Atlanta. "Maybe it all really was just a game to him. Why would he even think of compromising his crown and legacy for me?"

Maya snatches upright so fast she winces in pain. I lean over to help her, but she pushes her hands out to me, ordering me to stop. "Look, that's crazy talk. First of all, you're amazing. He's probably shit-faced over the fact you're not in his presence right now. Secondly, don't sell yourself short; you're worth a hell of a lot more than a crown. Lastly, if it was all a game, so what?! His loss. You will overcome it and find the love right for you."

I roll my eyes and let out a sigh. "Yeah, right."

Maya relents. "Yes, right! I was there when Marcus broke your heart and your confidence. I've been here these past three years to watch you systematically close off every entrance to your heart and convince yourself you don't need love. You hide yourself in that amazing home and your amazing work, scared men are going to bite. Well, guess what, they do. But sometimes, the venom is sweet, and no matter what happens, I'm glad Kofi bit you, because now you know you can fall in love and be happy."

"Right, I know that now. But I'm also sitting here alone, without him. What good did it do me?" I stand up and pace the room. "I should have never gone to Ghana in the first place."

"You're so dramatic, Ella. Look, did he ask you to leave? No!"

I interrupt her. "I had to! You know that!"

She shakes her head. "I know no such of thing. You left him. You left because you were scared to stick around and take a risk. Let's not get it twisted. You are here with my broken ass because you chose to be, not because he sent you home."

Her words hit me like a ton of bricks. She's right. I know it deep down. Fear is what has driven me here. It's driven me away from Kofi. No matter how much he tells me he loves me and needs me, I don't believe it. I do not believe he will choose me no matter what. So, instead of waiting by his side, I ran. I left him. He looked like an angry and broken man when he dropped me at the airport. For a second, I thought he might come with me. I wanted him to. I was mad he didn't. But now I know that wasn't the answer. He's a king and responsible for 11 million people. My work is a natural extension of the work he already does on a grand scale. It wasn't right for him to leave. It was wrong for me not to stay. The tears really fall now.

Maya hands me a tissue from her glass top nightstand. "Yep. Get it all out. Then get your ass online and book a ticket back to Accra."

I look up from my tissues. "Oh my God, Maya, you think he'll even want to see me? I can't just show up there, can I?"

She raises her hands and looks to the heavens. "Jesus, please give me strength with this one right here." Then she looks over to me. "Ella, what did we just talk about? Stop being scared. He loves you. You love him. Go! Do you need me to book the ticket? Shit, pass me my MacBook."

I go over and hug her shoulders. "No, I got it. You are an amazing friend, Maya Taylor."

She hunches her shoulders. "I know. I had to do something, because I was about to stab your Black ass if you tried to make me one more of those nasty ass smoothies. I'd rather have Adom—at least he feeds me junk food. This is my one chance to eat it with no guilt. I can't work out anyway."

I give Maya a side-eye. "Don't act like you only want Adom for chicken sandwiches and fries. You like him. Admit it!"

She crosses her arms over her chest and shakes her head from side to side. "I do not! He's annoying. I tolerate him because he really has looked out for me during all this. But we are just friends. You know Adom is not my type."

"Oh! So rich, tall, fine, and takes care of your every need is not your type? Since when?"

She smirks. "Since you are trying to delay going home and booking that ticket back to Accra. You can analyze my love life once you get yours together."

"Well, you can say all that. But I should let you know that with

Adom, it doesn't matter what your type is, because you're his. We both know that man is relentless in his pursuits."

Maya shifts uncomfortably in her seat. "That may be true, but I'm not his run-of-the-mill pursuit." She yawns. "Don't you have a plane to catch?"

"Fine!" I lean back down and kiss her cheek. "I'll go. I don't appreciate you kicking me out, but you know since I suddenly have shit to do, I'm going to let that slide."

"I ain't saying you got to go home, but..."

"Yeah, I know the rest." I grab my purse and wave as I head to the door. "Bye," I yell from the foyer as I exit Adom's house. Once outside, I feel ready to do anything. Maya is right. Kofi didn't want me to leave. I chose to out of fear. I hope he can forgive me. He better, because I'm flying home.

*

*A*s I turn on my street, I notice four black armored vehicles lined up across the street from my home. I wonder what rapper or athlete is visiting the area. They often rent the home across the street from mine. It's a secluded old mansion that offers luxury and privacy in a low-key area of the city.

I park in my driveway and look at the cars in my rearview mirror before exiting my car. Something about the cars feels off. First off, why are there four? That's a pretty big entourage for your average entertainer. Also, we usually get an email from the owners of the property if there is a big party renting it. I shrug it off and walk to my front door. I have plane tickets to book. I won't be here to complain about inevitable noise.

I continue to walk up my steps. Suddenly, the hairs on my arms start to stand up. I feel his presence before I ever hear him. I turn around and almost stumble in his arms from the shock. I start at his hair. Moisturized and perfectly trimmed curls as usual. Cocoa-colored skin the consistency of silk. A smile that makes my panties wet on sight. Tall muscular body making his black linen suit grateful for the chance to serve such a work of art. Then I hear the voice. It's honey and steel. Commanding me to attend to his words.

"Hello, Queen. I have missed you."

Chapter Thirty-Two

CAPTURE

Kofi

*B*efore I can say more, Ella is in my arms.

She holds onto me like she is afraid I will disappear if she lets go. Her hug is mixed with relief and desperation. Both reactions are unacceptable and tell me she actually thought it possible to lose me. She has no idea how far under her spell I am and have been since the day she cursed me for attempting to bring her to my home without her knowledge. Though it's only been five weeks since that tense car ride, I feel like an entire era has passed since then. My life is now seen as before Ella and after Ella. I'm so sure. Yet, she still doubts how much I am in love with her. That's why I am here, to relieve her of that foolish uncertainty. The only things I ever want her to feel for me are pure desire and expectation.

I give her a quick squeeze and kiss her forehead before pulling back. I do not release her arms as I step back. I crossed oceans to touch her, and I can't let go. She's magnificent. Her bronzed hair is swept up in a mass of curls atop her head, highlighting her strong cheekbones and the hazel in her eyes. Her lips are begging to be kissed. *Don't worry, I'm coming.* First, I need to get her inside the house. My entourage is nosy, especially Senya. He will never let me live down making out with my girlfriend in public. I hate that I had to bring him at all. However, I knew it was futile to fight him on the matter. He helped me move heaven and earth to ensure the press did not get wind. He surprised me with the team of 20 guards once I arrived. Only he and I flew on my jet.

I look at her. "May we go in?"

She shakes out of the enchantment my arrival has brought. "Yes, of course. Let me just find my keys."

She walks to the door and attempts to unlock her front door. She fumbles with the lock for a minute before I take the keys from her. She's clearly rattled. "I got you."

I manage to open her door. An open and clean space greets me. It looks like a page ripped from *Architectural Digest*. I only know this because Akua collects the magazine. She has for over 30 years. It's the only periodical I allow in Bonbiri, mostly because it's one I can guarantee I will not be scandalized in. However, Ella's home leaves me speechless. Everything oozes serenity and quiet. The muted grays and blues remind me of calming waters; no wonder she chose the river room at Bonbiri. It reminds her of her oasis here. I turn and watch her watching me. I grab her hand and lead us to a large gray sectional in the center of her family room. I sit down and place her on my lap. Tears start to fall.

I wipe her face with concern. "What are these for? I can't have my queen crying. Tell me who did it and I will fight them."

She gives me a faint smile. *That's better.* "You did it. Showing up without any warning, I'm overwhelmed."

I give a hesitant nod. "Is it OK that I'm here? When I called to check, Adom said you would be glad to have me come. I'll put him back on my shit list if he steered me wrong."

She laughs. "No, he is right. I am very glad to see you. But why didn't you call me? Why Adom?"

That's a good question. The best answer is because I'm a coward. I was scared she already moved on from me and my crown. I knew with distance, she migh realize the demands royal life would put on her, makes me not worth it after all. I was concerned she wasn't in as much pain as I was while we were apart. I figured Adom would be a reluctant emissary to ask on my behalf. He refused. He stated anything I had to say to Ella I must say in person, or I'm not worth her time. If he weren't my cousin, I would have let him know exactly where he could stick his opinion. However, if he weren't right, I would not be here at all. I'm grateful Ella has friends like Maya and Adom in her life. I decide to tell her some of that, but not all.

"Well, you were so disappointed when you left and, frankly, I think a little mad. I didn't know if you would want me. I couldn't bear coming here and you not letting me in. That would be tragic."

She nods. "Yes, I guess it would. I'm so sorry, Kofi." She looks at me. I don't avert my gaze. I cock my head to the side and let out a slow breath before responding.

"I know. You were scared. I also know that I was not doing enough to alleviate your fears. You never signed up for all of this. You came to Ghana to do your job and leave. You didn't plan to fall for an imperious king that rules halfway around the world. Knowing and understanding these things, I want you to understand that your apology is not necessary. You did what you thought was best for you at the time. I will never be mad at you for choosing to take care of you first. That's the only way you will be able to properly love me. The same is true for me. We can never be afraid to be who we are and answer the call of our lives as fully as we possibly can."

She breathes a sigh of relief. "Thank you. You're so right; I was fearful, and that was not a good place to support you from. I honestly don't know if there's anything you could say or do to alleviate the fear I had when I left Ghana. The fear wasn't about you. It was about me and whether or not I was willing to risk my heart again."

I nod. "I'm sure falling in love with a king that lives on an entirely different continent does not help your anxiety. But I want you to know I will close any distance between us to make this work. If we have to be bicoastal, so be it. I just can't lose you, and I don't want you nervous about anything. I want you happy."

Looking at her, I want to touch her and reassure her that no reign, position, or woman will ever be able to take her place as the most important thing in my life. She is the priority. Instead, it is she that positions her body to be closer to me.

She begins to speak. "Your position and geography were a smoke-screen for the fear." She grabs my hands and starts to rub them again. Her eyes scream, *make love to me*. I'm ready.

"But Kofi, I'm not scared anymore. I know that I belong with you in Bonbiri. No matter what the Ashanti council might say about who I am or what I do, if you tell me I'm who you want by your side, I will fight to be there."

Chapter Thirty-Three

PERFECTION

Ella

Kofi slips one hand away from my grasp and presses it against my right cheek.

"That's all I've ever wanted to hear you say to me since the moment I saw you stomp across that TED Talk stage telling the audience, '*We have cut out the tongues and closed the minds of half the world's youth through intentional miseducation, and we must now fight illiteracy like it is the last front in the War on Terror.*'"

I laugh at my words. It sounds exactly like something I would say. "And then you glared at your audience and bit your bottom lip to pause for effect." He takes his other hand and presses it to my left cheek. "It was in that moment that I knew I needed a queen like that. One who would not mince words. A queen that will inspire even the most reserved man to act! The Ashanti children need you, and so do I."

To punctuate his last word, he leans into my mouth for a kiss. It's nothing like the many kisses we shared over the past five weeks. It's not hot and steamy. It is gentle and lingering. It doesn't command me. It influences me. I start to undress.

"Come with me," I say as I break from his hold and stand. I take my shirt off and let him see my pink and black silk push-up bra. Then I turn knowing he's following me. As we walk down the hallway to my bedroom, I let my hair down and unzip my jeans, knowing he has a full view of my ass in the matching silk thong he picked weeks ago. Once we are in my bedroom, I turn around and face him. I slowly remove the bra and use my finger to motion for him to come to me. "I want you to remove my thong...with your teeth." His eyes go wide with lust. He starts to take his shirt off, but I stop him. "No, I want you dressed for this."

"Ella..." His voice is hoarse with need. "Are you commanding the king?"

"Call me Queen. And I'm not commanding—I'm asking you to remove my panties with your teeth and eat my sweet pussy like it's the last meal you will ever have, all while dressed like a proper king in this sexy ass black linen. Will you oblige me?"

He growls and hits his knees. First, he grabs my ass with his two hands and tugs at the center of my panties with his teeth, making sure to lick and tease me along the way. I almost combust before he gets started. "Kofi! I missed your tongue."

"Up!" He commands I lift my legs one at a time so he may fully remove the last barrier between his tongue and the center of me. He stands and lifts me up. I wrap my legs around his waist while he carries me to the bed. Once at the bed, he lays me down. "Push back and spread those pretty thighs for me, baby." I obey without caution. I sit up to watch his every move as he crawls onto the bed in between my legs. He pauses for a second and gives me a grin.

"My queen, may I remove my clothes now? I want us skin to skin." I nod my approval. He removes and discards his clothes quickly before delivering his mouth to my left nipple. As he nips and sucks, he uses his free hand to rub the pulsing bud between my legs. Round and round his fingers go as he moves his mouth from one breast to the next. When I arch my back off the bed and buck in plea-sure, he pauses his work on my breasts to watch me come undone. The look in his eye is pure want. "That's it my queen. Let go and give it all to me." *I do.* When I'm done, his tongue starts a new campaign between my legs.

He licks my centerfold over and over again like a cat licking his paw. Kofi is laying claim to my body, and I'm inclined to give it to him. After a final lick, he sucks my clit and kisses my center until I'm begging. "Please, Kofi, I need you inside me." He stops only to flip me over on my stomach. He slaps my ass twice before issuing his second command of the night.

"Get on all fours for me. I want you to feel every inch of me." I happily obey and feel his palm press the center of my back down so that my ass is as high and accommodating as possible.

The first thrust takes my senses away. After five days away from him, my body needs to adjust. I forgot how big my king is. He keeps his hands at the center of my back and pulls out to his tip before thrusting with full force into me again. I sink deeper into the bed as each push comes harder and faster than the one before. I'm pushed to a pleasure with no limits. I scream out his name. "Kofi! More, please more." He grunts his response and starts a punishing rhythm. I come and he doesn't stop. He acknowledges me by saying, "Good girl. Now come again," before pushing me to another peak.

"You will never leave me again, will you?" I'm so focused on the amazing dick taking my body over the edge that I don't answer. He slaps my ass, reminding me not to ever make him ask a thing twice. "Will you?" he breathes.

"Never," I scream out. Not only because I want him to hear it, but because my orgasm is fast approaching. He just continues to pound. Then I realize he's not crashing into me to chase his orgasm. He's trying to give me as many as my body will allow.

"You're mine," he whispers into my ear. "I won't have anyone else loving you or touching you. That's my duty." He speeds up and I know his release is coming. I reach back and grab his thighs as he slams into me for his final thrusts. I try to get as much of him in me as possible.

"Ahhhh, Ella, I'm coming, baby."

Just for fun, I come with him. I reach down and rub my clit with reckless abandon trying to catch up as he empties all the uncertainty and unresolved drama he brought with him across the Atlantic into me. At that moment, I know we're going to be OK.

When we finish, I collapse on the bed and he lies on top of me for a few minutes. When he finally rolls off, he rolls me onto him and lays my head on his chest. Grabbing my hand, he kisses the back of my knuckles. "I love you so much, Ella. My heart will burst if I love you any more."

I giggle. "Are you sure that wasn't your heart that just burst all inside of me a few minutes ago? You were in rare form, Asantehene."

He chuckles and picks my knuckles up for another kiss. "I waited six days to touch you again. I didn't even pleasure myself because I was determined to get back inside the woman I love. No matter what it took. So, you'll have to excuse my, um...enthusiasm?"

"That's a good description for it." I chuckle.

He lifts me off his chest and places me on my back. He then sits up on his elbow and looks down at me while drawing lazy circles around my left nipple. "What about you? You've never been that forward with me. What gives, Queen?"

I scrunch my nose and give a smile. "Maybe I'm happy you just saved me two thousand dollars?"

He gives me a curious glance. "How so?"

"I've been staying with Adom and Maya since I returned. I missed you too much to be alone. Today Maya finally talked some sense into me and kicked me out. I was coming home to buy a plane ticket to Accra. The first flight I could find, I was taking it."

He laughs a full laugh and pulls me back into his arms. "So, you were coming back to me, huh?"

"Yes, I couldn't take being away from you anymore. I love you, Kofi. I'm ready to start the rest of my life with you. No matter how long it takes to fix that foolishness with the Owusus, I know you're actively working to fix it. Plus, it's not like you're married. This can be fixed."

He kisses the top of my head. "May I take you to dinner? Let's go to your favorite restaurant!"

I sit up and look at him. "Now? Why?"

He sits up on both elbows. "Because I came all the way here to tell you something and I want to tell you in your favorite place over a bottle of your favorite wine."

I give him a careful glance. "Am I going to like this news?"

He tackles me until I am lying under him. He kisses me and responds, "It's going to be everything you've been waiting for."

Chapter Thirty-Four

FUFILLMENT

Ella

My adrenaline rushes from excitement and pure joy as we enter Two Urban Licks.

It is my favorite restaurant and the only place that serves candied Brussel sprouts the way I like them. In the lobby, I glimpse our reflection in the mirror behind the bar and confirm that we are indeed a stunning couple. I'm in a red silk strapless Valentino mini dress paired with nude four-inch Louboutins. My curly afro is perfection as it flanks my shoulders. Kofi complements me in a perfectly cut black suit paired with a black dress shirt opened at the neck. He looks regal without even trying. During the car ride to the restaurant, Kofi shared how Akua helped him win over the council. The good news along with the good man standing to my left makes me feel like I'm sitting on top of the world.

We decide to hit the bar while we wait to be seated. Kofi goes to order drinks as I take a seat. My feet are killing me, but my overall look is so worth it. The bar is full and I lose sight of Kofi as he presses into a crowded space a few feet from me to catch the attention of a bartender. *I bet he's never had to fight for his own drinks before.* There was no time to make a proper reservation at the type of place he is used to. Plus, he asked to take me to my favorite place, so here we are.

I am swiping aimlessly through my phone when I feel a hand squeeze my shoulder. I look behind me and freeze with shock. It's none other than Marcus Banks looking at me knowingly. He swallows and I keep my eyes on the apple inside his thick neck easing down and then up. "Ella! Wow, what a surprise to see you here!"

I cross my arms and flick my gaze upward into a sharp eyeroll. "This is my favorite restaurant, Marcus. It has been for 10 years. You just refused to take me here. I believe you said the crowd was too common. Remember?"

He laughs and flashes a cocky grin. "Did I say that? You must remember it wrong. I love the scene here—Keisha put me on to it years ago." *Why did he bring up that home-wrecking tramp?* Thank God I didn't know this sooner—the news would have put a bad taste in my mouth every time I visited. *I don't want to share anything in common with that bitch.* I wish he would just stop talking, but Marcus loves the sound of his own voice. God help him if he's still around when Kofi gets back. "You look good, baby. Have you been in the gym? I bet you're finally joining Maya for her workouts. I told you they would do you a world of good."

He's doing what he's always done—hiding his cruel intentions in carefully crafted *almost* compliments. Three years ago, I would dig into his comments and flip them around in my mind to determine his true meaning. I would spend weeks doing anything to get a real compliment from him. I craved his validation.

Now, I feel no need. He's still the tall, handsome man he always was. But none of it holds any appeal to me. He clearly isn't hitting the gym with his previous vigor. He's slightly softer around the middle. His hair is graying at the temples. His wine-colored tuxedo jacket and tight black jeans scream trying too hard on a Friday night. He's a 33-year-old man attempting to look 25. Must be Keisha's influence.

"Actually, no. I'm just a lot healthier now without the stress of three years ago." I slowly cross my legs and give him a peek at the

African tanned thighs I wrapped around Kofi earlier. He takes the bait and lingers a little too long. Got him! "Plus, my new schools in Africa keep me engaged in far more righteous pursuits than becoming a gym rat."

He narrows his eyes and sips his beer. *When did Mr. Dom Perignon start drinking Heineken?* "You have schools in Africa now? Congratulations. I know you always wanted to use your law degree to help the poorest of children. Of course, that doesn't really allow you to use it, does it? Who helped you get past the UN? You should have called me. I would have looked over the paperwork for you."

I don't bite. I eye Kofi out of the corner of my eye and decide to change the subject. "So, I heard you and Kiesha got married last year. Congratulations."

His smile is genuine, like a man in love. "Yes. I thought of inviting you, but I didn't want it to be awkward. You were always such an important friend. It felt weird not having you there. But I didn't want you to stress over it. I saw one of your sorority line sisters a few months before, and she said you were just throwing yourself into that house you bought." He gives me a look of pity. I want to punch him right in his stupid face.

"I do love my home. You made the right decision. I wouldn't have come to see you marry so far below your own false standards. Has Keisha finished her paralegal studies yet? I know you were paying for it. Or should I say *we* were paying for it, since that was actually during our engagement. It'd be nice to know there's some sort of return on my investment."

He grips his beer tightly and flares his nostrils. "Please. Your little charter network and child defense cases barely paid for the cars. I put Keisha through school and subsidized your lifestyle so you could play Mother Theresa. So don't give me your victim bullshit." The last part hits me like a bullet. As I hop off my barstool to give him a real piece of my mind, my royal escort arrives like a bulletproof vest.

"Ella, my queen, here is your drink." Kofi's deep African accent is in full force when he addresses me. Marcus stares at all six-foot-four of my African king. He's speechless. Marcus reaches his hand out and offers a handshake.

"Hello, I'm Marcus, Ella's ex-fiancé." Why he feels the need to evoke ancient history with that lame-ass title, I don't know.

Kofi silently stares at him and his weak hand before slowly taking a sip of his drink and smiling at me. I guess Marcus doesn't know you don't reach for the hand of the Asantehene.

"Marcus, this is King Kofi Ajyei. The leader of the Ashanti in Ghana." Kofi nods in his direction and continues to sip his drink.

Marcus' lips curl back into a tight line. *"King?* Since when is there a king in Ghana?" he says with a sneer.

Kofi turns to place his drink on the bar and winks at me before addressing him. "Since 1672, actually. And of course, we have had royalty since before Christ. Western nations actually stole the concept of monarchy from us. My bloodline has ruled since 400 A.D. If you would like a moment to Google and correct your assumption about the leadership of 11 million people, please do so. We do have time since our table is not yet ready. Usually, I would make a hasty retreat from such ignorance, but, as you said, you and my Ella were close once. I will not offend her."

Marcus stiffens. "That won't be necessary." He shoots a look at me. "I guess this is who helped you secure your UN contracts. I guess necessity makes strange...bedfellows." *I know he didn't just go there!* He's trying to say I slept my way into my contract! I step forward to give him what-for. But Kofi intercepts. First, he slightly touches my neck like, *don't move, I got this.* Then everything around me begins to move very quickly.

Kofi grabs Marcus by his tuxedo jacket lapel and the cheap fabric rips. He looks dismissively at the inferior piece of fabric and decides Marcus' shirt collar will do. Marcus tries to fight him off, but Kofi easily overpowers him and sits him on the stool I just vacated. He grabs Marcus' neck and presses his face to the bar. Kofi leans in so closely that his face is almost touching Marcus' and hisses in his ear, "Listen to me, you filthy piece of a jackal hide, Ella is a brilliant woman that secured the UN contract alone. But you surely know that."

He bends Marcus' arm behind his back and presses it up toward his shoulder blade. "You just want to hurt her, and now I will hurt you. If you ever see her walking down the street, look the other way. If you ever deign to speak to her, you'd better address her as Her Royal Highness or I swear to all my ancestors, I will rip you apart piece by piece until all that is left of you is the limp stick between your legs for your foolish wife to lick upon. Is that clear?"

Marcus doesn't reply. He is wild-eyed with anger and fear. Kofi bends his arm further. Finally, Marcus reluctantly nods his head. Kofi turns him around and grabs him by the shirt. *Lord, please don't hit him!* People are so engrossed in Kofi's display of physical dominance they start to crowd the area. I quickly feel strong hands pull me back and step in front of me. Quite naturally, Senya has made his way through the crowd.

"Your majesty!" he scolds. "Let go of the jackal now! We have no time for frivolous lawsuits."

Kofi doesn't budge. "Kofi, seesei ara!" he roars in Twi. Kofi obeys. Wow, I've never seen Senya have to do that before. It's amazing how quickly he calms him down.

Marcus leans back against the bar rubbing his neck and coughing, and Keisha pops out of nowhere looking disheveled. *I wonder what she was up to while her husband was getting his ass handed to him?* She fusses over him and starts talking about a lawsuit. Marcus shushes her and they slink away. He knows he does not want any more smoke with King Kofi Ajyei.

I stand and wait for Kofi to come to me. He smooths my hair and kisses my forehead. "I'm sorry you had to see that. I don't usually let my anger get the best of me, but it seems, Queen, since I met you, I have been forced to defend your honor on more than one occasion." I give him a side-eye before breaking out into a smile.

"Oh no, your majesty. Thomas Owusu's broken nose was on you."

He leans in and lands a kiss on my neck. "Trust me, all I cared about in that room was marrying you. He and his nose were in my way, so I broke it."

His breath on my skin sets me on fire. If Senya and what I now notice is half of the royal security team weren't staring, I would jump him right at this bar. They've moved everyone else out the way. Before I get a chance to lean in for a kiss, Kofi steps away and says something to Senya in Twi. Senya then hands him a small box. Kofi drops down on one knee and my whole world becomes him in that moment.

"Ella. My sweet girl. My queen. I wanted to give this to you at dinner, but I fear if I wait any longer to officially make you my queen, I will end up in another fight."

I hear Senya snort. "You got that right."

Kofi ignores him and continues. "You came into my world long before you ever physically joined me in Kumasi. I knew you were someone special from the moment I read your proposal. Getting to know and love you over the past few weeks has been the supreme joy of my life. I do not want to rule another day without you by my side. I call you queen because it is clear to me that you are my right hand, the mother of my children, and the keeper of my spirit. Lover, will you please do me the honor of marrying me? I will not go back to Ghana without knowing you will be my wife."

"Yes!" I yell. He stands and this time I do jump him, short dress and all. I kiss my king for all he's worth. He returns the passion and we try to become one at the bar of Two Urban Licks. Senya loudly clears his throat and I faintly hear the gasps and cheers around us. I guess Senya couldn't close the bar down for much longer. Not even for a king.

Kofi sets me down on a bar stool and finally opens the ring box. "This is for you, beautiful." It takes my breath away. The largest emerald-cut diamond I've ever seen is surrounded by a band of green emeralds set on a gold band that also has diamond baguettes. It's not like anything I've ever seen before.

"This was my mother's ring, and my father's mother's before her. Now it is yours." When he places it on my finger, it feels like a private coronation. He lands a kiss on my forehead and lingers while I take in all the ways my life has changed since falling in love with a king.

The End

Thank you for reading!
Sign Up at and be the first to read all about Kofi and Ella's lavish royal wedding in my September newsletter!
www.lovelouiselennox.com/stayconnected

STAY CONNECTED

Leave a Review!

If you enjoyed this book, please leave a review on Amazon or Goodreads!

Good reviews make an author's world go around! We can't build a reputation without you!

THANK YOU, THANK YOU, THANK YOU!

Subscribe to my Newsletter
www.lovelouiselennox.com/stayconnected

I send a monthly newsletter on the first of every month! It has updates, recipes, book reviews, free books by other authors, and much more! I also send the occasional email blast anytime I have a new release or sale. Other than that; I'm pretty quiet. You will not be spammed!

Follow Me!

I am in LOVE with Instagram. Keep up with all that goes on in my world; including exclusive content from upcoming books @authorlouiselennox!

We have a fun and active #HappyBlackRomance Readers Group on Facebook! Join Us! We discuss all things Happy, Black, and Romantic!

Join Us!

ACKNOWLEDGMENTS

It is crazy that I wrote this book during a pandemic!

We were sent home to work virtually on March 13th and I immediately thought...What will I do with the free time I gain from not having to commute 2 hours a day ? I decided to write a romance novel about Africa.

I love romance. I 've always been a writer. And, my beautiful husband is Ghanaian. Writing a book about an African King and his queen made sense to me! However I could not have done this without lots of help!

My Husband and Children: K...You already know what it is. Thank You for reading every chapter I write and providing feedback every night...until Midnight. You dear are the real M.V.P.

To my 2 babies: thank you for being you. You make me want to be better and do bigger!

My Parents: Thank you for convincing me I can do all things through CHRIST that strengthens me. Because of your teachings; I'm not afraid of a thing!

My Spelman Sisters: Our Spelman Moms group provides so much support. We are all so successful and busy; yet in our group, we can cry, yell, and laugh. Thank You for volunteering to be BETA readers. Thank You for being my ARC team. Thank You for starting me out on social media. Thank You for believing in me. We will forever remain #undaunted.

Thanks to every professional editor (talking about you Lauren and Sydnee!!), cover designer, and formatter. We did it!

God Bless,
   Louise

ABOUT THE AUTHOR

Hello, everyone! I am honored you chose my book and took the time to read it. Writing this story was a blast, and I look forward to releasing the two subsequent novels in this series.

Below is my official bio. I promise I do not walk around talking about myself in third person :-)

Louise Lennox is a fresh face in the romance genre. She is a freelance writer, blogger and novelist.

Louise writes books to provide Black women with a diverse presence on romance novel pages. The narrative of an unwanted, unloved, and unmarried Black woman is inaccurate.

In response, Louise writes #HappyBlackRomance. Her stories highlight the joy and undeniable sexiness of Black relationships.

Louise is a graduate of Spelman College, with a B.A. in English Literature. She also finished Loyola University Chicago with a M.A. in Education Policy.

She is a happy wife and devoted mother of two.

ALSO BY LOUISE LENNOX

Choosing a Chief

(Book Two of The Sexy Sovereign Series)

Adom and Maya's Story

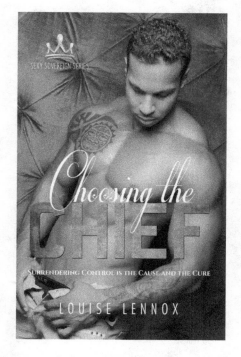

Releasing October 6th on Amazon.

<u>Pre-order it NOW!</u>

Surrendering control is the cause and the cure

Love & Lyrics (Book One of the Passionate Professors Series)

Get it now for free: www.lovelouiselennox.com

The Passionate Professors Series

LOVE & LYRICS
by Louise Lennox

Lesson One: Poets Bare All